WHEN EVIL CALLS YOUR NAME

JOHN NICHOLL

Chapter 1

Sunday 5, February 1995

I've been sitting here for almost an hour, trying to figure out where to begin: my name, perhaps, my location at the time of writing possibly, how I ended up in this miserable human dumping ground in the first place. Maybe, the awful entirety? Yes, that makes sense. If I'm going to tell you my story, why hold anything back. I've got absolutely nothing to hide. It's all a matter of public record anyway. What would be the point in trying?

This isn't going to be easy, but I think it's probably best if I introduce myself right now and get it over with. Please try to keep an open mind if you saw the numerous news reports relating to my case. Not everything they said was true. Not by a long shot.

Well, enough prevarication, here goes, time to bite the bullet, as the old saying goes… my name's Cynthia. Do you think that's sufficient, or do you require a surname? People often do for some reason. I suppose I may as well tell you now, and be done with it: Cynthia Galbraith. That's been my allocated label since my marriage to that man. So now do you understand my initial reticence? It was Jones, Cynthia Jones, before that. It's who I used to be. Someone I once was. A stranger from a distant far-off land I can never visit again. But then, I guess we all live in the shadow of the past to varying degrees.

I'm twenty-nine years old, by the way. I was twenty-six when I arrived here. That's three long years. Time tends to pass rather slowly here. No, that's understating the case, agonisingly slowly is more like it! Yes, agonising describes it very nicely.

But I'm getting ahead of myself. I can hear you saying it.
Shouting it conceivably? Or is that just my notoriously
overactive imagination playing tricks on me again? That
wouldn't surprise me. I get a lot of things wrong and make a
great many mistakes. He told me that time and time again. It
seems, such things define me.

Give me a second. Deep breaths Cynthia, deep breaths…
I'm writing this in my prison cell. There, I've said it! A
dingy eight-foot by six-foot enclosure illuminated by
intrusive overly bright, fluorescent-strip lighting that buzzes
constantly, and only serves to highlight how truly ghastly
every inch of this fucking place truly is.

My sincere apologies for the profanity, I hope you're not
offended. I found my fellow prisoners regular use of
'colourful' language hard to accept when I first arrived, but
it's amazing what you can get used to. And anyway, surely
it's just a word, a collection of letters, like all the other
words in this good, bad and indifferent world of ours. What
do you think? Tell me, please, I'll try not to take any
criticism personally. Obsession, control, bitch, murder, life.
It seems words can be emotive after all. What on earth was I
thinking? I should understand that more than most. Words
can hurt. They can have a substantial impact on our psyche.
They certainly did on mine.

But, I'm getting ahead of myself again. Now, where was I?
I need to press rewind and focus if I'm going to do my story
justice. Oh, yeah, I was telling you about my cell. I've
already told you the size. Small, that sums it up.
Claustrophobic? Most certainly, but I shouldn't complain.
Some say I deserve to be here. The judge clearly thought so,
given the length of my sentence. And then there were the
newspapers. I recall reading the Daily Mail at the time of my
trial. An evil woman, that's how they put it. An evil woman!
It sticks in my mind and eats away at me like a rabid dog.
Not an easy thing to read about myself, to be honest. I hadn't

thought of myself in that way until then. Stupid, yes, inadequate, yes, but evil? It was strange really: some journalists seemed to see me as villain, and others as an unfortunate victim of circumstance who rose from the ashes like a phoenix from the flames to smite my oppressor. How can different people, seemingly intelligent people, writers and the like, interpret the exact same events so very differently? I've given it a great deal of thought over the years without reaching an adequate resolution. You should make your own mind up. I think that's probably best. Perhaps one fine day you can provide me with an answer. I'd really appreciate it, if you could.

And back to the cell. I'll try my best not to go off at a tangent this time, promise. White peeling paint on walls pockmarked with multiple spots of black and blue mould, like a Jackson Pollock painting I like to think. A vivid imagination is a definite advantage in this place. It's my only means of escape when the walls close in on me. And then there's the bunk beds, of course. Not very comfortable, there's no denying that, but a lot of innocent people put up with a lot worse. There's a great many homeless people in this increasingly socially diverse country of ours. What have they done to deserve their fate?

Mine's the top bunk, by the way. That's truly significant here, it's the prison world equivalent of residing in Chelsea or Mayfair. Does that make any sense at all in your very different world? Well, yes or no, I've earned it after almost three years. Only thirteen more to go. Unlucky for some, eh? Unlucky for me, that's for sure!

I share my cell with Gloria, a skinny nineteen-year-old girl with fashionable short cropped dark-brown hair and a much older name. We've got nothing and everything in common, and very little to say to each other most of the time. We share occasional pleasantries, that's true. She asks me for tampons, toothpaste, toilet paper and other necessities on a

5

fairly regular basis, and she moans about the guards from time to time. But then, who doesn't? It's the national pastime in these parts. Most of them are okay, to be honest. The majority are just here to do a job, to pay the bills, and do the best they can within the confines of their role. But then there's the others: a seemingly different species, the right bastards who seem to take infinite pleasure in making my life as miserable as feasibly possible at every conceivable opportunity. They're the sort of people who like to pull the wings off butterflies. It seems there are good and bad people in all walks of life. I knew one of the worst, a monster, a man devoid of empathy or virtue, but it's far too soon for that. I'm not ready to address that particular topic just yet.

Pull yourself together Cynthia, pull yourself together. No need for tears. Get a grip girl and back to the story. That's about it really! I'd say Gloria has the potential to be one of life's good gals despite her current circumstances if given the opportunity. She was convicted of repeated multiple shoplifting offences to fund her drug habit, but I'm glad of her company most of the time. She fills a gap. I genuinely like the girl. She provides colour: a welcome distraction from the monotony of prison life.

Did I tell you about the bucket? No? Well, we, that's Gloria and myself, share a bright red plastic bucket which serves as our ensuite facilities, and a small rectangular window behind five dark steel bars, through which I can see the cold grey concrete exercise yard if I stand on tip toes, extend my neck to a maximum and peep over the sill. We get to spend an hour a day in the yard, three days a week, to breathe in the morning air, weather permitting, naturally. It's a welcome release, something I look forward to immensely: a time to cherish. I saw a small bird flying around there once, darting from one corner of the yard to another with effortless ease; a beautiful delicate creature so full of life and vitality. I think it was very probably a swallow, my bird, given the long pointed wings and effortless aerial gymnastics. But, I could be wrong, of course. It seems I often am. He used to tell me that all the time. Even now, after all this time, I sometimes feel his presence hanging over me like a malicious, spiteful spirit I can't escape however hard I try. As if he's here with me still.

Get a grip Cynthia, for goodness sake get a grip! He can't hurt you anymore. Except in your troubled mind, your invasive thoughts, and your nightmares.

Sorry for the distraction. I was telling you about my bird before becoming preoccupied yet again. It happens all too often, I'm afraid, but I'll try to control it as best I can. I used to think so clearly once upon a time in the distant past. I had an analytical mind, or so I was told by a respected academic. I need to focus on one thing at a time, rather than engage in mindless ramblings that I strongly suspect make very little sense to most of you.

I've kept a keen eye out ever since, a daily ritual born of hope, but sadly no more birds. Such a terrible disappointment! I think they avoid this place as much as possible. And, why wouldn't they? There are no majestic trees, no green fields, or hedgerows festooned with wild shrubs, no rolling Welsh hills that kiss the sea, or multicoloured flowers to delight the senses. I'd fly away and escape this place if I could. Wouldn't you?

What do I do with the other twenty-three hours? Is that what you're wondering? Well, it's lights out at ten every night and back on at six each morning, so it's actually only fifteen hours I have to fill. It could be a lot worse. Things can always be worse, as I know from experience.

I work in the prison laundry for eight hours a day, three days a week: that's Mondays, Tuesdays and Thursdays. Those are good days. For some reason I can't explain, work helps still my anxious mind. Not entirely, of course, that would be too much to ask for, but it helps. I guess it's a form of distraction therapy, like the tight elastic band I pull and snap against the soft skin of my wrist when he invades my thoughts.

I teach basic reading and writing skills to some of the other girls on Wednesday afternoons. Girls, that's a laugh! Women, most of them are women. Damaged, inadequate women in the main, who hit hard times, and paid a heavy price for their poverty, addiction, mental incapacity and disadvantage.

The class is the glowing highlight of my week. I actually feel I'm contributing something positive to the world; that my life's actually worth something. That he was wrong. That I matter. That I'm not just some worthless caged creature who, by definition has to be hidden away from decent people to protect their sensibilities. Do you understand what I mean? Do you know what I'm saying? Surely, you must do. We all need validation of one kind or another as we navigate our way through life.

One of the girls called me, 'Miss' a couple of weeks back. It still makes me smile when I think about it. I'm smiling now as I write these words, but for obvious reasons it never lasts. A smile tends to vanish as quickly as it appears in this place. I was planning to train as a teacher after completing my Law degree, in a different life, before I met the man who changed everything. Had I mentioned my ambition before? No? Well, I once hoped to teach in a Welsh rural comprehensive school near to where I grew up on the Pembrokeshire coast. And I would have loved it! Or at least I like to think so. Perhaps it would have been harder than I imagine in my recurrent fantasies. Maybe I'm wrong about that too.

And then there are Fridays. I see a prison counsellor at 2:00 p.m. every Friday afternoon, unless she's on one of her exotic holidays, or otherwise unavailable for one often unspecified reason or another. She's not a doctor or anything along those lines, but she seems to know what she's talking about most of the time. Or, at least I hope she does for my sake. I'm no expert in such matters, of course, but there's three rather impressive looking framed certificates on the office wall above her desk. I haven't actually read them, to be honest, so they could be just about anything now that I think about it. But, that said, there is a large colour photo of her wearing a purple mortar board and gown, in a stylish silver frame sitting on her desk next to her computer. She looks a lot younger, prettier and slimmer in the photo, so it must have been taken quite some time ago. Or has prison world aged her prematurely, as it has me? This place tends to do that to a girl.

There I go again, straying from the point as is my custom. I'll try harder to concentrate on one thing at a time. I didn't tell you Mrs Martin's name. But there you go, I've done it. Mrs Mary Martin: White Haven Women's Prison counsellor, wife, mother and countless other things of which I'm unaware, no doubt. That's the way of the world for women these days! I believe it's referred to as multitasking. Not having a minute to yourself would probably be a more accurate description. Maybe it's a male conspiracy: a cynical corruption of the right to equality. If you're female, you may have suspected as much. I have more than once.

On one occasion I called Mrs Martin 'Mary', when I thought I'd morphed from patient to patient stroke friend, but she didn't appreciate my newfound familiarity one little bit. I realised my mistake as soon as I'd uttered the words. She visibly stiffened, nerves taut, and adopted a sour expression which made her displeasure blatantly obvious. It's been Mrs Martin ever since. It seems best.

What does Mrs Martin actually do? Is that what you're wondering? Is such a service a reasonable use of hard-working taxpayers' money? Well, we just sat and talked until recently, really. Sometimes I did most of the talking, and

9

sometimes she did. That surprised me at first: her talking about herself, I mean. Perhaps she thought a caring, sharing approach would convey liking, and encourage me to be honest about my life? And I have been. So I guess it worked. Well, to a degree, anyway. I haven't been entirely frank. I've held a lot back up to this point. I think she tried what methods she could, and then realised that talking alone wasn't sufficient to illicit total honesty in my case. Who knows? I'm very probably making assumptions I'm not qualified to make.

Last week, for whatever reason, she suddenly changed her approach. That's why I've put pen to paper in the first place. Mrs Martin sat opposite me in her small cluttered magnolia office come consultation room, and suggested I write this journal. If I sound surprised, that's because it did genuinely surprise me at the time. Although, I've since begun to appreciate the potential benefits of the process. I'll try and remember exactly what she said to win me over; or at least recount her words as accurately as I can manage now that a few days have passed and the memory has begun to fade.

'Put down your thoughts on paper Cynthia.' That's how she began. I'm fairly certain of that. 'Talking can often help, Cynthia, but it's sometimes easier to write things down. It can prove both freeing and purgative. I think it's probably time for us to adopt that approach. Effective therapy is a bit like shaking a bottle of Champagne and pulling the cork out… Whoosh! The contents explode all over the place at first, but then what's left settles down very nicely. And that's what will happen to you. Your emotions will eventually settle. It will take time, of course. It won't be an easy process. There will be rocky ground along the way. But, we will get there in the end. It will be worthwhile. I promise! Writing a journal will help you come to terms with your past, and to adapt to and accept the unwelcome changes in your life that are largely beyond your control. Are you prepared to give it a try?'

I wasn't hugely impressed by the idea up to that point, to be honest, and my reticence must have shown clearly on my face, because she qualified her proposition with what appeared to be genuine passion. 'I implore you to keep a journal Cynthia. Write down your secret thoughts. The things you have never dared vocalise. Explore them on paper, as if telling the world. As if engaging in conversation with a million imaginary friends, all of whom are desperate to understand and help you.'

A little new age alternative for my tastes, perhaps, but I shouldn't laugh. I think Mrs Martin may well be a bit of a sixties hippy chick at heart: yoga, scented candles, joss sticks, flower power, vegetarian food and all that. But, I have to admit I was somewhat intrigued. The idea began to resonate with me for reasons I still can't fully explain. Maybe it was her enthusiasm, maybe her apparent desire to help, or possibly both.

'It will help you make sense of events Cynthia. You can bring the journal along with you each week. It will inform our work together. It will help address the invasive thoughts, the nightmares, the flashbacks, the mood swings and the occasional temper tantrums. You won't be entirely free of them, of course. Not totally! It's not as if I can cure you of a physical illness or repair an injury. The psychological scars will still be there, I'm not going to lie to you, but writing it all down, taking the cork out and subjecting the contents to the light will eventually help them fade.'

I would decline to swear on oath that those were her exact words, but my representation of our meeting is pretty damn close to what was said. If I've misrepresented Mrs Martin in any way, I can only apologise. It won't be for want of trying. And anyway, any such error would be of no particular consequence. Now that I've had the opportunity to think it through properly, I think I almost certainly responded to her refreshing honesty and enthusiasm rather than being persuaded by her argument.

Anyway, whatever the reason for my eventual accord, I agreed to give it a try, that's the crux of it. Maybe in the end I'd have bared my soul anyway. Who knows? Writing won't undo the past, of course. I fully appreciate that. Mrs Martin didn't pretend that it would, in fairness to her. Writing can't facilitate my physical freedom, or bring the lost back to life. That's certainly not going to happen. Not in this life, not in this world! But, if the process is in any way cathartic, it will have served its primary purpose and I will be extremely grateful for that.

I plan to write down my story from beginning to end, no holds barred. Even the stuff that keeps me awake at night. Especially the stuff that keeps me awake at night. Perhaps when I'm finished I'll try and have it published. Not for the money, but as a cautionary message: a red flag screaming: be careful who you trust. Be very careful who you trust.

I may have done myself a disservice a line or two ago. I regret mentioning money at all now that I've done it. Some thoughts are better left unsaid, wouldn't you agree? I need to take this seriously if it's going to mean something; if it's going to achieve anything. Money is of little if any value to me given my current predicament. The prison provides its guests with complementary food and board. It's all-inclusive for the criminal classes. Not five star of course, there's no pool, sauna or room-service, but you can't have everything in this life.

Sorry, there I go again, making light of my situation. I guess I'm just trying to alleviate my melancholy mood. It's a constant battle, to be honest, fighting the creeping shadow of despair that haunts me. Slaying demons is never easy. In all seriousness, I fully intend to give this my best. I'm fully committed to the process. I've got all the time in the world, and very little, if anything, to lose.

Chapter 2

Are you sitting comfortably children? Then I'll begin.

If you're not of a certain age, you may well be thinking I've lost the plot completely at this point. The phrase resonates from my early childhood, but may well mean nothing at all to you. I have no way of knowing. But, if that is the case, not to worry, it really isn't important. I think I was simply attempting to delay the inevitable. I had absolutely no idea just how terrifying a blank sheet of white paper has the potential to be. I'll get a grip and make a start.

Memories don't come in straight lines. My head is full of situations and stories, events I need to address in a meaningful sequential order if I'm going to do this process any justice at all. I think I'll begin with my childhood. That seems logical. Nothing very remarkable, I'm afraid. No suspense, mystery, or intrigue, or anything as exciting as that. But, that's what makes what happened subsequently all the more surprising. All the more shocking! The contrast, that's what I'm talking about. The dramatic, black and white, yin and yang, good and evil contrast. I don't think I can make it any clearer than that.

I left the comparative safety of my mother's womb and entered this big wide world of ours, with all its many pleasures and dangers, on the 15th of June 1966. I was born in a tiny cottage hospital, in a small Welsh seaside town built on a windy headland, surrounded by dark granite cliffs, wild green seas topped with galloping white horses, and pale, pepper-pot-yellow bucket and spade beaches. Nature's majesty on my doorstep, so to speak. Not a bad start in life, I'm sure you'd agree. My parents claim it was a glorious, bright, summer day with a cloudless powder-blue sky and a warm golden glow. The very best that the Welsh summertime can offer. I only have their word for that of course. I have no memories of events prior to the age of four. Some people claim to recall the trauma of birth, but I'm not persuaded, to be honest. It seems highly unlikely to me. But I could be wrong. I recall mentioning that I often am.

I continued the 'small' theme and arrived prematurely, weighing in at just two pounds and three ounces. My dad took a black and white photo of me lying next to a bag of Tate and Lyle sugar with his Olympus Trip 35 mm camera at the time. It seemed like the right thing to do, apparently. Mum and Dad used to show the photo to anyone and everyone who was willing to look at it. Or, at least, that's how it seemed to me as I grew up in that happy place. Mum still carries it in her handbag to this day. It's somewhat creased and faded these days, but she still seems to cherish it. She showed it to me once during one of her increasingly infrequent visits, as if I were seeing it for the first time. Perhaps it reminds her of better times. That would make sense, wouldn't it? Yes, of course it would. There are things I'd choose to forget, if I could. I'm sure she's not so very different.

When I was about six-weeks old, I finally moved from the hospital ward to my new home in Tenby, with parents who loved me, and a three-year-old brother called Jack, who didn't. Or, at least not at first! I think they call it sibling rivalry. Mum tells me that he was insanely jealous for a time, which is understandable when you think about it. He'd been the sole focus of his parents' love and attention for his entire life up to that point, and all of a sudden there I was invading what he considered his territory. Things improved, of course as we became used to each other's company, and our relationship swung back and forth between adoring and detesting one other, as is often the case.

15

The four of us lived in a two-bedroom terrace house, with a back yard that served as a childhood playground. I have no recollection of those early years, as I mentioned earlier, but I've seen photographs and atmospheric flickering cine films, lovingly produced by my dad with his much prized hand-held camera. We're all smiling in those films, the sun was shining, and I was dressed in immaculate princess dresses, brightly coloured hair bands, and shiny black patent leather shoes that still make me smile. We all look happy in those celluloid representations of the far-off past, and I have no reason to think that our reality was any different. There must have been trials, of course, there always are in this life of ours, but in the main we were happy. And why wouldn't we be? No wonder Mum likes to focus on times gone by, rather than the current grim reality. No wonder her eyes sometimes go blank when she sits across the table from me in the visiting room. It can't be easy for her. It certainly isn't for me. But, as long as she keeps coming when she can, as long as she brings my girls to see me occasionally, I'll have to be satisfied with that.

When I was just four years old we moved from our small terrace home to a new build three-bedroom red-brick semi, of the type much beloved by the aspiring middle classes striving to solidify their respectability in the eyes of a judgemental world. Our new home was part of a relatively small housing estate, located a mile or so from our lovely walled medieval town. The house had the distinct advantages of an extra bedroom, meaning I no longer had to share with Jack, and a pleasant back garden, where Dad proudly cultivated prize-winning red, white and yellow chrysanthemums, and planted various vegetables, which we invariably enjoyed with our Sunday roast. I remember the small rectangular lawn being absolutely immaculate. Like a bowling green, as the predictable cliché goes: not a single weed, not a blade of grass out of place. I sometimes wonder if such things give us humans the temporary illusion of control, until God laughs at our plans.

There I go again, letting my mind wonder aimlessly. Perhaps I should consider studying for an Open University degree when I eventually finish laying the details of my life at your feet. I must learn to discipline my intellect and focus on the specific task in hand. My Cardiff University tutor used to say much the same on a fairly regular basis before my life fell apart. It seems I'm still to learn that particular lesson. I've started meditating each evening before attempting to sleep despite the pervasive human anguish that invades the darkness. It's another of Mrs Martin's bright ideas. You just close your eyes and focus on your breathing, apparently. Can it really be that easy? Mrs Martin claims it's backed by scientific research, and I have no reason to doubt her word. Maybe it will help. One can only hope. I'll let you know how I get on, in case you want to try it yourself.

It was onwards and upwards for the Jones family. I feel a resounding trumpet fanfare would be appropriate at this stage of the story, were such things possible outside my head. Dad had been promoted within the county council's planning department, and Mum was working part-time in a local shoe shop for pin money, as she liked to put it. I started school at Jamestown County Primary, a dark Victorian building with an external toilet block, and a canteen we had to walk to for ten minutes or more, hand in hand, each lunchtime come rain or shine. It's an odd reality that the school which seemed so large to a young child, was actually small and compact when I attended a charity coffee morning as an adult. To my surprise, one of my old teachers was still working there. That was a nice surprise. For me at least, I'm not so sure about her. Maybe I reminded her how much time had passed. Ageing seems to come as a shock to us all, despite its inevitability. I very much hope they were happy years. Shall I tell you a bit about her? No? You're probably correct. It's not as if she's a particularly significant part of the story.

There I go, straying off the point again. I absolutely loved it. Education, I adored it. That's what I meant to say. As a child, not so much as an adult, with the inevitable pressures of scrutiny such things involve. I loved school as a child. What the hell's wrong with me? Why didn't I just say that in the first place? I have a tendency to make things so much more complex than they need to be. I'm sure you'd already realised that for yourself. That's if you've bothered to continue reading. It's one of my many failings, I'm afraid. Please bear with me if you can.

I've established that my primary years were a happy time. A cherished time, that I can look back on and smile. If only I could say the same of my adult years. I left primary school at the grand old age of eleven, along with the rest of my fellow classmates. Some of us were destined to attend the local comprehensive, me included; and others the much in demand Welsh education secondary school, which had recently opened in our area. Both were good schools, or at least that's what the headmaster told us on our last day of primary education. We were, he said, 'On an exciting journey, the outcome of which would depend on how much effort we made in our new educational establishments.' If only it were that simple! Sadly, life has taught me that attempting to determine our future is something of a lottery. We can try, we should always try, but there are no guarantees. That's the point I was aiming for. Phew, I got there in the end. I'm going to run out of ink at this rate. It would be nice if we could determine the outcome of our lives with some degree of certainty. But, of course, we can't. Life's not like that. I put a lot of effort in. I really did. I worked hard. But, then I met him. Fate or random chaos intervened. I'm not sure which. But, look where my efforts got me. If life's a lottery, I think it's fair to conclude that I'm one of the losers.

 The headmaster may or mayn't have believed his own words. He could conceivably have been saying what he thought we all needed to hear. Who knows? But, whichever it was, I took his words as sacrosanct at my tender age. Influential authority figures possess such power over their young and impressionable charges. If he'd told me I was to attend a school on the moon, I would have believed him without question. That's the sort of man he was. That's the sort of child I was. I was an innocent growing up in a dangerous world.
 The long hot summer betwixt my final day of primary school and entering the land of comparative giants, seemed a period of never ending childhood bliss. If only… What's the point in saying it? It was a lovely time, I should focus on that and be done with it. We travelled to the Vendee for two glorious weeks in August: Saint-Jean-De-Monts, in case you're interested. Dad drove our ancient green and rust Volkswagen Passat estate car packed with childhood memories, and festooned with family bikes, GB stickers and yellowed headlights, from Wales to France via the Dover ferry. It must have been a horrendous journey, now that I think about it, but such things seem unimportant when reminiscing, wouldn't you agree? The journey becomes blurred, and the good times come into sharper focus. If only everything in life could be like that. We can only focus on the positives when life allows us that luxury. There aren't many positives in prison world.
 We stayed in a spacious comfortable Eurocamp caravan with all the mod cons, near to a seemingly infinite windswept Atlantic beach, backed by rolling sand dunes

decorated with intermittent green tufts of hardy seaside grass, that provided an ideal childhood adventure playground. The site had spacious pitches with carefully positioned privacy trees and bushes, a pleasant club house with a table football game, a children's club, which for some reason I refused to attend, a restaurant which served delicious hot buttered crepes for breakfast, and a large swimming pool, where Dad and Jack were forced to wear minuscule Speedos. I've no idea why. I think it's a French thing. They seem to do campsites so much better than us Brits. Have you ever been? If you have you'll know what I mean. And the cakes! Oh boy, the cakes! I remember eating an eclair filled with caramel custard and topped with caramel icing. Wow! That's all I need to say on the matter. What I wouldn't give for one of those now. Maybe one fine day I'll enjoy one again. With a double espresso, enjoyed in the company of a mysterious Frenchman who knows nothing of my dubious past. That would be a gratifying experience. I think I'll stay in a bijou boutique hotel next time, if I can afford it, that is. There's a lovely looking one as I recall, in the town, near to a church with a tall steeple, and a red-tiled roof. I know what you're thinking, but it really could happen one day. There's an online petition against the length of my sentence. My self-indulgent homage to my happy childhood may become more than a desperate female fantasy. One day, it really could happen. I'll be one of life's lucky winners one fine day. Or at least, I like to think so.

I'm a little out of breath after all that. Please give me a second or two to calm my breathing before I continue. Slow deep breaths through the nose and out through the mouth. That's more like it. Thank you for your patience.

Dad often used to bemoan the closure of the grammar schools because, and these are his words, 'It represented the ill-informed destruction of the greatest facilitator of social mobility that existed in our great country.' He may have been correct. He may have been wrong. You can make your own mind up on the matter. I don't really think I'm equipped to judge. But, what I do know is that attending a comprehensive school certainly didn't do me any harm. After the initial shock of transferring from the prestigious heights of top class to the ignominy of the lowest, I settled in relatively well. I made friends quickly, happily engaged in various extracurricular activities, represented the school at hockey, and achieved reasonably good grades. This is the point in the story when I get to blow my own trumpet, and confirm that I did in fact do rather well. I don't think that's unreasonable. My self-belief needs all the help it can get. I obtained ten O Levels: six grade As and four grade Bs. Not bad, eh? I had already decided I wanted to train as a solicitor, and I planned to study for a Law degree at Cardiff University. I joined the sixth form, with those admirable aims in mind, the following September. But, as you know, good intentions don't always bear fruit.

Mum and Dad were over the moon when I achieved excellent A-level results shortly after my eighteenth birthday. I think two As and a B were better than they had hoped for. But, I'd worked hard, and to be honest, I was expecting nothing less. If anything I was a little disappointed not to achieve three As. I very much hope that doesn't make me sound in any way big headed. I wouldn't want that. If I'm going to be entirely honest, that has to relate to the positives as well as the negatives. God knows they're in the minority. I passed my exams, me, I passed, that's the way it was. Occasionally there's still some justice in this world. It's important to acknowledge that. But, to put my results in context, I've achieved very little of note since. Actually, that isn't strictly accurate. I've achieved nothing worthwhile since, with the exception of bringing my two wonderful daughters, Elizabeth and Sarah, into the world. And what a dark world they entered. But, more of that later; the girls apart, writing this journal, for what it's worth, is probably my biggest achievement since that time. What a thing to admit to yourself, leave alone, share it with others. I hope you don't judge my many failures too harshly when you know the full story.

My apologies for wallowing in self-pity yet again! It can't be an attractive spectacle. I'll try to hold it together as best I can from here on in. My tears are beginning to smudge the ink in places, and that can't be a good thing. Sorry! Sorry! Sorry! And, as if that isn't bad enough, my self-indulgent melancholy literal ramblings weren't even an accurate record of events, now that I come to think about it. I did actually go to university. I didn't finish the course. I didn't actually achieve a degree. But there were very good reasons for that, and getting there in the first place was worthy of note, wasn't it? I'll tell you a little bit more about it as my story continues.

Chapter 3

We were a close family unit back then: Mum, Dad, Jack and me, in those far-off days, and I feel compelled to tell you a little about each of them before continuing my narrative. It seems somewhat churlish to do otherwise. I'm sure I'd feature heavily, were they writing memoirs of their lives. I'd like to think so, anyway. I'll tell you about Dad first, as the nominated head of the family, then Mum, and finally my big brother. That seems to be the natural order of things in my head. So here we go, Dad first. But, before I start, I should point out that I very much hope you don't read anything into that, because it really could have been Mum first, or even Jack, were I so inclined. I have to start somewhere, so why not Dad? It certainly wasn't Dad who destroyed my trust in men. That came later. Much later when I met the man I eventually married.

Dad was something of a traditionalist. An old-fashioned man, if you like. Certainly not a new man, of the kind favoured by some feminist types I've met over the years. But, I wouldn't want to give you the impression that he was a caveman who didn't pull his weight. Because he did. He absolutely did! At least, in my eyes he did. He enthusiastically maintained the house, he did the heavy lifting, he looked after the garden, he took responsibility for the refuge, and he brought in the bulk of the money that paid the bills and for our camping holidays each and every summer. Mum sometimes says that there is danger of confusing equal opportunity with being fundamentally the same. I never really understood what she meant when I was younger, but I've had a lot of time to think since. Work as a team and play to your strengths, I think that was what she

23

meant to say. Anyway, whatever she meant, they were clearly happy with the way things were. It worked for them.

I've just realised that I've been talking about Mum and Dad as a couple. No, that's not really what I mean. I want to get this exactly right if I'm going to say it at all. I'm talking about them as if they were a single entity, rather than focussing on each as individuals. I considered redrafting this section of the journal to address the issue, but I think the blurring of the lines is inevitable given the length and strength of their relationship, and so I've left it as it is. They were childhood sweethearts, you see, and two had become one. They finished each other's sentences, and read each other's thoughts right up to the time Dad died shortly after I was sentenced. He was a fit fifty-eight year old who played golf, drunk alcohol modestly, and hadn't smoked for years. Where's the justice in that? He died of a broken heart, of that I'm sure. Broken by Jack initially, and then by me: his little girl! I blamed myself for a long, long time. Mrs Martin has repeatedly tried to convince me that events were largely beyond my control. Sometimes I believe it, and sometimes I don't. Shouldn't I take responsibility for my actions? I very much hope this process clarifies matters. Let's wait and see what conclusion you eventually come to when you know the full facts.

Mum was absolutely lovely. No! What on earth's wrong with me? I'll start again, and get it right this time. Mum is lovely, that's what I should have said: Mum is lovely! That's how I should have put it in the first place. She's still with us, you see, although a part of her died along with Dad. I think that was almost certainly the reason for my error. It's an easy mistake to make, but I really should be more careful when referring to those who mean something to me. They may read this one day, and details matter. Details can matter enormously. The trial taught me that.

My mum was an old-fashioned mum: looking after us all brilliantly, caring for the home equally well, keeping it clean and tidy, transporting me to ballet, Brownies and piano lessons, baking cakes and the like. As good a mum as I could have wished for. And she seemed happy. I like to think she was fulfilled. I've never thought about it in any depth before, to be honest. Is that selfish of me? Should I know what she actually thinks of the life she's lived? Perhaps I'll ask her one day, if I think she's up to answering and I can deal with her answer.

And then there's my once wayward brother Jack. Where on earth do I begin? Jack! Jack! Jack! He's one of life's free spirits. I think that's probably the kindest way of putting it. Others would have called him a rogue or worse. A lot worse! I recall Jack telling me that a local police officer called him a cunt on one drunken Saturday night escapade. It took me almost a week to get over the shock. That really was how innocent I was in those days. I'm sure I could write an entire book just about Jack, if I were so inclined. But, I hope you'll agree it isn't the primary purpose of this exercise. This is supposed to be about me. What would Mrs Martin say if I failed to do my homework properly? I will tell you about Jack, but I'll attempt to keep it brief.

After a relatively uneventful and promising childhood, culminating in three reasonable A-levels, Jack became what Dad referred to as a disappointment. He went off the rails long before my spectacular fall from grace. While I was studying for, and passing my O-levels, Jack attended Exeter University, enthusiastically indulging his hedonistic instincts to the nth degree. Drugs became the most important thing in his life for a time, and we, Mum, Dad and I, became a virtual irrelevance, unless he needed money. It was pot to begin with, no real harm in that you may think, but it was quickly followed by LSD, and ultimately heroin. By the third year of his course he was missing more lectures than he was attending, and dealing drugs to other like-minded students to pay for his burgeoning habit. Mum and Dad reached out to him repeatedly with the offer of help, but he determinedly rejected their loving efforts. I tried myself, once or twice, but like him, I was way out of my depth. Maybe I should have tried harder. I like to think I would have, were I a little older and worldly wise. But, there's no way of knowing with any certainty.

Jack drifted away from us all, and lost touch altogether after his predictably unsuccessful finals. He did send Mum and Dad a postcard from New York a year or so later, with a colourful picture of the Statue of Liberty on the front and a prominent red banner saying: 'THE BIG APPLE!' as if that wasn't blatantly obvious to everybody. Jack told them he was okay, but to Mum and Dad's consternation, he didn't include an address or contact number. If I'm feeling generous, I put his selfish behaviour down to the unattractive self-focus of youth. But, I have to admit that at times, particularly when Mum's distress was betrayed by her face, I thought that the police officer had it spot on.

Maybe Jack broke Mum and Dad's heart long before I did. I'm not trying to minimise my responsibility. Either way, the outcome was much the same. What on earth did my gentle loving parents do to deserve their awful fate. Was it karma? Were they very different people in a previous life? Or is it simply that life isn't fair? Who knows? Answers on a postcard addressed to Cynthia Galbraith care of prison world.

I could happily have slapped Jack, and slapped him hard, given the opportunity. But, I didn't actually see him again until he arrived at my Cardiff door, unannounced, and full of heartfelt apologies a few weeks before my nineteenth birthday. This may well seem highly unlikely, but I really didn't recognise him at first. He'd grown a scraggy unkempt beard that dominated his features, his long auburn hair was tied back in a bohemian-style ponytail and parted in the middle, he'd gained about two stone in weight which he carried well, and he was wearing round gold metal prescription John Lennon glasses, that didn't suit him at all in my humble opinion. He told me that night, over a couple of drinks in the students' union bar, that he'd beaten the drugs. I was understandably dubious at first, addicts are notoriously prone to lies, as I'm sure you're aware. But, to my surprise and pleasure, it turned out to be true. He'd been rescued, that was the word he used, by his evangelical born again Christian girlfriend, who had loved him unconditionally, introduced him to her faith, and proactively facilitated his ongoing recovery. To her credit, she had it seems, acted as counsellor, nurse, jailer and lover, until he finally stopped injecting destructive poison into his veins, and survived weeks of pain, nausea, stomach cramps, sweats, anxiety and all consuming cravings until the heroin eventually lost its insidious power over him. I haven't met Marie, that's her name, but one day I'll thank her in person for returning my big brother to his family.

Anyway, I think that's probably sufficient to give you a flavour of each of them. I very much hope you agree. I've read and reread my musings, and I've come to the certain conclusion that nothing that happened prior to my meeting that man contributed in any way to my current predicament. There is nothing whatsoever that my parents or brother could have done to predict, let alone prevent the misfortune that later befell me. Nothing! And on that note, I have decided to move on with my story.

Chapter 4

I've got almost an hour before lights out, and so I'll crack on and make the most of the time… If I hadn't passed my A-levels, if I'd chosen to attend a different university, if I hadn't met Steven, if I hadn't dyed my hair platinum blonde, I'd probably never have met the man who brought so much misery into the world. If, a tiny word with potentially limitless implications! I've gone over and over it a thousand times in my anxious mind in an attempt to explain events adequately, or to create a fictional parallel universe with different happier outcomes. But, such things are not possible in our physical world. Sadly, we cannot rewrite our past, however much we desire to eradicate selected memories from our minds. We can't wipe the tape clean. I've tried. Believe me, I've tried.

But I really mustn't forget the positives. Because there were positives. It wasn't all doom and gloom. I can't let what occurred subsequently pollute and eradicate all that was good. Cardiff was a truly happy place when I first moved there. Actually, now that I think about it, I was happy for the first three months or more. Blissfully happy at times. I think it's probably best if I start at the beginning of my journey from comparative naivety to experience, and proceed gradually from there.

Mum and Dad transported me from my comfortable west Wales home to the first year female halls of residence on the day before the start of my first term. We travelled in a car packed with everything an independent girl could conceivably need to settle into her new abode. It took the three of us almost an hour to transport everything from the car to my small single room with its single bed, wardrobe, desk and sparkling white porcelain sink. The move inevitably resulted in a degree of anxiety at my tender age of eighteen, but my apprehension was largely overridden by my excitement, and the friendly persona of the other girls sharing my experience, who seemed equally keen to make new friends. University represented freedom, it represented self-determination, it provided the opportunity to stand on my own two feet in a safe environment. I liked the idea of semi-independence, in that privileged temple to learning, and, to be honest I couldn't wait for my parents to leave and let me get on with it.

I was in two minds about revealing that fact. The bit about wanting my parents to go, I mean. Do you think it reflects badly on me, or is it understandable given my youth? It certainly didn't mean I loved them any less. I simply wanted to spread my wings and fly. Fly like my bird, with the big wide world, or Cardiff in my case, and seemingly endless opportunities on my doorstep. Does that sound a little pretentious or a tad romanticised possibly? I would completely understand if you reached that conclusion. I wouldn't hold it against you. But, I really was that kind of girl in those long gone days. A little immature, sure, somewhat naïve, unquestionably, pretentious, on occasions, I'll admit to that. But, as I've explained, I was young, I was carefree and above all I was happy. I like to think I was one of life's romantics. Others may well have a different word for it. But, that really is how I saw myself in those days of seemingly endless summer. If only I could turn the clock back and inhabit the past forever. If only! I wonder sometimes if I'll ever experience happiness again.

Well, back to the story, and not before time I imagine you're thinking… I walked with them as far as the car, parked in the busy tree-lined street directly outside the dorm, and waved enthusiastically as Dad started the tired engine on the third turn of the key and drove off in the direction of the M4, with Mum hanging head and shoulders out of the passenger-side front window like an overheated dog panting for oxygen. She stared at me with a frozen unconvincing smile on her lips, that strongly suggested she was courageously swallowing her sadness to protect my feelings. Was I concerned by her reaction? Did I consider her sensibilities for a solitary second? Not really, if I'm honest. I was excited about the future with that self-focus of youth I've already mentioned, and I told myself I was moving a few miserable miles down the road, not emigrating half way around the world as Jack had. Was I really that selfish? I have to admit that the answer is, yes. We look on things differently as we get older. Or at least, I do. I can't speak for you, of course, but I suspect it's universal.

As soon as I lost sight of their car, I rushed back upstairs to the second floor, two or three steps at a time, and was met by the sound of loud female chatter and nervous laughter. I strongly suspect that the departure of other moping or celebrating parents was almost certainly the catalyst for the virtual frenzy, and that my reaction to my parents departure wasn't so very different to that of the other young women. There! That makes me feel a little better about myself. I knew there had to be a good reason for going into so much seemingly unnecessary detail. Maybe Mrs Martin was correct all along.

'A place for everything, and everything in its place.' I tidied away and rearranged my possessions with my Mum's advisory cliché playing in my head like a cassette on a loop. Not bad advice in fact, when your room is as minuscule as mine was. Swinging cats and all that! I don't have to worry about such things these days, of course. Not because my cell is any bigger than my first student accommodation, because it's not. It may even be smaller in fact. I just don't have that much stuff anymore. Gloria hasn't either. Nobody here has. It's just not the way of things in prison world.

That evening, after unpacking, feathering my newly acquired nest, and going from room to room befriending anyone and everyone who was receptive to my tentative approaches, we, that's my newfound acquaintances and I, agreed to meet in the communal lounge at 7:00 p.m., before making our merry way to the student union bar to do the things we thought students aught to do on their first night of freedom.

I showered at about 6:15 p.m., applied what I like to think was subtle makeup, and took what I would now consider a ridiculous length of time to choose an outfit which I felt best reflected my new cool scholarly status. How ridiculous is that! The self-obsession of youth strikes again.

When I joined the other girls at just before 7:00 p.m., it seemed blue jeans, tee-shirts and flat shoes were the order of the day. Not the usual teenage garb. Not what I would have chosen for a night out in Tenby only days before. But, I guess it was a uniform of sorts, an attempt to fit in, tribal behaviour, if you like. Most of us want to belong to something, so it's not really that surprising when you think about it. Perhaps I wasn't so ridiculous after all. Maybe I was just being human, with all the frailties and insecurities being human involves. Yes, I think I'll forgive myself that particular weakness. Others won't be nearly so easy to pardon.

The twelve of us sat at two tables directly opposite the hectic student bar, and spent the first hour or more drinking far too much cheap alcohol subsidised by the tax payer, trying to communicate above the sound of the pounding rock music, and flirting outrageously with any boy in our immediate vicinity, whatever their appearance and degree of interest. And then it happened. On that first night! How unlikely is that? There are moments in life, moments that pass long before we realise their significance, moments that change our lives forever. I can say with confidence that this was one of those glorious moments. I glanced towards the bar and noticed him immediately, despite the seething mass of people, despite his diminutive build, as if he were standing alone in a glaring white spotlight on a West End stage. And the remarkable thing was that he had noticed me as well. We stared at each other, and became the only people in the room. Was it destiny? Was it fate? Or was it simply the evolutionary drive to find a mate and continue the species? At the time I didn't care a jot. I just had to meet him, I had to touch him, and this is probably going to sound utterly ridiculous, I had to love him.

I can picture the scene now, as if it were yesterday: Steven, that was his name, walking towards me for the first time in faded skinny jeans, a red sweatshirt with the Cardiff University logo on the front, and battered white leather Adidas trainers that had long since seen better days. I can picture the unkept shiny black curly hair framing his angular face, and the brown doe-like eyes that penetrated my soul. I can tell you without question that love at first sight is a reality. I know it can happen, because it happened to me. It was the best of times. The happiest of times. I had never smiled so much. I had never laughed so much. Heaven really was a place on earth. Or at least that's what I thought at the time. If only it could have lasted.

We left the student union building together within ten minutes of first meeting and walked the pleasant streets of Cardiff, hand in hand, until we found a quiet bar and sat in a corner getting to know each other a little better. Steven was from Plymouth, a seaside city in Devon on the Cornish border, which regrettably, I still haven't visited. He told me he'd originally visited the Welsh capital to watch England play Wales at his beloved rugby union, and, or so he claimed, he formed an immediate bond with the place that remained unbroken. He liked the ambience, he liked the amicable people and he liked the Brains bitter ale. I think it may well have been the beer that swayed him most, although he would very probably deny that if he could. Perhaps I'm doing his memory a disservice. I don't mean to be unkind. I really wouldn't want that. He was the love of my life. Why would I?

Steven was studying for a postgraduate degree in Psychology after completing a first degree at Manchester University. He was a little older than me, a little more mature possibly. But then girls tend to grow up a lot faster than boys, wouldn't you agree? Some of them seem to remain children forever.

We began a heated, passionate, all consuming love affair that first night, and I quickly grew to love everything about him. He became my world, my soul mate.

I suspect that the more cynical amongst you may conclude that what I saw as Steven's engaging idiosyncrasies would have become irritating habits given sufficient time, but I genuinely believe that our love could have endured for an eternity given the opportunity. But, that's not the way it worked out. I can't rewrite history: not for the sake of the story, not for the sake of your sensibilities, not in the interests of my sanity. What happened, happened. I dearly wish it hadn't, but it did. I set out to tell you the uncensored truth, and that's exactly what I'm going to do.

Please give me a second or two to collect my thoughts and to wipe away my tears before I continue. These things are never easy. I've only got about two minutes before the bastards flick the switch and all becomes unwelcome darkness. I think it's probably best if I stop writing now and place the notebook under my mattress for safe keeping. I need to brush my teeth before saying goodnight to Gloria, closing my tired eyes, getting my head down, and trying to

33

dream of Steven. Whether I'll succeed, however, is debatable. I certainly wouldn't bet any money on it. He doesn't make many appearances these days. If only I could drive what happened subsequently from my mind.

Oh, there is one last thing I should tell you before bringing this session to a timely close. He was there that night. At the students' union bar, and later at the pub. I didn't know that at the time, of course. I knew nothing of his existence back then. If only it could have stayed that way. If heaven can be a place on earth, then sadly so can hell.

Goodnight for now, I'm going to give the meditation a try against my better judgement. Say a short prayer for me if you're so inclined. I'd like to think God is a far more proficient demon slayer than I could ever be.

Chapter 5

I didn't have a great night last night, to be frank. It was my own fault really. Thinking about that evil bastard just before trying to nod off to sleep is never a good idea. What was I thinking? Even thoughts of Steven were a lost cause after that. You'd think I'd have gotten used to the recurrent nightmares by now. It's been almost four long painful years and he still haunts my dreams like an omnipresent malevolent spectre hovering over me and spewing hate and destruction from every pore. He brought nothing but suffering into this world. He damaged so many lives. What on earth was wrong with the man? I could potentially tell you a bit more about him at this early stage, but I think it's probably best if I address that thorny issue at the logical time in the story. I may simply be putting off the inevitable, but there's no point in leaping ahead months at a time. Or at least that's what I'm telling myself. If you try hard enough you can justify almost anything.

There is one more thing I wanted to mention before I refocus on the past. It hasn't been all bad news here in prison world, despite my earlier observations to the contrary. Gloria's gone! I don't mean she's died, or anything awful like that. Gone isn't one of those ghastly platitudes for death that people resort to, to save each other's sensibilities. She's been moved to an open prison to prepare for her eventual release back into the world at large. That's all I meant. I'm glad I can still be happy for other people when such a response is warranted. I'm happy for her. I really am! The poor girl was dealt a poor hand from a very early age. No lucky breaks for her. No silver spoon in her mouth. She's due some good luck for once in her sad life. Perhaps some of it will rub off on me. You never know. Or have I already received my allocated share of luck for one lifetime?

I met my new cellmate this morning when one of the nicer guards brought her to what is now our cell: Sheila Davies, forty-three years old, and English or so she claims, despite the blatantly Welsh surname. I haven't presumed to ask what she's in for yet, or for how long. It's not the done thing. Prison etiquette and all that. But, my first impressions are fairly positive. We seem to have things in common, and I'm hoping we can share more than a cell. I'm not talking about anything sexual, it's men only for me I'm afraid. Women just don't do it for me, which is something of an issue here in prison world. And so, I'm not looking for sex. I'm talking about companionship: close bonds born of shared adversity, that sort of thing. I don't think that's too much to ask for, even in this hell hole. Do you think I'm being over optimistic given my circumstances? I'll let you know how things turn out when a few days have passed and I've had the opportunity to get to know her a little better. That's more than enough mindless gossip for one day. I was telling you about Steven.

Well, after that first night of unbridled passion, things went from good to better. Such things really can happen in the physical world. We became instant soul mates and spent every available moment in each other's company. You'd think such a relationship would quickly burn itself out or become as claustrophobic as my crowded cell. But it didn't, it really didn't. I'd never been so happy, I'd never experienced such contentment, and I'd never been more alive.

What did we do with our time? Is that what you're wondering? Apart from the obvious which I'll keep largely to myself. Well, we did a lot of things. We went for long walks through the parks and city streets, he introduced me to an eclectic range of books I had never heard of, let alone read, we relaxed and danced and listened to his varied music collection, and on occasions, on my insistence, to boy band musical abominations that he truly loathed. We went to the cinema once a week, whatever was on, and ate ridiculous amounts of sticky toffee popcorn that stuck to our teeth. And we attended concerts of one kind or another when we could afford it. I could go on, but I think you get the gist of it. We had a good time. No, we had great time. Oh, and we worked as well, of course. It may not have sounded like it, but we worked hard when we needed to. Steven's thesis exploring the psychological development of identical twins progressed well, and I was achieving good grades despite, or perhaps due to our love affair. I think we're at our most productive when we're happy. There really were no downsides that I can think of. That's not selective memory, honestly; life was good. It really was good. I feel blessed to have known him for as long as I did.

Within about two months of our first lightning bolt meeting Steven asked me to move into his shambolic one-bedroom Canton flat. Or at least I think he asked me. It may have come about by osmosis. Yes, now that I think about it, that's how it happened. I was spending more and more time in the flat prior to the move, and many of my student possessions had moved in long before I did. Maybe my memories are fading. Maybe they aren't as sharp as they once were: not as bright, not as big, not as loud. Maybe the pictures playing behind my eyes are blurring slightly at the edges. I very much hope that's not the case. I really don't want to lose any more of Steven than I already have. Perhaps now that I've written things down I can better hold onto what's left of him. Maybe my journal can become a form of personal insurance policy against further loss. Do you think it's possible to amplify the good memories whilst eradicating the bad along the way? Does that make any sense at all, or are you beginning to doubt my sanity? I wouldn't blame you in the slightest if you were. I wonder about it myself sometimes.

We, that's Steven and myself, had already been living together for a month or more when I eventually built up sufficient courage to tell Mum and Dad about our relationship. Actually, it was Mum I told during one of our regular Sunday evening catch up telephone conversations. She told Dad all about it later when she thought the time was right, and then let me know the following week when we spoke again. I was absolutely dreading the conversation, but to my surprise they didn't appear to disapprove as I expected they would. Not in the slightest! Not even Dad, whom I had assumed would choose to hate Steven without taking the trouble to meet, let alone get to know him first. Isn't it strange how we tend to put people into metaphorical boxes, often on the basis of wild, ill-informed assumption or prejudice. To my shame, that's what I did to Dad. Even people we know well, or at least think we know well, are subjected to our outlandish presumptions. Why do we do that? Why did I do that? I think it's probably a mechanism we humans use to make the world a simpler place. Or maybe not? If Steven was here I could ask him. He was well versed in human psychology. It's the sort of question he'd know the answer to.

On the Sunday, following my revelation, Mum and Dad invited us, that's Steven and me, to stay with them at their home for the first weekend in November. That was a turn up for the books, I can tell you. Personally, I had no qualms about going, but I feared that Steven may well have a very different take on the matter. It wouldn't have been that surprising in the circumstances, would it?

I tried to mask my astonishment, and told Mum that I'd love to come, which was true, but that I'd have to find out if Steven was free that weekend, which wasn't. I knew he was free, I just wasn't sure if he'd agree to go. I'm sure Mum must have read me like a large print book, looking back on it now, but at the time I naively believed that I'd pulled the wool over her more experienced eyes.

Steven arrived back at the flat after one of his regular three mile runs around the streets of the city and along the banks of the Taff about twenty minutes after the call. I made him a large plate of cheese and tomato on toast, smothered in copious amounts of his favoured Branston Pickle, whilst he showered away the sweat, and poured him a glass of chilled German lager from the fridge in a highly transparent attempt to solicit his agreement to the trip.

I use the word transparent advisably, because he came into the kitchen with his wiry body wrapped in a large fluffy white bath towel, sniffed the air, smiled broadly from ear to ear and said, 'What are you after?'

What could I say to that? I have to admit that I chose to resort to appealing to his basic instincts, knelt down in front of him and pulled off the towel with my pearly whites rather than plead my case. It was easier, much more effective, and a lot more fun. I'm not going to torture myself by outlining the intimate details of our lovemaking. In my restricted world of insurmountable want, this sexual dessert, that would be far too much to bear. But, suffice it to say that by the end, he would have agreed to virtually anything in the interests of securing an encore. He did attempt to wriggle out of it the next day when he'd indulged his erotic desires to the full, as men seem prone to do, but I was never going to let that happen. Not on your life! I still had a capacity for assertiveness back then. I was a lioness, a self-confident woman, not a mouse. The mouse was born later in my tale.

Twelve days later, at 5:20 p.m. on a wet and windy autumn afternoon, Steven and I were standing on platform three at Cardiff's bustling-with-life railway station, and waiting for the next train to the sprawling seaside city of Swansea, which had risen after the destruction spawned by Hitler's

Luftwaffe in World War Two. Or at least that's what Dad told me when we went shopping there for a school coat, when I was thirteen or fourteen. He was usually right about such things. I can hear him saying it now, in that supercilious, know-it-all way of his, with his glasses resting on the tip of his nose. He would have put it more succinctly than my recollections suggest, of course. He had a skill with words that, regrettably, it seems I haven't inherited. It annoyed the hell out of me at the time, like most things my parents did or said to my teenage self, but I miss him terribly every single day. He was one of life's good guys: a ray of bright sunshine in a dark foreboding world. Perhaps he's looking down on me right now and smiling. Maybe, he's encouraging me onwards with my pen and ink adversity. I'd like to think so anyway. And, so you see, I can be optimistic after all.

Steven was more nervous than I'd ever seen him. Crazy really, if you think about it. All he was going to be doing was meeting two people who were new to him. Two people who cared for me, as he did. Two ordinary, unremarkable wonderful people who'd brought me into this good and bad world of ours. And the strange thing was, I was as at least as nervous as he was, more if anything, despite my passionate but less than persuasive denials to the contrary. I kept proactively adopting a pensive expression and repeating the same predictable statement, 'I'm not nervous, Steven, really I'm not! They're my mum and dad, why would I be nervous?'

I kept repeating it, less and less convincingly, and each time he'd laugh in that infuriating sexy boyish way of his, and say something along the lines of, 'Yeah, yeah, you never were a very good liar Cynth. Who are you trying to kid?'

It made me so very cross! Unjustifiably cross. Which he seemed to find even more hilarious. What a wind up merchant! I recall it as if it were yesterday. A bit of a cliché I appreciate, but it's absolutely true. It's almost as if I could reach back in time and touch him. I really wish I could.

Mum and Dad met us at Swansea Station, in the busy heart of Wales's second city, and walked toward us as we negotiated the ticket barriers with the help of a friendly, overweight guard, who opened the disabled access gate to allow Steven and his large orange student rucksack through the more generous gap. Isn't it strange how the smallest of details can sometimes stick in our minds like ghosts from our past. They resonate and bring the people and events back to life for a time.

Dad stepped forward first and shook Steven's hand warmly, before turning away and giving me a generous hug. Mum smiled, said, 'Hello, love,' kissed me on the cheek, and then hugged us both in turn, as Dad began walking purposefully in the direction of his newly acquired Citroen ZX, which was parked in a disabled bay directly opposite the station's entrance.

He, Dad that is, opened the spacious boot to allow Steven to put the rucksack in the back, and made a throwaway humorous comment in reference to the size of our luggage. Something along the lines of, 'Are you staying for the weekend, or were you planning on moving in?' Those may not be his exact words, but they're near enough. I'm sure you get the idea. He was attempting to lighten the mood. Mum asked me about our journey whilst Dad spoke to Steven. She did that sometimes. Making conversation I guess, and I wasn't really paying attention to the men at that precise moment. Anyway, his exact words are of no real consequence. Mum and Dad were both making an effort to make a potentially stressful situation as easy as it could be. That's what I'm trying to convey in my cack-handed way. They really did make an effort to be nice. I appreciated that, and so did Steven.

We chatted and listened to seventies music, as Dad drove west down the M4, through the rolling green hills of rural Carmarthenshire, which stretched to the horizon and touched the sky in the light of the half moon, and towards the majestic Celtic coastal kingdom of Pembrokeshire. It took us another forty-five minutes to reach Tenby, or Dinbych-Y-Pysgod, as the town's known in the lyrical Welsh language. The Port Of The Fish, if you were wondering.

Dad made a quick circuit of the town to introduce Steven to its impressive medieval walls, scenic picture-postcard beaches and impressive harbour, before heading in the direction of the house. Steven observed that the place reminded him of St Ives in Cornwall, another much loved place he intended to take me, but never did. That was high praise in his eyes, the comparison with the West Country, and he was right, of course. His words of approval were entirely justified. Even my familiarity with the place hadn't dulled my appreciation of its picturesque allure. It's as pretty as a postcard. If you haven't been there you should make the pilgrimage one day. But avoid the school holidays if you can. You won't be disappointed.

If I close my eyes tight shut, and concentrate hard in the semi-isolation of my late night cell, I can picture the four of us staring at the tall angular pastel painted houses that frame the scenic harbour, through the windows of Mum and Dad's new car. But the mirage quickly fades and vanishes back into the unreachable past. The reality of what happened subsequently is all too powerful, all too dominant, and it ruthlessly drives the happy times from my troubled mind with such force that it leaves me giddy. Things can change so very quickly in our uncertain world. In the blink of an eye! If only we'd stayed in Cardiff. If only!

Oh, there is one thing I've neglected to mention or subconsciously chose to forget. Maybe it's a self-preservation thing, yes, that's very probably it. Anyway,

42

when we were sitting overlooking the harbour on that first evening back in Wales, Steven thought he recognised one of his Psychology lecturers passing alone in the driver's seat of a bright red convertible Saab with a black canvas roof. He waved, but the man didn't respond, probably due to the fact that he appeared to be staring at me. Steven wasn't one hundred percent certain of the driver's identity at the time, and it didn't really seem to matter a great deal. I gave it little if any thought, to be honest. I often sparked male interest as a young woman. I wasn't a bad looking girl in those days, before life happened, and blunted my edges. Maybe I should have taken note. Perhaps if I had, things may have worked out differently. Or maybe the story was already written, and it would have happened anyway.

Dad suggested picking up a takeaway curry before finally heading for home. I was never one to turn down the opportunity for a chicken dopiaza, and Mum and Steven seemed equally keen on the idea of readymade spicy sustenance. They could have been going with the flow in the interests of cohesion or an easy life, but that definitely wasn't my impression at the time. Dad and Steven went into the restaurant and made the order, whilst Mum and I talked about life. Mum said she liked Steven from the moment she met him. She said he had a pleasing demeanour and gentle soul, and she was right. He was a kind thoughtful boy with an appreciation of the arts, and an inclination to try and see the best in people whatever their propensities. Mum was an excellent judge of character in those long gone days. We all make assumptions on first meeting, based on appearance, mode of dress, and so on, but hers usually proved to be correct. A rare skill indeed! But, not any more sadly; these days she's suspicious of everyone, even me. Her world has become a darker more frightening place where dangers lurk in the shadows, and trust has to be earned. Not surprising, really, I suppose, in the circumstances. I've tried to help.

I've told her repeatedly that there are still good people in this world of ours despite our experiences, but her perceptions have changed, I suspect forever.

Steven held open the door for Dad to leave the takeaway first, carrying two large brown paper bags filled to the brim with curries, yellow pilau rice, deep fried onion bhajis, crisp popadoms and what would prove to be delicious complimentary hot lime chutney. What I wouldn't give for that meal now. My mouth's watering as I think of it. The prison kitchen hasn't won very many culinary plaudits as far as I'm aware. There are no Michelin star restaurants in this resort. Not surprising when you think about it. Why would they waste good food on the residents of prison world? Some might say that feeding some of us at all is more than we deserve.

I'm a little concerned that my recent lighthearted comments may have given you the impression that I'm superficial and not taking this seriously. I really wouldn't want that. I don't know why it matters to me quite so much, but, I can tell you that it does. If it were a choice of gourmet meals each and every day for the rest of my life, or one more minute with Steven, or Dad for that matter, they'd win every single time.

The four of us sat around Mum and Dad's Victorian stripped oak kitchen table to eat, drink imported German lager, and give Mum, Dad and Steven the opportunity to get to know each other a little better. Conversation was somewhat stilted at first, given the inevitable British reserve, but by the time Dad opened the sixth bottle of beer, the alcohol was oiling the conversational wheels very nicely. When Dad and Steven discovered their shared love of rugby union, their relationship was sealed. Within the hour, Mum and I were watching a mildly amusing but ultimately pointless rom-com in the lounge, whilst the men plotted an overnight trip to Twickenham to watch Wales play the old enemy England in the annual championship.

We were all up surprisingly early on the Saturday morning, probably due to the unexpected bright November sunshine flooding through the thin bedroom curtains. After generous helpings of delicious local salted bacon, free-range eggs and ground Kenco coffee, served up by Mum at her enthusiastic motherly insistence, we decided to take advantage of the unseasonal temperate temperature, and take a walk through the quiet town, around the headland, past the lifeboat station, the bandstand and St Catherine's Island, towards the majestic sweeping south beach, with its fabulous views of offshore monastic Caldey. It was a happy morning, filled with laughter, friendly chatter and smiling faces. Or at least that's how I remember it. We treated ourselves to delicious fish and chips for lunch, and sat on a bench overlooking the fishing boat harbour with its small church and accompanying beach, to savour them whilst large grey and white seagulls screeched, and soared, and swooped, and dived effortlessly to skim the waves with the beat of a majestic wing. I wonder if the gulls appreciate such glorious freedom? I like to think that they do.

We returned to the house together sometime after lunch, and spent a quiet afternoon reading newspapers, and listening to the radio. At about 3:00 p.m., Steven became somewhat restless, and asked it I minded if he went for a run. Why would I object? Can you think of a reason? It was something he did every single day, after all. It was something that defined him. Something he loved. Something he needed to do. Mum and Dad didn't see a problem with it either. If they'd thought it was ill-advised, surely they would have said so at the time.

Anyway, Steven got changed into navy shorts, a white replica England rugby union shirt that irritated the hell out of Dad, and his well-worn Adidas running shoes, before leaving the house in the direction of the town. I watched as he jogged casually down our tree-lined street, so full of youthful energy, so full of the joys of life, and I thought nothing of it at as I eventually lost sight of him and closed the front door. If I'd known then, I would have stopped him. That goes without saying. I would have called him back. Of course I would. But, as I think we've established, life's not like that. How could I possibly have known what would happen next? I couldn't. I really couldn't! Maybe we all have inescapable destinies. I think some believe that's the case.

I didn't actually begin to wonder where Steven was until almost two hours had passed. I feel guilty about that now. He usually returned from a run well within the hour. I guess I must have been distracted by the convivial company, or assumed that he was taking his time, and enjoying the unseasonable sun-drenched Pembrokeshire coast whilst he had the opportunity.

When I finally looked at the gold metal carriage clock on the mantle above the gas fire, I began to wonder if Steven had lost his way on returning to the house. He was new to the area, he didn't like asking for directions, it would be entirely understandable if he had. After putting on a pair of shoes and grabbing a jacket, I found Dad reading a fishing magazine in the small conservatory overlooking the garden at the rear of the house. Dad grinned initially, when I told him, but in fairness he reacted immediately when he saw the irritation and concern on my face.

Dad rose from his chair, pulled on a thick woolly Arran jumper, retrieved his keys from a hook in the hall, and headed to the car with me following close behind. He reversed out of the drive, preformed a rapid U-turn in the road directly outside the house, and headed for town with me acting as lookout in the front passenger seat. I can't tell you exactly why, I can't put my finger on the precise cause, but for some inexplicable reason I had an undeniable sense of foreboding. How do you explain such intuition? The sun was shining, but there was a dark, barely perceptible shadow hanging over my beautiful hometown. Don't ask me how, but I knew that something had gone horribly wrong.

I kept a close eye on both sides of the street with nervous darting eyes as Dad drove slowly around the town whilst repeatedly uttering words of reassurance. He must have thought I was overreacting. Why wouldn't he? But if he did, he was wrong. Horribly, appallingly wrong.

As we entered the esplanade, oblivious to the uninterrupted scenic view of the ocean and the monastic island beyond, a single dark wind-tossed cloud moved slowly across the sky and masked the sun, as if God were mourning humanities many failings and frailties. I unfastened my seatbelt urgently, leant forwards in my seat with my nose almost touching the windscreen, and froze statue-like, as I stared at the scene unfolding directly outside The Atlantic Hotel. The wide one-way street, lined by tall houses and imposing pastel hotels, was blocked by a stationary ambulance and two Dyfed Powys police cars with blue lights flashing. Three uniformed constables and a young paramedic were standing watching a second older paramedic who was attempting to resuscitate a young man lying on the cold tarmac. I couldn't see the boy's face, but I knew. I just knew. Life had changed in an instant. In a shake of a lamb's tail.

If recounting these events is intended to be therapeutic, it's certainly not working just yet. I could quite easily tear up my notepad and hurl my pen at the wall at this stage, to be honest. Maybe I'm at the shaking the bottle stage Mrs Martin mentioned. Maybe I'm agitating the liquid within with my emotive reminiscences. Maybe the bubbles are rising. I can't say that I'm looking forward to the whoosh when the cork finally fires out. But, on a positive note, I should get to the settling down stage soon after that. No pain no gain. Or at least that's what I've been led to believe. It would probably be easier to do what most of us girls do here, and escape reality via one illicit drug or another. Drugs are surprisingly available in prison world. But, I've made a commitment and I'm not one to give up easily. I plan to soldier on and see how things progress before resorting to a self-inflicted chemical lobotomy.

Dad parked half on and half off the pavement, and the two of us jumped from the car and slammed the doors shut with a look of trepidation on our faces. I took a step or two in the direction of the incident, but then I stopped dead in my tracks and watched along with a small crowd of gathering spectators, as the older of the two paramedics steady rhythmic hand movements slowed and then stopped altogether, as he looked up at his colleague and nodded three times as he panted for breath. Even at a distance I knew instantly that it was my Steven, despite the neck brace, despite the oxygen mask covering his lovely face. And then I noticed his hair, as if it were magnified, big, bright and sharply in focus. His beautiful black curly hair was matted with dark red congealed blood. So much blood! And his gentle doe-brown eyes appeared to be staring into space but seeing nothing at all. It was the worst moment of my short life. A terrible split-second that will be forever etched on my mind. My legs buckled and I stumbled forwards to throw up in the gutter at the side of the wide pavement on the sea side of the road. Please don't die, Steven. Please don't die.

Dad placed a supportive arm around my right shoulder, helped me upright, and handed me a paper tissue taken from his trouser pocket as we walked forwards together, staring unblinking as the two paramedics carefully rolled Steven onto his side, slid a stretcher under him, lifted him from the road and carried him towards the open rear doors of the ambulance. Please don't leave me, Steven. Please don't go.

I pulled free of Dad's urgent grip and ran forwards, as a somewhat dowdy female sergeant who must have been in her fifties, appeared from behind the ambulance and turned towards me with a concerned expression on her world-weary face. She strode towards me purposefully with both arms held wide as if in exasperation at the ghoulish onlookers, and shouted, 'Slow down little lady. Let them do their job.'

Dad caught up with me and held me tightly as I responded to her instruction, and stood just ten feet or so away and watched as the ambulance men lifted Steven into the waiting vehicle. For some reason I still don't fully comprehend, my frantic emotional appeals to accompany him on his journey to hospital, were repeatedly refused. In the end Dad took my arm and pulled me away as I became increasingly irate and the sergeant approached us for a second time.

'Do you know the young man love?'

I opened my mouth as if to speak, but then closed it again, unable to find the words.

Dad, to his credit, took control as best he could, and said something to the effect that we knew the patient, as I cried, attempted to deny reality, and desperately clutched at nonexistent straws. 'He is going to be all right, isn't he?'

'Are you a relative love?'

'I'm his girlfriend, we live together. We're going to be married.'

The officer focussed on the road for a moment or two, before slowly raising her head and meeting my pleading eyes. 'Come on love, let's take a seat in the back of the police car. We can have a chat there. Your dad can come too if you like.'

I grabbed Dad's hand, and dragged him towards the white Ford Escort parked on the other side of the road, as the Ambulance began its urgent journey towards Withybush hospital in nearby Haverfordwest. I recall reassuring myself that they were doing things quickly. The siren was blearing. The blue lights were flashing. Those had to be good things, didn't they? Maybe I was kidding myself. Maybe I was in understandable denial. Unconvincing but determined denial.

The officer opened a rear passenger-side door, waited for us to get in and closed it after us once we were safely seated in the back. She got into the front passenger seat stiffly, and turned sideways to face us before speaking again. I remember her smiling thinly and briefly before the expression left her face. 'What's your name love?'

'Cynthia, Cynthia Jones, but what about Steven? What about Steven?'

She made a quick note in her pocket book with a yellow biro, and said, 'There's no easy way to tell you this love. The young man stopped breathing about twenty minutes ago. The paramedics managed to resuscitate him, he began breathing again, but he didn't regain consciousness.'

Dad tightened his grip on my hand.

'But, b-but they're taking him to hospital, the doctors will...'

Dad turned to face me and placed a hand on each of my shoulders. 'Look Cynth, let's just follow the ambulance and talk to the doctors when we get to the hospital. He's going to the right place.'

His commonplace platitude was well intentioned and I clung to it like a limpet. I didn't say anything in response, but nodded twice. What else was there to say? What else was there to do?

Dad provided the kindly officer with our full names and contact details on being prompted, and asked if it was okay for us to make a move. As we were leaving the vehicle he turned back, swallowed hard and asked, 'Do you know what happened to the boy Sergeant?'

'Steven, his name's Steven!' Why on earth did Dad's failure to use his name upset me so very much? Maybe I was hitting out to alleviate my angst.

'I know love. I know.'

'Not as yet Mr Jones, the boy had some serious head injuries; it's likely he was hit by a car, but I don't want to jump to any conclusions. They'll tell you more at Withybush. Can you give me the name and address of the boy's parents before you head off? A telephone number would be useful.'

'I've no idea, to be honest, but Cynth…'

I can recall suddenly realising that I had absolutely no idea where Steven's parents lived, or how to contact them. I remember the realisation hitting me in the gut like a physical blow. I didn't even know their names for goodness sake. I knew Steven was from Plymouth, and that was about it. Steven was the love of my life. How could I have been so ignorant of his history? I felt I'd let him down. I loathed myself for it at the time, and it pains me even now. I tell myself that I was young and carefree, that I was living in the moment, but it seems a feeble somewhat desperate excuse for my obvious shortcomings. I took him to visit my mum and dad. He knew all about Jack. He knew so much about me, and I knew so little of him. What does that say about me? I'm not really sure, to be frank, but I don't like myself very much when I think about it now. Maybe it's best if I stop pontificating, move on, and tell you what happened next.

Dad drove a lot faster than was sensible on my insistence, and we caught up with the ambulance just beyond Kilgetty roundabout, about five miles from Tenby. I can remember having mixed feelings about the urgency with which we travelled. The ambulance negotiated the Welsh country

51

roads with surprising speed. On the one hand I was relieved that Steven would soon be in hospital with the skills of the doctors at his disposal. On the other, what was the urgency? It had to be serious.

We arrived at the hospital in a little under half an hour, and watched from the car as Steven was transferred from the ambulance and into the busy casualty department. I had never felt so utterly helpless. I was acutely, terrifyingly aware that there was absolutely nothing I could do to influence the outcome of events. Nothing, absolutely nothing!

Dad finally found a tight parking space a minute or two later, and we rushed together into reception just in time to witness Steven being rushed away on a trolley bed by a young porter seemingly covered with poor quality tattoos, and two attendant staff nurses in light blue uniforms, who appeared genuinely concerned for Steven's welfare. At least he was getting immediate attention. That's what I told myself. That was something, wasn't it? Or did it mean he was in serious danger? I felt conflicted, and very close to panic. Please don't die, Steven. Please don't die.

Dad spoke to the overtly officious middle-aged twinset and pearls woman standing behind the reception desk, but she couldn't tell him very much at all despite his best efforts. It annoyed the hell out of me at the time, but looking back I now realise that she was simply a gatekeeper with little information and even less authority. In the end, as a result of my desperate pleading, she resorted to saying, 'Take a seat, and I'll try to find someone to speak to you.' I had never felt so ridiculously grateful for being treated with basic courtesy. If she'd handed me a cheque for one million pounds, I couldn't have been more pleased.

Dad and I sat in the small WRVS cafe adjoining the waiting room, drinking unappetising excessively sweet lukewarm tea, and waited, and waited, and waited. I paced the floor, tugged at my hair, checked my watch repeatedly, and wondered why the hands were moving so very slowly. About forty minutes later a nervous young Asian doctor dressed in green theatre scrubs appeared, and spoke briefly to the reception assistant who pointed in our direction. We stood as he approached us with a sullen look on his face, that told me what he was about to say before he opened his mouth to speak.

'Take a seat, please. I need to talk to you.'

Dad grabbed my arm as the room became an impressionist blur of bland colours, and guided me towards a seat a few feet behind me. It only took the young doctor a minute or two to shatter my world. He told it like it was. What other choice was there in the circumstances? He spelt it out in clear unequivocal words that I will never forget: 'I am sorry to tell you that your partner is dead.' You see, words are important. Just ten words, and my life was devastated. Steven was dead. There was no room for hope, no room for bargaining, no room for denial and no room for pleading. A light had gone out and would never shine again.

But why? I needed answers. What happened? He was out running. Just running! How on earth had he died? A thousand unwelcome questions invaded my mind. For some reason I still can't explain, I wrote down everything the doctor said, word for word, when we arrived back at the house an hour or so later. I read it and reread it so often, that I can still recount his words without effort, like a dark poem learnt by heart for an exam.

This is what he said: 'I regret to inform you that Steven suffered a ruptured spleen as the result of a severe blow to the abdomen. We operated, but he had already lost a great deal of blood. There was nothing we could do to save him. He died on the operating table. I am very sorry for your loss.'

And that was it. It really was as simple as that. One minute he was alive, breathing, with his heart pumping and the blood surging through his veins, and the next he wasn't. He was gone. I'd lost him. Steven had left this world forever, and I would never see him in the flesh again. If there is a heaven, I know he's there. He has a gentle soul as Mum observed. Whether I join him, however, is far less certain.

Give me a moment, I need to calm myself before I write something I later regret. The last thing I want to do is offend Mrs Martin. I know she's trying her best to help me and can't work miracles. But, open the box when you're ready to deal with the contents. Really? How on earth do I keep the lid on until then? What do I do in the wee small hours when I relive the nightmare as if it were happening in real time? Surprise surprise, she didn't give me the answer to that one. Do you think she'd have an adequate answer if I asked her at my next appointment? No? I didn't think so. I feel a little better now that I've got that lot off my chest. I'm going to take a break at this point. I need some time to rest my thoughts in the interests of my mental health. To be truthful, I'm struggling. This part of my story wasn't easy to immortalise on paper. It makes it all the more real, somehow, writing it down. If that makes sense. All the more emotive, as if it all happened only yesterday. I was beginning to wonder if writing this journal was such a good idea after all, but maybe, just maybe, lifting the lid and peeping in will help me in the end. I'm not particularly optimistic by nature these days, but I'm repeatedly telling myself it will. There's a lot more to say, of course. A great deal more happened, and I will recount it all when I'm ready, I can promise you that. But now is not the time.

Chapter 6

I've learnt a little more about Sheila. Not directly from her, as she remains tight-lipped despite my repeated efforts to communicate. It's reliable information, however, sourced from a needy guard, who I've got to know pretty well over the years. She's one of those people who wants to be liked. The guard, I mean, not Sheila. I get the distinct impression that Sheila doesn't give a toss what people think about her.

  Anyway, it seems that Sheila and I haven't got that much in common after all. She's a lifer, like me, that's true. We share that unfortunate reality. Not so very different up to this point, I can picture you saying. But I like to think that the circumstances that led us here were extremely dissimilar. Sheila poisoned her mother and stepfather in an unsuccessful attempt to obtain her inheritance, as the sole beneficiary of their rather generous wills. She was hoping to spend her life living in perpetual sunshine, but instead she's sharing a concrete room with me, care of prison world and the British government. A small restricted claustrophobic box where neither of us can escape the other if we need to. And that's a problem! It's a real problem. She makes me nervous. Very nervous! She's a cold, calculated killer. Everything I did was in the heat of that moment. For good reasons. There was no planning, no calculation, no potential material gain. Do you think that makes us different, or are we two sides of the same coin? I hope that when you know more, you will empathise with my actions, and agree that people convicted of the same crime can carry varying degrees of guilt. I'll leave you to think about that whilst I continue my story.

Mum and Dad were very supportive on the evening of Steven's death: they expressed their sympathy, they asked what they could do to help, and they showed me they cared with empathetic words and repeated offers of sweet tea. They really did try their best, but in reality nothing they could have said or done would have alleviated my sorrow even to the slightest degree. I was despondent, dejected, desolate and the world was a colder, darker, lonelier place.

There was no rationale to my grief fuelled rage. I was angry with God, angry with Steven for leaving me, angry with my parents for existing, for living, angry with everyone and everything. I smashed things that mattered to them, I smashed things that mattered to me, and I said things they didn't deserve to hear, things I soon regretted, but could never take back or delete from their minds. Grief can have that effect on people. I actually said that I wished it was them who had died rather than him. What a ghastly thoughtless thing to say to people who love you. I hope they understood that my destructive actions and harsh words were the product of an acutely traumatised mind. I like to think that they did.

I retreated to my tiny childhood bedroom at some point during the evening, and wailed helplessly into my pillow until exhaustion eventually intervened, and I slept fitfully until I was awoken early the next morning by the shrill sound of the doorbell ringing. I listened with only half interest as Dad opened the door, and entered into conversation with a man whose gruff Welsh voice I didn't recognise. I was about to close my eyes again in a further attempt to escape my gloom, when I heard the man say Steven's name. It was as if a bolt of electricity were surging through my body. Why was a stranger talking about my love?

I leapt from bed, quickly pulled on a pair of old Wrangler blue jeans and a white cotton tee-shirt, and hurried downstairs on my bare feet, two or three steps at a time, just as two men were following Dad into the lounge. Dad was inviting them to sit and offering tea or coffee in his usual convivial manner when I rushed into the room.

This is a critical part of my story, and I think it's probably advisable if I outline who said what and to whom, as best I can, in the style of a novel, rather than attempt to select what I consider important, and potentially inappropriately prioritise some facts above others.

Dad looked at me with a forlorn expression on his face as I walked into the lounge and said, 'Good morning love, these two gentlemen are from the local police.'

I ignored Dad's well-intentioned greeting, and stared at the older of the two officers, a disheveled looking individual of fifty-something, wearing an aged Harris Tweed jacket, stained tie and brown slip on shoes that were urgently in need of polish. Despite everything, he had an easy air of authority about him, and I correctly surmised that he was the senior of the two men.

He met my gaze, rose to his feet, held out a hand in friendly greeting, and said, 'You must be Cynthia, I'm Detective Inspector Gravel, local CID, I'm here to talk to you about Steven's death.'

We shook hands and sat, whilst Dad called to Mum, who had retreated to the kitchen, requesting four coffees.

My mind was racing, my head was pounding, and I was desperate for answers. 'Do you know how the accident happened Inspector?'

DI Gravel scratched his deeply lined forehead, and adopted a reflective expression, which suggested to me that he was choosing his words carefully. 'We aren't entirely sure what we're dealing with as yet. The investigation is ongoing, to use the jargon. This may seem a strange question, but did Steven have any enemies that you know of?'

Enemies? Why on earth was he talking about enemies? Surely it was an accident. It had to be an accident. I moved to the very edge of my seat. 'No, no, of course not. He was a student. Just a student! Everyone liked him. Why would anyone want to hurt him?'

I must have sounded more than a little irate, because the younger man, who I later discovered was Detective Sergeant Clive Rankin, smiled thinly, and said, 'We're just covering all the bases love. There are some unusual circumstances surrounding the boy's death. You do want us to get this right, don't you?'

I felt like screaming, I felt like stomping around the room like a petulant two-year-old child, and tears of angry frustration welled in my eyes and ran down my face. I tried to control myself, but my grief got the better of me and I shouted, 'Yes, yes, of course I do! Why wouldn't I? What the fuck are you talking about?'

Mum appeared from the kitchen carrying a silver plated tray of coffees and a plate of dark chocolate digestive biscuits reserved for visitors. She had a look of genuine shock on her face, and I remember thinking that she looked suddenly older. Extreme stress can sometimes do that. One of the women here literally went grey overnight when told her son had died after a late night bar brawl. I don't think I would have believed it had I not seen it with my own eyes.

Anyway, Mum offered the refreshments to the two officers, and glared at Dad, imploring him to say or do something to alleviate the obvious tension.

Dad stood, approached my seat, placed a supportive hand on my shoulder and patted my back gently. 'What's the answer to my daughter's question Inspector? She deserves to know the truth.'

I could have hugged him! But I just sat and stared at the inspector, waiting for his response.

DI Gravel cleared his throat, took a gulp of coffee, wiped the milky moustache from his top lip with an already grubby sleeve, and said, 'Steven was hit by a vehicle. I say vehicle because we don't know what type it was as yet. There's no cameras in the area, and up to this point no witnesses have been identified. The driver, whoever he or she was, didn't call an ambulance or the police. We know from the severity of Steven's injuries that he was hit at speed. He was obviously very badly hurt. It was dry, there was excellent visibility, the esplanade is a one-way street and there were no skid marks left on the tarmac, which strongly suggests the driver made no effort to slow down before hitting him.'

I shook my head incredulously. 'What? Why would anyone do that?'

'It's early days Cynthia, enquiries are ongoing.'

'I know Tenby's quiet at this time of year, but somebody must have seen something, surely?'

The inspector drained his mug. 'Either the driver was lucky, or they chose their moment carefully. One of our young constables patrolled the street at just after three. He didn't see Steven at any point. A local man, walking his dog found Steven lying at the side of the road directly outside The Atlantic Hotel, and called for an ambulance immediately. Where were you at that time?'

Dad tightened his grip on my shoulder. 'What the hell is this Inspector? Are we suspects now? That's absolutely ridiculous!'

'We've got to cover all the bases Mr Jones. There are things I have to ask you. The quicker we do this, the quicker I get answers, the quicker we can leave you in peace and get on with the investigation.'

'She was with me all afternoon. She was with me! Is that good enough for you? Cynthia became concerned that Steven was out running for longer than usual, and thought he may have got lost somewhere in the town. It was his first time in this part of the world. We drove around until… well, you know the rest.'

'Spell it out for me Mr Jones.'

'I turned right onto the esplanade and we saw the ambulance. What more do you need to know?'

'And you'd be happy to make a written statement to that effect?'

Dad looked increasingly frustrated,'Yes, of course, anything that helps.'

'Then you won't have any objections to us taking a look at your car?'

I could see by the expression on Dad's face that he was as irritated by the line of questioning as I was. He patted my back again in demonstration of his ongoing support, stood, walked towards the hall, and said, 'I'll get the keys,' without hesitation.

The police didn't find anything when they looked at the car. But, then you already knew that. Of course you did. There was nothing to find. Dad came back into the house alone after a few minutes, closed the front door behind him, and joined Mum and myself in the lounge. He took a deep breath, sucking the air deep into his lungs. I could see the strain of events on his face, and he made a show of rubbing his eyes, saying that a wayward lash had scratched his conjunctiva. I had never seen him cry before and I never did again.

'What else did the police say Dad?'

'Give me a second, I'm just popping to the toilet.'

He returned a couple of minutes later, looking a little fresher. I think he'd splashed cold water on his face because his retreating fringe was damp. I remember being unjustifiably angry with him at the time. Anyone who hasn't experienced the extremes of emotion that surround the death of a loved one may find that surprising. Grief, as I discovered, can affect us in such diverse ways. I can say that

60

with certainty. I've been there, seen it, done it, got the tee-shirt. I felt that mourning Steven's passing was my prerogative and mine alone. Looking back now, I realise that Dad was very probably feeling my pain, and reacting to that. It was empathy as opposed to self-indulgence. I was wrong about that as well. Do you recognise a theme?

'So what did they say Dad?'

He slumped in his chair with the persona of a much older man, blinked repeatedly, and blew his nose noisily into a white cotton hankie before responding. 'They've contacted the university for Steven's parents' contact details. Devon and Cornwall police will be giving them the bad news.'

'Today?'

'Yeah, I've asked DI Gravel to pass on our telephone number.'

'Good, but…'

'What's worrying you love?'

I told him there was nothing, but that was far from the truth. If Steven hadn't met me, if he hadn't loved me, he wouldn't have died. I think we often look for someone to blame for the catastrophes that touch our fragile existence. If I blamed myself, why shouldn't Steven's parents do likewise?

Dad kept staring at me, but suddenly looked away. Mum made us another comforting hot drink, handed us our mugs, and stood directly in front him with her hands on her hips. 'What is it Gareth? There's something bothering you.'

Dad looked increasingly uneasy, averting his eyes and shifting uneasily in his seat, but Mum wasn't going to let him avoid her question that easily. 'Come on Gareth. I know there's something! Spit it out.'

Mum wasn't usually that assertive, but It was hardly surprising really. She was under pressure like the rest of us. Dad nodded, and repeated that he'd asked DI Gravel to pass on our contact details.

'Come on Gareth, there's something you're not telling us.'

Dad's face appeared to visibly crumple, and the tension was almost palpable.

'Gareth?'

'There's going to be a postmortem. It's unavoidable in the circumstances. And an inquest as well. There'll be an inquest as soon as the coroner receives the pathologist's report. I'm sorry Cynthia, you had to know the truth. It's better you hear it from me than somebody else.'

I recollect thinking that the world had gone completely mad. What if it wasn't an accident? Who would want to kill my Steven? Run him over in the street, as if his life were worthless. How was I supposed to accept that he was lying in a morgue? How was I supposed to accept that... Well you know the rest. Things were changing too quickly, much too quickly. I found myself wondering if life could get any worse. Well, believe it or not, I later learnt that it could. It really could.

Chapter 7

It's been a truly momentous day here in prison world. I received a letter from Jack first thing this morning, and I had a few minutes to read it after slopping out and taking a communal shower with some of the other women. What I wouldn't give for some privacy. Nobody can stop me dreaming.

Anyway, back to the letter. One of the older guards passed it to me through the bars at about sixish. I couldn't quite believe my luck at first, but there it was in my grubby little hand. It had been opened, of course. All our letters are opened before we receive them. It's one of the many rules that I theoretically understand the need for, but that drives me to distraction nonetheless. Does that make any sense in the world beyond the bars? Bureaucracy, red tape, I'm sure you know the sort of thing I'm talking about.

I recognised Jack's terrible scribbled handwriting immediately, and pulled the letter from its thin envelope with such urgency that I very nearly dropped it in the toilet bucket. It missed by just a fraction of an inch and looked up at me asking to be read. I picked it off the cold concrete floor with trembling fingers, and clutched it tightly, as if my very life depended on it. And in a round about way it did. Occasional contact with loved ones takes on an immeasurable importance in prison world. Support networks are essential for psychological, and if I'm honest, physical survival. I think most of the women here suffer depression from time to time, sometimes with tragic results.

And back to the letter. I must try to enjoy the positives when I can… I scrambled onto my recently acquired lower bunk, ignored Sheila's crude mumbled obscenities, and focussed on the cheap white writing paper held out in front of me to accommodate my deteriorating eyesight. I read and reread the first paragraph three of four times, before it finally sank in. Jack, my previously wayward brother, was conforming to tradition. Jack and Marie were engaged to be married. How about that! I just wish Dad could have witnessed Jack's metamorphosis. Maybe it would have helped heal his broken heart. I like to think it would. But, there I go again, trying to rewrite the past. Dad's dead, I'm partly responsible and no amount of self-indulgent pontification on my part is going to change that painful reality. Maybe somewhere in infinity there's a parallel universe where Jack didn't discover pot, and where Steven didn't die. Perhaps in that alternative world Mum and Dad will live happily into old age. I'd really like to think so anyway.

Jack and Marie are to be married in a presbyterian church in the Californian summer sunshine. Life can be so utterly unpredictable for good or bad. He says he wishes I could be there. I wish I could be there! That's one of the worst things about prison world: the earth keeps turning, your loved ones' lives move on, but you can't be a part of it, not really, not in any meaningful way. You can't share in their merrymaking, or offer succour at times of crisis. I see Mum and my girls once a month at best and Jack not at all.

He's promised to send me photographs of the wedding, and I'm grateful for that. He's well intentioned, but in a strange way, I'm dreading viewing them. Does that seem ridiculous to you outside the walls? I think it probably would have to my pre-incarcerated self. I'll take pleasure in my brother's celebration of love and commitment. Truly I will. But even now I know it will be a sweet sorrow.

Oh, there is one more thing I wanted to mention before continuing with my story… I've made a formal written request to the governor for a cell of my own. Sharing with

Gloria was sometimes tedious, but generally tolerable. She was a nice enough girl. Cohabiting with Sheila, however, is a little different. I have learnt that not every female prisoner is a victim of circumstance. Some are evil bastards, just like he was. Sheila has little if any empathy for anyone, whatever their circumstances. Except for herself, that is. She feels her own distress with an obvious burning intensity. Such a basic lack of humanity is not solely the preserve of men, as I had previously surmised. My naivety surprises even me at times.

Lifers shouldn't have to share a cell. That's what the official guidance says, apparently. Or at least I believe it does. Someone said it once, but I haven't actually read it for myself. I've appealed on that basis, rather than cite Sheila's objectionable personality traits. I hate to think what would happen if she knew what I truly thought of her. I find her utterly repugnant. Repugnant and frightening! She has an unequivocal air of menace about her. Like he had. She's one of life's predators. I've seen evil up close and personal in the past. There's a coldness about her that's hauntingly familiar. If she recognises my weakness, if I let my mask slip even for a moment in her company, I fear she may feed on my fragile emotions like a vulture feeds on rotting flesh. Such a happy thought. It seems such things define me.

I'm very much hoping for a positive response to my request, but I won't hold my breath. This place is horribly overcrowded. The prison authorities aren't going to concede any time soon, and that's if they do at all. I'm probably clutching at straws and deceiving myself that there's any hope at all. There just aren't the cells available, even if they wanted to help, which seems unlikely in itself. What on earth was I thinking? Like it or not, I'm stuck with the woman, and she's stuck with me. I'll add it to the ever growing list of the unpleasant inconveniences that dominate my increasingly unpleasant life here.

I think I've said all there is to say regarding my recently acquired accommodation crisis. I can't think of anything else of significance for now. I'm sure you don't want to hear about the horrendous smell of human waste and desperation, or the incessant ear splitting noise that pervades every nook and cranny of this place. And so it's back to my enforced reminiscences. Tenby, beautiful Tenby, here we come again…

Steven's father phoned and spoke to Dad on the evening after the two police officers' visit to our home. Dad said that Steven senior sounded incredulous that his son had died in such circumstances, in a seaside town he'd heard of at sometime or other, but never visited. Steven's mum and dad planned to take the train from Plymouth to Tenby later in the day. They needed to see where it happened for themselves. They needed to be nearer to their son. I thought it macabre at the time, but what was I thinking? Why wouldn't they want to see their child?

Dad invited Steven senior and Moira, Steven's mother, to stay at our home, but to my relief, he declined. I think the expectation of social interaction with people who, at the end of the day were strangers, would have placed an intolerable burden on all of us despite our shared adversity. I think they must have felt much the same way, because he wouldn't be persuaded despite Dad's best efforts. They'd booked a room in The Atlantic Hotel with its uninterrupted view of the deep ocean. In any other circumstances I'm certain they'd have had a marvellous time. But, of course, circumstances are everything. I pictured Steven's bruised and battered body laying on the cold hard tarmac, and hoped the authorities had washed away his blood. I didn't want them to see it. I prayed they wouldn't see it.

Steven senior phoned our home at about 4:00 p.m. the following day, to say they'd arrived at their hotel about half an hour prior to his call. I answered the phone, but to my relief he asked to speak to Dad, rather than engage in conversation with me. I think that was best for both of us at that point. After the usual inane pleasantries regarding the journey, Dad arranged to collect the couple at 7:00 p.m. that evening for a welcome meal at our modest home. Mum spent the next two hours or more in a whirl of activity, preparing delicious fresh local lamb for us all, whilst I followed her instructions and hoovered, wiped and dusted the entire house in preparation for their eventual arrival later that evening. I recall thinking it was utterly pointless initially, but keeping busy was surprisingly therapeutic in the short term. I'm not saying it changed anything, because of course it didn't, but it provided a degree of welcome distraction for a time. There was less time to think, less time to cry and less time to mourn.

Mum sent me upstairs to change at about 6:40 p.m., and disappeared into the ground-floor bathroom to wash and tidy her already immaculate permed hair. I understood that she wanted to make a good impression, because it mattered to me as well. I wanted Steven's parents to like me. I wanted them to think he'd made a good choice. I wanted them to understand that I truly loved their son.

I heard Dad's car pull up on the drive at about half an hour later. I peeped out from behind the unstylish but functional net curtains in the lounge whilst Mum switched the kettle on, and saw a visually unremarkable couple in their forties getting out of the car and following Dad towards the front door. There was an unmistakable sadness about them that resonated with me, and caused me to look away urgently as the intensity of our shared grief suddenly became too much for me to bear.

I heard Dad turn the key in the lock, open the door, and invite Steven's parents into our private world. I was still standing by the curtains, trying to work out what to do or say on our first meeting when Mum suddenly appeared from the kitchen, touched my hand gently with hers, and said, 'Come on love, let's say hello.' Simple uncomplicated words that I needed to hear.

I was disproportionately pleased by her kindness and encouragement, and took her hand in mine and squeezed it between my fingers, before meeting Steven's parents in the hall where Dad was taking their winter coats and hanging them on the Victorian hall stand.

I stared at each of them in turn, wanting to say something meaningful, but failing to find the words. Steven's lovely mum stepped forward, and threw her arms around me, as if greeting a long lost friend or much loved prodigal daughter. She was crying uncontrollably, and I felt her warm tears on my face and neck. We clung on to each other as if for dear life, and sobbed together. Deep all-consuming sobs that caused our chests to heave as we struggled for breath. I don't know exactly how long we stood there in each other's arms, but I recall a powerful sense of affinity born of all-consuming grief. She was mourning as I was, and our shared empathy appeared to validate my crushing loss in some indefinable way. We shared an immediate bond that would prove to endure. She still keeps in touch occasionally. These days not as often as she once did, to be honest. But, I still receive a card at Christmas, and a sympathetic heartfelt letter on the anniversary of Steven's untimely death each and every year. It seems she can't escape the past any more than I can.

Do you think I'm in danger of over sentimentalising the events of that evening? I've concluded that those rare moments in life, when we are truly touched by another's kindheartedness, or feel completely understood as individuals, resonate with us throughout our lives, particularly at times of intense emotional reflection or adversity. But, maybe I'm overcomplicating this and our relationship was at least in part self-serving, rather than entirely altruistic. Let me know what you think if you get the chance. Do we humans do anything at all for purely unselfish reasons? Am I sounding more than a little world-weary? A tad cynical? Probably! Please ignore my negativity. It's all too easy to see the worst in people in this hellhole. Prison world does that to a girl. It's an unavoidable consequence of incarceration.

Mum and Dad made an admirable effort to make what was always going to be an excruciating evening as bearable as possible. Mum ushered us all from the hall into our comfortably furnished family lounge, and sat each of us in our designated places before hurrying into the kitchen and quickly reappearing, balancing five white bone china cups of coffee and a large plate of assorted biscuits on that glittering silver plated tray I've already mentioned.

We all sat sipping our drinks, nervously nibbling on biscuits, and engaging in the usual glum small talk that tends to dominate such painfully emotive situations. Dad asked about their train journey from the West Country, Mum asked about their hotel, and repeatedly offered further refreshments they clearly didn't want but felt compelled to accept. Anything to avoid another painful silence I suppose, and I certainly don't blame them for that. I think I sat in virtual silence struggling with my thoughts and searching for something worth saying. And then, after about forty minutes or so, Dad actually said something meaningful. Something that went to the very heart of the matter, and I silently sang his praises to the rafters. He placed his cup and saucer carefully on a coaster on Mum's treasured teak veneered G Plan coffee table, looked at each of Steven's parents in turn, meeting their eyes, and said, 'I am so very sorry for your loss. Steven was a wonderful boy.'

Steven's dad swallowed hard, and blinked repeatedly as his eyes filled with salty tears. Moira took a white paper handkerchief from her handbag, and dabbed at her red bloodshot eyes. Dad looked concerned at their initial reaction, but he visibly relaxed when the fleeting hint of a smile momentarily played across Moira's face, and she said, 'Thank you so much Gareth. It was good to hear you say our son's name.'

Yes, words really can matter. They certainly did that night. We spent the next hour or more talking about Steven. His mum and dad told us cherished stories from his childhood, about his sporting triumphs, academic achievements, and future ambitions. And I told them how much I loved him, and about our happy life together in Wales's wonderful capital city before his death.

I think that's enough of wallowing in the past for now. I'm tired, and just can't face writing about the funeral at the moment. It was a major turning point in the journey that is my troubled life, and I want to do the memories justice. I'm going to put down my pen and paper, say goodnight to Sheila, who may or mayn't grunt in response, close my tired eyes, and try to fly away to a happier far-off place in my dreams. Fly away Cynthia. Fly away like that glorious bird of yours and find happiness, however fleeting.

Chapter 8

I haven't put pen to paper for a couple of days, not by choice, but due to uncontrollable circumstance. Our esteemed governor: Mr George Thompson OBE, no less, deemed to grant me a week in solitary confinement. What a generous man! It was intended as a punishment, naturally, but, to be honest, I'm rather enjoying the imposed isolation. It's only day three with four to go, but so far so good. How come I'm allowed to write again? Is that what you're wondering? It is unusual, I'll grant you that. But, apparently, the circumstances are exceptional. Or at least that's what Mrs Martin argued on my behalf. Continuing my journal is absolutely essential to my effective long term rehabilitation, apparently. I'll forgo my weekly counselling session, it seems she capitulated on that small matter in the interests of professional harmony, but when she appeared at my cell door early on Tuesday afternoon with my pen and paper in hand, there was an undoubted air of the victor about her. She had a definite skip in her step. Three cheers for Mrs Martin… hip, hip, hooray and so on!

Why do I find myself in solitary in the first place? It's a fair question that deserves an honest answer. I was seriously considering glossing over the reason for a time, but after an hour or two's soul searching, I eventually decided to come clean. If I started censoring my writing, what would be the point of continuing? That's a rhetorical question by the way. Honesty is everything. I would make one plea, however, before throwing myself on your mercy. I implore you to take my exceptional circumstances into consideration when judging my actions. Picture the worst of childhood bullying: the vilification of weakness or dissimilarity, and then magnify it a hundred fold in your mind. Picture it and inhabit that reality. That may give you a flavour of how unpleasant life here can become for those who choose not to, or are unable to stand their ground when such a response is demanded. It's survival of the fittest in prison world. Sink or swim. Do or die. I don't think that's over dramatising the case.

Right! I've set the scene as best I can. My statement of mitigation is at an end, for what it's worth. And so I'll tell you what happened in my own words, no holds barred as I said previously.

At about 8:15 p.m. on Thursday evening I was lying on my bottom bunk trying to relax when Sheila leant down from above with her greasy brown hair dangling around her face: angry, sullen and hating everything and everyone. She demanded some toothpaste. Not in the spirit of mutual sharing; she didn't ask without expectation as Gloria would have. She demanded in that hateful way of hers: 'Where's your fucking toothpaste bitch?' Bitch! Now that's a label I detest with a blazing intensity. Bitch! It resonates from the past like no other word. I've heard that withering label a thousand times or more and hoped never to again.

I lay there unmoving at first, frozen on the unforgiving mattress by my fear and indecision, hoping the moment would pass quickly. I tried to placate her, I tried to reason with the unreasonable, I tried to diffuse the tension as best I could. And it's something I'm good at. I've had a great deal of practice, after all. But she just smiled sardonically, and fed on my weakness as he used to in that sadistic patronising way of his, and I hated her for it. I really hated her for it.

Sheila lowered herself to the grey floor with an audible manufactured sigh, and stared at me with unblinking eyes, relishing her perceived dominance. I looked down, avoiding her gleeful gaze, expecting the situation to deteriorate at any second but desperately hoping it wouldn't. And it did, it really did in an explosion of hostility. She bent forwards at

72

the waist, and reached towards me with her filthy jagged finger nails, clutching the front of my delicate powder-blue blouse six inches or so below its lace collar. I was startled, and urgently pulled away towards the cell wall at the very edge of my mattress, but, she tightened her steely grip with those bony hands of hers and dragged me off the bunk and onto the cold hard floor, which I hit with a painful dull thud as a stab of pain exploded in my coccyx. She suddenly released her grip, stood upright and loomed over me: menacing, threatening, spiteful, triumphant. 'Toothpaste bitch! Now!'

I decided when I first arrived in prison world never to be a victim again if there was anything at all I could do to prevent it. A personal promise I fully intended to keep to the very best of my ability. I'd already been victim enough for one lifetime. I did anything and everything to please that man. The monster! I strove to meet his every whim to the umpteenth degree. But nothing worked. Nothing helped. Nothing was ever good enough. He never failed to identify my failings, and punish them, again and again and again. Never again! His profile appeared before me as Sheila's face distorted and took on his features in my mind's eye. Not this time Cynthia, there'd be no running, not this time.

I grabbed her lower leg as she kicked out at me, lifted it sharply, causing her to lose balance, stumble backwards, and collide with the wall directly behind her. I utilised the bed frame to lift myself unsteadily to my feet: very close to panic, sweating, and with tears running down my face, as her face took on an animalistic snarl of the type I'd witnessed many times before. I took a step or two backwards on unsteady legs, searching for the right words, desperate to appease her, with both hands held out in front of me in cautionary acknowledgement of her capacity for evil. 'There's no need for this Sheila! Surely we can talk like reasonable people. There's no need for violence.'

And then she stopped, rather than hurl herself at me as I'd expected. I thought for a glorious irrational second or two that reason had prevailed. But then she stared at me with a dismissive sneer, turned and looked pointedly at my photos proudly displayed on the cell wall next to the bunk, reached out with those filthy fingers of hers, peeled off my favourite photo of my beautiful daughters, and tore it in two pieces. She held it out in front of her at arm's length, and tore it slowly and deliberately, obviously savouring the moment. The cow, the absolute cow, how dare she do such a thing.

As I stood, incredulous, horrified, with both distress and anger rising within me, she threw the pieces to the floor, cleared her throat, spat on them, and ground them into the concrete with the sole of her right shoe.

And then it happened. I lost control, leapt forwards and bit her! I lunged at her with all the speed and power I could muster, sank my front teeth deep into her right tricep, and worried at the flesh like a dog gnawing at a favourite bone. I didn't enjoy it, I want to make that perfectly clear. I didn't like the salty taste of her blood in my mouth, or the metallic stink of it in my nostrils. It was a far from pleasant experience. The assault was born of enforced necessity, rather than pleasure, an instinctive reaction to extreme adversity. Winning or losing can be the difference between life and death in this dog eat dog world of ours. I actually considered snapping at her face and biting her nose, very briefly. What an awful thought! But, I stopped myself. I took control and I'm proud of myself for that. None of us truly know what we're capable of, until faced with life's extremes. I found that out on the day that led me here. It's fight or flight, and flight isn't always possible. Don't fight unless you have to, but if you have to, win, that's my advice born of experience. Where do you run to when you're locked in a cell with your antagonist or in a cellar deep below your home? And so please don't be too quick to judge. If anyone had told my student self what I would later do, I would have found it impossible to believe. You may learn similar painful lessons yourself, one fine day. That's assuming you haven't already, of course.

Sheila required twenty-two stitches, or at least that's what I've been told by one of the long-serving guards who actually seemed quite chuffed by what I'd done. I'm expecting a visit from the local police sometime soon, but that doesn't really concern me a great deal, to be honest. What's the worst they can do? I'm already locked up here, that's not going to change. And Sheila's not going to provide a statement or press charges or anything as ill-advised as that. It's not the done thing in prison world. Being a grass is considered the lowest of the low, and so she'll keep her filthy mouth well and truly shut for fear of punishment by the mob. Of that I'm entirely confident. I'll have to watch my back for a while, of course, but I don't think she'll be keeping my top bunk, borrowing my toothpaste or tearing up any more of my treasured photos anytime soon. Well, you wouldn't, would you? The mouse has turned and become a roaring lioness again.

That's it, enough said, I'm going to leave it there and beg your mercy. I've got nothing more to say on the matter. If the police do turn up, I may provide you with a brief update. But don't hold your breath on my account. They're busy people. It may well be a very long wait. I think I'm ready to write about Steven's funeral now that I've got that unpleasantness out of the way, and so I very much hope that you're ready to read on. I've given it a great deal of thought, and I need you to understand just how pivotal the events of that day were to the incessant downward spiral of my life that followed. It was a swirling whirlpool dragging me down, lower, lower, lower: a black hole from which I could never hope to escape. But, of course, I didn't know that at the time. I was focussed on my loss, and nothing more. That terrible realisation would come much later in my tale.

Steven's mum and dad decided to hold the funeral service at the Pembrokeshire crematorium in the green rolling hills near the small pleasant town of Narberth, just a few miles from our home, rather than transport his body back to the West Country of his birth. He'd told them he had grown to love Wales, and so, it seemed appropriate. I was grateful for their decision.

It was early December by the time the legalities related to a suspicious death were finally concluded, and the surprisingly temperate weather of the previous month had been replaced by freezing Siberian temperatures and a dusting of scenic snow that covered the countryside in a blanket of white, creating a beautiful chocolate box vista that seemed at odds with the unrelenting solemnity of the day. The circle of life can be very hard to accept when you're on the receiving end. Anyone who has faced the death of a loved one will no doubt know exactly what I'm talking about. I wouldn't wish it on my worst enemy.

We joined Steven's mum, dad, younger sister, maternal and paternal grandparents at their hotel at about 10:30 a.m. on the morning of the funeral. The grief was almost palpable as we stood together in a black clad depressed huddle on the icy seafront pavement, as a gleaming black Zephyr Hearse and a second funeral car I couldn't identify arrived to transport the immediate family to the crematorium. I clearly recall that my first sight of Steven's light oak coffin adorned with polished brass handles and vibrant green and red winter wreaths made a profound emotional impact on me, as if I were being told of his untimely death for the first awful heartbreaking time. He was so very young, as was I, and death up close was extremely hard to bear.

I elected to accompany Mum and Dad on the short journey to the crematorium, after declining Steven senior's kind offer for me to travel in the relatives' car. I made an excuse to the effect that the car was already full, but in reality I needed the constant support of my parents, and particularly my lovely mum, to navigate the entire dreadful experience.

There were about twenty people in the crematorium when I entered the room and sat at the front. Several of Steven's university friends had made the trip from Cardiff and I was grateful for that. He'd have wanted them there. I'm certain of that much. One suggested I join them that evening for a drink to honour Steven's memory but I politely declined. They were fond of him, I loved him dearly, and that's a significant difference. It may seem harsh, but I didn't want or need their company.

The service, which only lasted about half an hour or so, passed surprisingly quickly with the usual inevitable mix of hymns, prayers, eulogies and tears, culminating in the coffin slowly disappearing through a red velvet curtain on automated rollers to the melodic sound of A Whiter Shade Of Pale, one of Steven's favourite songs. Dad squeezed my hand as Steven made his final journey in this material world of ours, and reminded me that his spirit had long since moved on to a better place. I welcomed his well-intentioned words of reassurance at the time, and I still find comfort in the thought of an omnipotent creative life force and an afterlife to come. It has to be better than this one. I like to think that one day I'll see Steven again, despite my conviction, and that we'll continue where we left off. I think I hear his voice sometimes, whispering words of encouragement and timeless love in my ear. I've sought his advice more than once, before choosing my words carefully and committing them to paper for posterity. Does that sound ridiculous to you? I'm in no doubt that some of you will think so. I guess that's inevitable, but some will understand

77

and sympathise. Maybe it is absurd, or maybe it isn't. At the end of the day we live on a tiny rock travelling through space with apparent infinity stretching in every conceivable direction. How much do we really know of reality? If we were as clever as we like to think we are, encyclopaedias wouldn't have to be constantly revised, would they.

What on earth is wrong with me? I was telling you about the funeral before delving off in another direction. I really need to control my thoughts and focus if I'm to stay on track and get this finished within a reasonable timescale.

As I was leaving the service, and receiving various well-meaning words of regret from friends and relatives, a man I didn't know approached me. His slightly greying sleek black hair, neatly trimmed sideburns, and gun-metal aviator glasses seemed strangely familiar somehow, but I couldn't think why at the time. It was one of those slightly awkward moments when the other person clearly knows you, but you just can't place them however hard you try. I'm sure you know what I mean.

Anyway, he smiled engagingly, met my inquisitive gaze with piercing steel-blue eyes moist with tears, and said, 'Please forgive my impertinence.' He reached out a hand to shake mine gently, holding it for just a fraction of a second longer than was comfortable, and continued, speaking in a soft erudite south of England accent that led me to conclude that he was privately educated. Isn't it strange the things that cross our troubled minds at times of stress. Why on earth would I consider such inconsequences at such a moment? I can't begin to explain it.

There I go again. I should simply have told you what he said and left it at that, rather than picturing the scene and magnifying it in my mind. I'll try and be more succinct, but

I can't promise success. And maybe it doesn't matter anyway, given the primary purpose of my discourse. Back to the story. For goodness sake, girl, get back to the story…

As I was saying a second or two ago, he smiled, and then said, 'My name is Dr David Galbraith, I had the privilege of being one of Steven's Psychology lecturers. He was a truly wonderful student, and more to the point, a wonderful person. But I don't need to tell you that. I am so very sorry for your tragic loss. If there is anything I can do to help facilitate your return to student life, please don't hesitate to let me know.' He placed a comforting hand on my right shoulder and smiled engagingly again, before turning and walking away.

I can remember thinking on first impression that he was a rather pleasant man, good looking in a mature sort of way, and empathetic, those had to be good things, but his use of the past tense when referring to Steven, distressed and unjustifiably angered me: 'Steven was a wonderful student. Steven was a wonderful person.' Was, was, was! Why did the word hit me so very hard? I'd just sat through his funeral. I'd stared at his coffin for almost forty toxic minutes, picturing him lying still, stiff and cold in his dark white satin lined box. Why did a single word drive reality home so effectively when death was all around me?

I understand that the doctor's offer of assistance was akin to something people say in such unfortunate circumstances, with absolutely no intention whatsoever of honouring their overture. But, and I can say this with absolute certainty, I gained the distinct impression that he was entirely sincere. I still can't identify any single factor that gave me that unlikely impression, but sympathy and understanding appeared to ooze from his every pore. He was a complete stranger to me, and yet I felt instinctively that my well-being mattered to him despite our unfamiliarity. I instantly believed he was one of those rare people who put the feelings of others ahead of their own. I fully appreciate that that's a peculiar statement to make, particularly when he said so very little on our first meeting, but it's undoubtedly true. I would happily swear to that on oath in any court in the land. Maybe I was overemotional at the time. Maybe I valued his status as Steven's mentor. Maybe I was looking for comfort in what seemed a cruel world. But, whatever the reason, I welcomed his kind words, and thought he was the sort of man I would like as a friend despite the glaring age gap between us. First impressions count. They're often wrong, of course. But, they count nonetheless. Steven once told me that psychological research suggests we take one-tenth of a second to form a first impression. That seems ridiculous when I think about it now. We reach them all too quickly to simplify our complex world. If only I'd taken more time.

Chapter 9

Dad sat me down and spoke to me regarding my potential return to university on the morning after the funeral. He said, 'Life has to go on,' and argued passionately that Steven wouldn't want me to give up my studies as a result of his leaving this world. Tired clichés I know, but he meant well, and it probably needed saying. If your loved ones can't tell you what you need to hear, who can? I knew that Dad was correct on both counts, although I still think he would have been well advised to delay speaking to me for a few more days. It was far too soon for me to take what he said on board.

I fully appreciated that returning to Cardiff would have been the sensible thing to do, but I just couldn't bring myself to do it, or at least not so very soon. After half an hour or more of talking and drinking seemingly endless mugs of sweet and black instant coffee, we reached a reluctant compromise that we could both live with. I would resume my studies sometime after the Christmas holiday. To be honest the idea terrified me. Cardiff without Steven's company wouldn't be the happy place it had so recently been. His ghost would inevitably inhabit everywhere I went. I could all too easily have stayed at home indefinitely and hidden from the world. But, where would that have got me? Life had to go on.

Our preparations for Christmas were unusually muted, which I guess was inevitable given the circumstances. Mum and Dad made a half-hearted effort to go through the motions of turkey and all the trimmings, but what with my mourning and the painful reminders of Jack's absence brought into sharp focus at a time of intended family reunion and celebration, our transparent lack of any real enthusiasm was blatantly obvious to anyone. Why wouldn't it be? At times I began to ponder if I should have delayed my return to Cardiff after all.

A few days prior to the great day, a Christmas card addressed to me arrived at the house in a high quality pale-blue envelope. I can clearly recall Dad collecting the post from the hall, and commenting on the immaculate slanted and looped copperplate handwriting as he handed me the card. Even in my depressed state, I have to admit that my interest was sparked by its impressive artistic flourish. As I opened the envelope and took out a card portraying a young smiling Victorian boy playing in pristine white snow, a letter written in the same style as the address fell to the floor at my feet. I picked it up from the multicoloured lounge carpet, and looked at the name at the end of the letter before reading the contents. I was genuinely surprised to see that it was from Dr Galbraith, and signed, Best wishes, David. A card would have been thoughtful in itself, but he'd taken the trouble to write. That genuinely touched me.

Rather than attempt to summarise the contents of the letter, I think it best to recount it word for word, as it was written. I have read it so many times over the years, searching for any suggestion of what would follow, that I know every single word by heart. I've decided not to attempt to mimic his presentation, as I don't have the necessary skills. I don't think it really matters, although you may disagree.

This is what he wrote:

22, December 1985

Dear Cynthia,

I hope I find you well, despite the awful events that led to our first meeting. Have you given any further thought to

82

resuming your studies? I can understand that returning to Cardiff for the first time since Steven's tragic death must seem an almost insurmountable task, but I would implore you not to abandon your academic pursuits. I know that Steven placed an extremely high value on education, and I feel certain that he would wish you to continue despite his leaving. I would be both delighted and privileged to offer you any support you require on a practical, academic or personal level. Perhaps we could meet for a bite to eat to talk about your future. I have one other matter I would very much like to discuss with you, and I feel this would be better done face to face, rather than in writing.

I hope to receive your response very soon. I won't wish you a happy Christmas given the situation, it seems inappropriate, but I can assure you from painful experience that time can be a great healer. You may not think it now, but you will experience joy again in the future.

Kindest regards,

David Galbraith

What do you think of the content? How do you think you'd have reacted if faced with a similar scenario? I'm interested to know. Really, I am. The letter seems simple enough to me. Any hidden agendas? Any alarm bells? I didn't think so.

When I recount his written words now, all these years later, I think he comes over as somewhat pompous and elitist. But, I was young, I was vulnerable, and to be honest, somewhat naive and impressionable. I didn't read between the lines. Steven's death was the first significant crisis of my short life. But life happens, things change, and not always for the better.

I think it's fair to say that when I first read that letter, I interpreted the contents as being from an intelligent, sophisticated and super-sensitive individual who felt and understood my emotional pain. Maybe that was his intention. Maybe I was actively seeking what I found. Who knows? I certainly don't! I can only put it down to my relative youth and inexperience. I'd like to travel back in time and shake my young self and scream, 'Don't be such an idiot, you stupid girl! He's after something, they're always after something.' But even if some well-intentioned individual had said something along those cautionary lines, I probably wouldn't have listened anyway.

I considered writing back over the Christmas period, but I didn't actually get round to putting pen to paper. In fact, as far as I can recall, I didn't give the doctor much thought until I answered the phone at about 7:15 p.m. on a dreary dank Welsh New Year's Eve, and heard his distinctive instantly recognisable accent on the other end of the line.

Despite my initial reticence at the start of our conversation, I was genuinely surprised to find myself glad he'd rung. Not because I felt any physical attraction to him, far from it, it was far too soon for such thoughts, but due to his obvious fondness for Steven's memory. He didn't really say anything very different to what he'd said that day at the crematorium, but the simple fact that he was willing to talk about my loss, rather than avoid the subject as most people tended to do, meant a great deal to me. The bereaved want to talk of their loss, they need to talk of their loss, and to share fond memories of the dead. I know I did.

Towards the end of what I now realise was a rather contrived, somewhat convoluted conversation, with him asking trigger questions and me doing most of the talking, he returned to the subject of my interrupted studies. In all honesty, it wasn't something I really wanted to think about, but he suddenly suggested I consider changing my course. It wasn't something I seriously considered, or at least not initially, but I agreed to think about it, more to get him off the phone than anything else. It seemed the easiest option.

Two days later, as I was sitting on a high stool by the kitchen window, watching spellbound as large snowflakes floated slowly from a luminous grey sky and disappeared almost instantly on hitting the warmer ground, the phone rang out loudly in the hall. For some instinctive reason I can't begin to explain, I knew that it was Dr Galbraith as soon as I lifted the receiver from its wall mounted cradle. This time, after asking me how I was coping with my loss, he got straight to the point: 'I would like you to consider studying Psychology my dear. I believe you'd find the subject far more rewarding than your erstwhile legal studies.'

I was taken aback at first, unsure of how to respond, and so I remained silent.

'Hello, Cynthia, are you still there my dear?'

I nodded once and said, 'Yes, still here.'

'Well, what do you think? Is it something you'd be willing to consider?'

'Steven said much the same thing, but I always thought that Law was the right course for me.'

'Look, I'm in Pembrokeshire on Saturday, visiting a relative who's a bit under the weather. How would you feel about meeting for a meal that evening? My treat: It would give us the opportunity to discuss your options properly.'

It felt wrong to be talking about the future with a virtual stranger so soon after Steven's death, but for some reason I can't properly explain, I reluctantly agreed to meet him. Maybe it was his elevated status, maybe his magnetism. Or maybe I was utterly fed up with being back home with Mum and Dad, after getting used to a more independent lifestyle. I think I'll delete this paragraph if Mum ever considers reading this, although she might understand. Isn't life complicated. It seems total honesty may not always be such a good idea after all.

I agreed to meet Dr Galbraith, or David, as he repeatedly insisted I call him, at the very same Indian restaurant from which my family had purchased Steven's last supper. Does that seem callous? To my never-ending shame, I strongly suspect that it does. Perhaps I'm the heartless shrew described by the more right-wing newspapers after all. If you've reached that conclusion, please keep it to yourself. I don't need to hear any further criticism. There was more than enough at the time.

I began getting ready at about 6:00 p.m. on the following Saturday evening, and was showered, made-up, dressed smartly but casually in black cord Levis jeans and a modest navy jumper, and watching the clock nervously by 7:15. Mum and Dad were pleased I was going out into the world of the living, and even more pleased that I was meeting an esteemed lecturer, who seemed hell-bent on facilitating my return to academia.

Dad encouraged me in the direction of the car as soon as I was ready, and dropped me off directly outside the restaurant five minutes or so before the allotted time, with the strict instruction to ring him when I was ready to be collected later in the evening. What a lovely man: nothing was ever too much trouble and he always seemed to have my best interests at the forefront of his mind.

The doctor was sitting and waiting at a table for two at the back of the warm atmospheric restaurant, decorated in suitably garish red and gold flock wallpaper, when I opened the door and hung up my coat. He stood and smiled warmly as I walked towards him, and pulled out a chair to allow me to sit opposite him. Now, that was something I wasn't used to. He was always so very polite in public situations. Always charming, never a harsh word, the perfect English gentleman.

For some reason, as he handed me a menu and smiled I noticed that his neat hair was trimmed to perfection with a precise side parting fixed in place by just the right amount of shiny hair wax. In fact, everything about him was precise: his styled hair that I've already mentioned, his faultlessly manicured nails, and his expensive looking navy suit, white shirt and silk tie. He had the look of a man who valued the impression he conveyed to others. I later learnt that my initial impressions were spot on.

I recall looking at the menu for several minutes, carefully noting all the available options on offer, before placing it down on the table and choosing what I always chose: chicken dopiaza, or chicken with extra onions for anyone who's interested, pilau rice, onion bhajis, crisp popadoms, and sweet mango chutney. I'm nothing if not predictable.

Dr Galbraith chose a medium vegetable curry with boiled rice, and drank glass after glass of Perrier natural mineral water from distinctive green bottles, despite ordering a carafe of white house wine which I later realised he didn't touch the entire evening.

I in dramatic contrast, welcomed the chance of a large glass or three of reality numbing vino, and willingly accepted as soon as it was offered. I can clearly recall that he refilled my glass each and every time it reached the half way point, which I'm afraid was rather too often. He made polite conversation, and asked how I was doing, but didn't address the subject of my future until I was pretty much intoxicated. Do you think that was a deliberate ploy on his part? Or, was he simply oiling the wheels of conversation in the interests of a convivial evening? It's hard to tell. That's the point I'm making: it's very hard to tell.

You may well have spotted a theme developing by this point in my journey. I'm not the most decisive woman in the world, or even in prison world for that matter. I pontificate almost constantly, and on most matters: even those of no particular consequence to my life. Deciding whether or not to put sugar in my unappetising watery prison porridge in the morning, for example, can seem an insurmountable problem on occasions. Does that sound ridiculous? Does it sound pathetic, to you? I'm guessing it does, and that I probably do too. But, don't be too quick to judge. I wasn't always like that. If you're called stupid often enough times, you start to believe it and doubt your judgement. I'll leave you to think about it whilst I carry on writing.

About an hour or so into the evening when we'd finished eating, the doctor ordered two Irish coffees topped with wonderfully thick cream, that felt like a decadent extravagance to a girl who'd so recently become used to the enforced frugalities of student life. He ordered me a second, but nothing more for himself, before finally asking me if I'd made a decision regarding my studies. 'Have you given any thought to your academic future as the evening's progressed my dear girl?'

'I haven't, to be honest Doctor.'

'David, please call me David.'

I nodded, and kept nodding nervously until he spoke again.

'I should probably explain that the majority of my time is spent working as a consultant child psychiatrist with the Department of Child Adolescent and Family Psychiatry in Caerystwyth. I lecture at the university on a part-time basis. I think it important to share my knowledge with the next generation of potential therapists. I see that in you Cynthia: the potential to help others deal with their emotional distress. It's an extremely rare gift that I've no doubt you possess.' And then a gleaming toothy smile that unnerved me. 'I believe you to be a very special person.'

I think he must have seen the uncertainty in my eyes, because he continued to take the lead, asking guiding questions, uttering words of empathetic encouragement, making his case, and pointing me back in the direction of Cardiff and psychological studies as opposed to Law . I don't know if that makes what actually happened that evening any clearer, but I suspect not. I'll try and give you a flavour of the ongoing conversation, although my memories may be clouded by the alcohol. 'Have another my dear girl! Why not, it will help you to relax. How about a Tia Maria my dear, it will complement your coffee beautifully.'

'Why don't you join me Doctor?'

'I'd love to my dear girl, but regrettably I'm driving. You have another though. I insist. Down in one. That's it!' It was something along those lines. And anyway, I'm sure you get the gist.

He looked at me across the table after a couple of hours had passed, smiled warmly, revealing those flawless white teeth I mentioned, and said,'Now then my dear, it's been a marvellous evening and I feel we've got to know each other a little better. Tell me, have you reached any conclusions regarding your studies?'

I shook my head repeatedly despite realising he wasn't inclined to let it go. My memory may be playing tricks on me, but I clearly recall his concerned expression, as if it really mattered to him, as if he really cared. I think it's fixed in my mind because I was genuinely surprised by the implied level of his concern. He shook his head slowly, took off his grey-metal rimmed glasses, placed them carefully on the white linen table cloth in front of him, and looked deep into my eyes, holding his gaze for a second or two before speaking again. When he did finally speak, his words were clearly enunciated with passion. 'I fully appreciate that you have been faced with the greatest crisis in your young life. You have lost a wonderful young man. A truly wonderful young man with infinite potential. I can understand why you're struggling to think about your future when your focus remains on the past. You're looking behind you, and at this stage of the grieving process I'm afraid that's inevitable. As I said in my recent letter, I want to help. I'm keen to help. I know from my own painful experience of loss, just how difficult it can be to get your life back on track. Even the simplest of decisions can seem insurmountable. It would be all too easy for you to reach the wrong conclusions or make no decision at all. I want to help you ensure that doesn't happen. I owe that much to Steven. As I said, he was a wonderful boy. I was so very fond of him.'

To my shame, I remember enjoying the unrelenting attention he gave me. That reality embarrasses me all these years later. Was I really that shallow? Was I really that easily influenced? Was I really that gullible? Or, was it understandable given my brittle state and his engaging style. I'm not really sure. If this process of self-examination is intended to help me reach conclusions about myself, it's not happening as intended quite yet. I plan to talk to Mrs Martin about it at our next meeting. I suspect she'll tell me to persevere, but let's just wait and see. Who knows, she may have other ideas.

The doctor's eyes suddenly moistened and filled with tears, as he told me that his wife of eight years had died in the April of the previous year, in a faltering voice resonating with what seemed genuine emotion. He took a black leather wallet from an inside pocket of his tailored jacket, and handed me a small colour Polaroid photograph of a beautiful young woman with dark shoulder length hair parted in the middle and an engaging smile, sitting on the deck of what looked like a car ferry somewhere in the warm mellow Mediterranean sunshine.

He seemed reluctant to tell me how she died, but I reached across the table, touched his hand and asked again. I understood his initial reticence when he eventually lowered his eyes, seemingly focusing on the table cloth and told me that she'd taken an overdose of analgesics and alcoholic spirits, after what he described as an extended period of severe depression.

I tightened my grip on his hand feeling we had grief in common.

'I tried to help her. Believe me, I tried desperately. I utilised my full range of therapeutic skills, but in the end it just wasn't enough. She was rushed to hospital and they did what they could: they pumped her stomach and it looked hopeful initially. But the damage to her liver was irrevocable. She died the next day.'

His statement came as something of a shock, not due to how she died, but because the mode of her death seemed strangely at odds with the seemingly happy full of life young woman in the photo.

He took a pristine white cotton handkerchief from a trouser pocket, and dabbed repeatedly at his reddening eyes, before looking up at me and forcing an improbable smile. I apologised for causing him such obvious distress, but secretly thought that his experience of grief equipped him to help me deal with my sadness.

He raised a hand in the air in the style of an assertive police officer stopping traffic, and said something along the lines of, 'Enough of the past, enough of my problems, we're here to help you make the right decisions regarding your immediate future.'

I smiled, nodded once, and said, 'Thanks Doctor.' Or, at least that's how I remember it.

He placed the photo back in his wallet with the utmost care, pushed the wallet to one side, and smiled engagingly. What on earth did he say next? I'm trying to get this right, really I am, but as I indicated earlier, some of my recollections of the evening feel like alcohol-fuelled dreams or the product of my subconscious mind, rather than memories of real events. As the evening progressed I drank more, and as I drank more… Well, I'm sure you get my point. Maybe you've been there yourself in the past.

He spent the next half hour or more enthusiastically expounding the reasons why I should return to Cardiff, and perhaps more importantly, why I should study Psychology under his expert tutelage when I got there. I think that by the end of the night I must have succumbed, because as drunk as I was, and as persuasive as he was, I suspect I'd have agreed to almost anything.

He paid for the meal in cash, gave the waiter an overly generous tip he didn't deserve, helped me from my seat with a strong supportive arm, and laughed despite my embarrassment, or perhaps because of it, when I suddenly turned away and hurried towards the toilet on unsteady legs.

I repeatedly washed my mouth out with copious amounts of cold water and splashed my face at the sink in a well-intentioned but ultimately unsuccessful attempt to stop the room spinning uncontrollably. I'm not sure how long I was in the ladies, but it must have been quite a while because he knocked reticently on the door and crept into the small dimly lit room to find me propped up and swaying in one corner, with tears streaming down my forlorn mascara-smeared face. What a state I must have looked. It doesn't bear thinking about. I'm usually so meticulous when it comes to my appearance.

He smiled, uttered words of encouragement and reassurance, assisted me in the direction of the exit and helped me into my warm green woollen winter coat, which had been hanging on a hook near to the door. 'Come on my dear girl, let's go for a nice stroll before contacting that father of yours.' And then a joke to lighten the mood. 'He's going to think I'm a bad influence if we don't sober you up a bit… What do you say? I'd be in serious trouble.'

I can distinctly recall pausing mid-step as the freezing weather stung my face on being led out of the restaurant and into the quiet out of season night-time street. I'm not sure which direction we took, but by about 11:30 p.m. I found myself sitting on a hard wooden bench almost directly opposite WH Smiths in Tenby's main street, with a glorious view of the picturesque harbour and Amroth beyond, painted by the subtle light of the early January moon. Like it or not, the world keeps turning with or without us, seemingly oblivious to our existence.

My slightly disjointed reminiscences remind me that we need to make the most of the good times while we can. Those we love can leave us all too quickly. My advice, for what it's worth, would be not to take anything or anyone for granted, but I'm sure you knew that already. I'll bring my brief sermon to a close and continue…

By the time Dad pulled up alongside us in his modest family car about twenty minutes later, I was absolutely freezing, shivering uncontrollably, and very glad of the opportunity to take advantage of the vehicle's comparative warmth. Dad thanked the doctor for entertaining me, or it may have been looking after me, that's probably more like it, and then looked at me with a questioning look on his face when he noticed the telltale signs of my earlier excess. Dr Galbraith smiled sympathetically and waved enthusiastically as Dad drove off, and quickly disappeared from my view as Dad negotiated the first bend.

Dad repeatedly asked probing questions about the evening during our short journey back to the house, and I recall thinking it felt more like an interrogation than a conversation. It annoyed the heck out of me at the time, but I've since realised that he was simply trying to establish if anything positive had resulted from the evening. He had my best interests at heart as usual. He wanted the best for me, and that was his cack-handed way of showing it. In all honesty, I can't recall what he asked me exactly, or what I told him in reply. That conversation would take place the following evening, when despite my sobriety he still wouldn't receive any meaningful answers.

I reluctantly dragged myself out of my warm comfortable bed at about 10:30 a.m. the following morning, and after the shock of looking at myself in the brightly lit bathroom mirror, never a good idea after an excessively boozy night, I headed downstairs and into the kitchen for a much needed glass of cold water and two soluble aspirins, which gradually went some way to alleviating the horrendous headache that felt as if my brain were attempting to force its way out of my skull through my ears.

Mum tried her best to feign concern when she first saw me slumped at the kitchen table, but her true feelings were quickly betrayed by the smile that played on her lips as she turned away on the pretext of performing some household task or another. I didn't say anything in response, but I think she must have realised the game was well and truly up, because she said, 'Sorry love, can I get you a nice cup of tea?'

'Please, Mum.'

I sat at the kitchen table, trying to make small talk, with the embarrassing events of the previous evening gradually materialising in my alcohol-ravaged mind. Mum poured boiling water into a favoured blue porcelain mug and added a tea bag and a splash of cold soya milk before handing it to me with a grin. 'How did it go last night love? Did you have a good time? Dad said the doctor seems like a nice man.'

'Yeah, it was okay in the circumstances.'

'So what did he want to talk about?'

'He wants me to go back to university.'

She sat more upright, animated by the news. 'Well, Dad and I have been saying much the same thing. Life has to go on.'

'Yeah, but he wants me to change courses.'

She swivelled in her seat and looked me in the eye with a pensive expression on her face. 'But what about your Law degree love? You seemed so keen before…' She looked away. 'Well, you know what I'm saying.'

I nodded reticently. 'He thinks Psychology would suit me better. He says I have a God given talent I wasn't aware of.'

'Really, what do you think love? I suppose he must know what he's talking about.'

'Steven loved it.'

'So, what did you say?'

I shook my head and silently cursed my hangover. 'I can't remember, to be honest. But I need to give it a lot more thought.'

'It sounds like a good idea to me love.'

I took a large gulp of the fast cooling liquid. 'Maybe you're right Mum. Maybe you're right.'

Chapter 10

The last seven days have passed all too slowly as they tend to here, and my period of enforced isolation is finally at an end. You may recall me saying that I rather enjoyed the experience initially, particularly once Mrs Martin had facilitated my continued writing, but the novelty eventually wore off. Towards the end of the week I began to struggle, both physically and mentally. I'm sure it's a phenomenon that must have been researched at some point by one university psychology department or another, but I've never read anything on the subject. It's perhaps a tad overdramatic to say that the lack of human company withered my fragile soul, but that's how it felt by the last day. I don't know how else to put it. My head was banging, I felt physically sick, my thoughts were becoming increasingly dark and invasive even for me, and I badly needed a shower to wash away my increasingly stale sweat. If there's a hell somewhere in infinity and I find myself there for eternity, I fear I'll be alone in permanent darkness with not even a hint of light and no one to talk to even for a single second. Hopefully I'll find redemption somewhere along the way and avoid such a fate. I'd like to think so anyway.

Right, I'll pull myself together as best I can and try to be more positive from here on in. That wouldn't be a bad idea, I'm sure you'd agree. I'm back in my cell and very glad to be here. Now, that's one sentence I never envisaged myself writing. I guess it's the lesser of two evils. And wonder of wonders, I've got yet another new cellmate: the third in a matter of weeks. That may be some sort of prison world record, but I can't see me featuring in the Guinness Book of Records any time soon. There you go: I'm thinking more positively already.

You may be thinking that there's little if any point in me telling you about the new woman in my life if she's likely to move on as quickly as the previous two. But in reality, Gloria and I shared a cell for quite some time. It's just that I began writing this shortly before her recent departure to what's hopefully a happier place and eventual freedom. And Sheila, well, you know as much as I do about Sheila. Sheila was an abomination. I don't think it's in anyone's interests to raise that regrettable debacle again.

My new cellmate's name is Emma. Emma St Bride, a highly unlikely label for a resident of prison world. I immediately assumed that she'd turn out to be some spoilt minx who'd unwisely entered the dirty world of illicit drugs, or a greedy needy professional pen pusher who'd embezzled money she didn't need. But I turned out to be wrong on both counts despite my earlier cautionary words regarding the folly of jumping to conclusions on the basis of fleeting first impressions. I really should have learnt that particular lesson by now.

It turns out that Emma, despite the name's misleading persona of upper middle-class respectability, grew up on a large solidly working-class council estate in Halifax in the north of England. Nothing wrong with that, of course. We can't all be born with silver spoons and all the advantages that entails, but for me her name invoked a privately educated debutant type with an annoying pebble in the mouth south of England accent. How did this seeming inconsistency occur? How did the label cross the class divide? Well, it turns out her father was a fan of the Avengers, and particularly high kicking Diana Rigg in a tight black leather cat suit few men could resist. It seems males are visually rather than emotionally stimulated. I read that in a book once upon a time in a previous life. They're Mars to our Venus: simple uncomplicated creatures that are easily pleased. Or at least, most of them are. His tastes were far more sinister.

Emma, it still feels strange to call her Emma, was very willing to volunteer why she's here. She just spilt it out without me saying a word. Maybe she was too willing; it's some distance from the norm. She told me she's a single mother of twenty-three years, who grew up in virtual poverty, and misses her four-year-old son Gary horribly, as if mourning his death. He's been taken into local authority care and placed with foster parents. She hasn't seen him for months, apparently. I'm beginning to wonder if there's something she isn't telling me.

Emma, it seems, was convicted of theft after repeated offences to feed her drug habit which led to a period of incarceration along with the rest of us miscreants. If that's the winding path she followed, she isn't the first and she certainly won't be the last. But, there's something that doesn't fit. Something that leaves an unpalatable taste in the mouth. She seems nice enough on first meeting, but if she's here after a bit of thieving, why is she sharing a cell with a lifer? That's just not how things work here. I could be charitable and put it down to the chronic overcrowding, but rumours are she's serving a five year stretch. She hasn't told me that herself, naturally. It was the one matter she seemed reluctant to discuss. If it's true, she's hiding something. If I find out what, you'll be the first to know.

I'm scribbling this nonsense whilst sitting on the top bunk passing some time before breakfast. I neglected to mention that. I'll be heading to the canteen in a few minutes, and so I'll need to bring this session to a close soon. I'm seeing Mrs Martin later today, and I can honestly say I'm quite looking forward to it for a change. She's one of the few who seem genuinely on my side. Perhaps she can do something to make Emma's life a little easier. I think she probably deserves that, whatever her crime.

.

Chapter 11

I've still got about half an hour or so before lights out, and I'm keen to tell you as much as I can about my therapy session before darkness prevails once more. I'll try my best to close my ears and ignore the incessant drone of Emma's pitiful sobbing. She carved her son's name into her arm in inch high letters at some point during the day, for some reason I can't comprehend. Such things are not uncommon in prison world and nothing much surprises me anymore. I've become used to the night-time weeping chorus of others. I've had to. What other choice did I have? It was that, or lose my fragile grasp on sanity. I can shut it out most of the time, the white noise for the criminal classes, with my rough grey blanket pulled tight around my ears. But it still gets to me sometimes. There's only so much sorrow anyone can bear.

Mrs Martin had just returned from a weekend's break in Bath with her second husband, Fredrick, as she insists on calling him. She said they had a marvellous time. And why wouldn't they? I would, given the opportunity. I'm sure most of us would; it's a lovely city after all. I'm pleased for her, honestly I am, but did she really need to tell me all about it in such enthusiastic minuscule detail? She even recommended a bijou vegan restaurant in North Parade Passage. I could all too easily have slapped her, but I stayed firmly in my seat and sat on my hands. For an experienced woman who's supposed to understand the many complexities of the human psyche, she seems a tad insensitive at times, wouldn't you agree? It's going to be a very long time before I go to Bath, or anywhere else for that matter. Perhaps I should take a closer look at those certificates of hers.

When she'd finally finished torturing me with details of her romantic interlude, she did eventually ask, 'How are you finding the reflective process Cynthia? I hope it's not too arduous.'

'It's okay I suppose, at least it's giving me something to do.'

'Tell me more.'

'Well, I guess it's helping me focus on my life.'

She nodded and smiled momentarily without parting her lips. 'I'm glad you're finding it useful. Do you mind if I read the first few pages?'

She held her hand out towards me, but withdrew it quickly when I clutched the notebook tightly to my chest.

Her face took on a contemplative expression, as if she were deep in thought and choosing her words carefully before speaking again. When she did eventually speak she moved to the very edge of her seat, leant towards me, and placed a hand on my shoulder. 'I'm not here to judge you Cynthia. I'm here to help. There's very little I haven't heard before.'

I averted my gaze and said, 'Okay.'

'It's important to take responsibility for any mistakes you've made in your life and learn from them.'

I took a deep breath and handed her my precious notebook open at the first page.

'Thank you.'

As she began reading I assured her that I had no desire to minimise my responsibility, but I realise that in reality I was simply saying what I believed she wanted to hear in the interests of an easy life. I do feel guilt, and it torments me at times, but I'm not ready to tell her that just yet. I was hiding behind my brief defiance. It seems an admission of weakness would be unwise in my dangerous world where strength is a distinct advantage. I'm finding it a lot easier to write the truth than to speak it face to face. I don't really think that's dishonest, as Mrs Martin anticipated it would happen, and she'll read the whole truth and nothing but the truth at some point in the not too distant future anyway. If she thought I'd tell her everything willingly and easily, the journal would be entirely superfluous. That seems obvious. I think she knows exactly what she's doing. This was always going to be a lengthy process, rather than a miraculous instant fix all.

At the end of our one hour session, Mrs Martin smiled warmly, and told me to keep writing. I was expecting some sort of caveat, but that was it. She said nothing more, other than reminding me that the hour was up. Doesn't time pass quickly when you're enjoying yourself. Please forgive my flippant sarcasm, but her to-the-second timekeeping never fails to surprise and frustrate me. She seems to have a built in clock, like an experienced boxer who knows instinctively when a round is near to its end and throws a flurry of punches to impress the judges.

Keep writing! It seemed somewhat dismissive when she said it, but now that I think about it, it's all she needed to say. And so, that's what I plan to do: keep writing and see where it takes me.

Chapter 12

I recognised Dr Galbraith's flowing pen and ink script as soon as Dad handed me his second letter on the 3rd of January. I found myself pleased that he'd bothered writing again, and eager to know the contents. I grasped the letter tightly in one hand and hurriedly retreated to my childhood bedroom to recline on the comfortable single bed and read it in peace. I prized it carefully from its now familiar envelope, and unfolded it next to me on top of my pink and white striped winter quilt.

The letter began with the expected platitudes, which I read with only passing interest, but then it became much more interesting. At this point I can either try and summarise the salient points, or recreate the letter again as I did last time in an attempt to avoid bias. That's probably best, although I can't promise that my representation won't be influenced by time passed and flawed memories. For some reason, I don't recall the second letter with the same photographic clarity as the first. I can't explain why, because if anything its contents were even more significant to my future. I didn't read it as often, that's the obvious explanation, but it seems far too simplistic a statement. Maybe there were clues. Clues I missed. Why didn't I read it as often? That's the real question. Perhaps you can work it out. I've tried and failed miserably.

Anyway, I was in the process of telling you what he'd written. I've given it my best shot, but I just can't picture the single page in my mind. I'm going to have to resort to summarising the key points after all. I hope that's okay with you? Overcomplicating matters can be a very effective delaying tactic.

In short, it seemed I'd already agreed to resume my studies when the post-Christmas university term started again on the 24th of January. That didn't come as a total shock, as I suspected I may have made that commitment on that drunken night. What did surprise me, however, was that I'd be studying Psychology, rather than Law! I knew I'd agreed to consider changing courses, but I was almost certain that I made it clear I needed more time to think. He'd already spoken to the relevant lecturers, he'd made the necessary arrangements, it was a done deal.

I felt very close to panic. Going back to Cardiff at all wasn't easy to face, but the thought of a new course, with a new group of students who'd inevitably be well ahead of me in their studies and relationships was truly daunting. I'm one of life's worriers. Headaches become brain tumours, boils become cancerous tumours, and common colds pneumonia. Or at least in my head they do. I know it's stupid. I know it's counterproductive. But it seems that's the way I'm made and there's little, if anything, I can do about it.

I lay back on the bed, shaking my head slowly and trying to come up with a viable escape strategy. My mind was filled with unwelcome questions I couldn't answer. It seemed a fait accompli. It was all happening much too quickly. I'd lost control.

As I read on, reaching the final paragraph, I threw my head back and fought the impulse to vomit. It seems I'd agreed to him collecting me and transporting me to Cardiff on the 17th of January. It seemed I'd agreed to stay in the Riverside flat he owned in the city, and it seemed I'd agreed to him taking a few days off work to tutor me in the psychological basics. Really? I'd agreed to all that? Why not the halls of residence? Why not point me in the direction of the relevant text books? Why a full week before the beginning of term? Had I really agreed to all that? Maybe I did and maybe I didn't. I could have, I suppose. It's a possibility. I've done some pretty stupid things when intoxicated. But then, haven't we all!

Chapter 13

Emma's son is dead. It seems she killed him. Just two years old and his short sad life was over. What a tragedy, what a terrible reality! Life can be so very cruel. Let's hope he's in a better place.

She didn't tell me herself. Why would she in the circumstances? That want-to-be-liked guard who we'll just call 'Needy Guard' in the interests of her anonymity, whispered it to me at lunch time as I stood waiting to be served with a plateful of unappetising slop masquerading as food. She pulled me aside and spewed it out, relishing the telling like a gossiping fish wife spraying her poison to all and sundry. I feigned interest initially, keen to bring the unwelcome interaction to a rapid conclusion, acutely conscious of the staring eyes and cocked ears of other nearby prisoners, but I quickly wished she'd kept the information to herself and hadn't told me anything at all. It would have been easier that way. I didn't want to know. I didn't need to know. I've digested enough human misery for one lifetime. For a hundred lifetimes! And I'd actually started to like Emma and her various idiosyncrasies. We weren't friends, that would be an exaggeration, but I think we could have been in different circumstances. I really do. I knew she was fragile. I knew she was haunted by memories she'd much rather forget. But so am I, so am I! She could have been victim rather than perpetrator. I can't be the only one, can I? I so wanted that to be the case.

I saw the same plump middle-aged guard skulking in the corridor about half an hour later, all bleached blonde hair, dark roots, over-tight uniform, stale body odour and red chipped painted fingernails, as I made my weary way back towards the laundry from the canteen of hell. I approached her reticently this time, rather than her approaching me, and she turned away at first, making a point before eventually turning to face me as I knew she would. 'Oh, so now you want to talk to me.'

And I did. I wanted to know more. I needed to know more. Not because I was naturally inquisitive or wanted to self-indulgently wallow in my cellmate's suffering, but because I was hoping that the detail would alleviate Emma's guilt to some degree. I just didn't want to hate her. I had to share a cell with the girl after all.

'You said Emma killed her son. What actually happened?'

She gestured with a subtle tilt of her head, and led me into a restricted brightly lit side corridor leading to various staff offices I hadn't seen before. 'So, what do you want to know?'

'Emma, what happened to her son?'

She lifted a hand to her face and adjusted her fringe with chubby fingers. 'I've had my hair done. What do you think?'

She wanted validation, searching for compliments. She had all the power. I said it looked good with as much conviction as I could muster. What else could I do?

She smiled thinly, seemingly doubting the sincerity of my response.

I took a step backwards as she drew closer and her stench filled my nostrils. 'There were too many snooping eyes in the canteen. You know what it's like in this place. People can get the wrong idea.'

She looked genuinely upset. 'Ah, so you don't want to be seen talking to me. And I thought we were friends.'

'You know how things are. I can't be seen to be too close to you however much I want to.'

She nodded, seemingly satisfied with my explanation. 'She poisoned the boy, slowly, over a period of months. She fed him honey laced with salt. Watched him suffer, the cruel bitch!'

She was gleeful, drooling, aroused by the illicit sharing, and I hid my revulsion as best I could. 'Why would she do that?'

Her face broke into a sneer that defined her. 'It's something called Munchausen Syndrome by Proxy. I've been reading all about it. She craves attention. She's desperate for attention. I thought you'd have known that, what with your psychology background and all.'

I just stared at her with my mouth shut. What was the point in saying anything at all? Why play her games?

'The bitch poisoned her little boy for the attention it gave her: Concerned doctors rushing around, test after test, repeated hospital admissions. She took him to three different casualty departments a total of nineteen times. Fucking bitch!'

Suffer little children. His words echoed in my mind, and I gagged, resisting the impulse to vomit.

'Didn't the bastard you killed do something similar?'

A single tear ran down my cheek and I noticed I was trembling. 'It wasn't the same.'

'What did you say? You seemed to be whispering. If you've got something to say, just spit it out.'

I wiped her warm spittle from my face with the back of one hand, and repeated myself, louder this time, whilst fighting my tears. Why did I let her get to me? I should not have let her get to me.

She shook her head incredulously and laughed, head back, multiple dark amalgam fillings in full view. 'Two murderers together, I'm sure you'll get on famously. So much to talk about. So much in common!'

I turned away, ignoring the provocation. We're different. Surely we're different. 'Does everyone know?'

She broke into a smile that lit up her face. 'Not as yet, but they will. They definitely will. The bitch deserves everything that's coming to her.'

'She needs professional help. The woman needs help.'

She formed her right hand into a tight fist, and shook it in the air at eye level. 'I know the kind of help I'd like to give the bitch.'

That word again. That hateful word. I'd heard enough. More than enough! Another crisis to ponder in my confined world of woe. I do care about the people around me, really I do. I'm not antisocial by nature or devoid of empathy like some others I've mentioned, but I need to focus on my writing. Too many distractions, typical inevitable unwelcome distractions time and time and time again. I turned and walked away as she called after me: angry, resentful, radiating spite. I'd pay for my insubordination, but it felt so good at the time. I think it was probably worth it.

Chapter 14

I watched from the lounge window as an impressive shiny black Daimler sedan pulled up outside our modest Tenby home at about 11:30 a.m. on the 17th of January. Dr Galbraith made a superfluous adjustment to his strangely out of place cartoon tie on exiting the vehicle, and hurried down our fragmented concrete driveway just as the ominously darkening sky began to fill the air with freezing winter rain, swirling in every conceivable direction at the bequest of the coastal wind.

Dad opened the door on the second knock, and welcomed the doctor into our small white painted hallway with a firm handshake, as Mum scurried to the kitchen to prepare refreshments worthy of our esteemed visitor. I stood and smiled coyly as the doctor followed Dad into the lounge, and found myself wondering if he always wore a tailored suit. He was always stylish, always immaculate, always charming, and he wore it well. He really did. The man glowed. He made an impression wherever he went. There was no denying it.

Dr Galbraith approached me confidently, touched my arm briefly with an outstretched manicured fingers and asked, 'Are you ready for your big day my dear?'

I was pondering my response, unsure of the honest answer, when Mum appeared, carrying that same 'meant to impress' recently polished silver tray loaded with best white porcelain crockery, a stylish Portmeirion coffee pot, and a tin of assorted biscuits decorated with a stereotypical country scene that for some inexplicable reason I disliked intensely.

The doctor directed the somewhat stilted conversation for the next half hour or more, oiling the conversational wheels with a friendly smile, empathetic words or a timely question or comment, as we sipped coffee and nibbled biscuits. Such contrived social situations are never easy to bear, particularly following the loss of a loved one, but the doctor somehow made the experience bearable. It was something he was good at. Something in which he excelled. Saying the right thing when the situation dictated. Making the right impression when it mattered. A Svengali at the very peak of his powers.

Even the doctor's conversational skills were beginning to flag by 12:15 p.m. He glanced sideways towards my suitcase standing alone in one corner of the lounge, and said, 'Right then young lady, are you ready to make a move. We've got a long drive ahead of us and I'd like to reach Cardiff before the light fades and it starts freezing.'

I did't move an inch, but Dad stood, approached my chair, reached out a hand and helped me to my feet. 'Come on love, the doctor's right. You want to get there safely, don't you.'

'David, please call me David.'

Dad looked towards him and nodded, as I headed into the hall to pull on the surprisingly fashionable warm winter weight green wool Jaeger coat received from my maternal grandmother as a Christmas gift. He appeared next to me with my overburdened suitcase in hand, as I fastened the last of three buttons against the anticipated winter chill.

I don't think Dad ever did call him David. Not that it matters. It's of no real relevance. It just came to mind and I mentioned it in passing.

Dad opened the front door, reached for my suitcase, and led the way towards the doctor's limousine, walking quickly, head bowed and shivering against the cold. The doctor unlocked the car with the press of a button, and held open the front passenger side door for me to quickly escape the stinging rain. Dad put my case in the cavernous boot and hurried back to the shelter of the porch, where he stood and watched hand in hand with Mum as the doctor started the engine with one turn of the key and manoeuvred expertly into the road.

I was impressed by the Daimler. Why wouldn't I be? All that soft supple grey leather and polished walnut. I'd never been in a car like that before: an extravagant car, a car shouting success, and so quintessentially British. And I have to admit that at least a part of me was looking forward to the journey. Steven was gone, he wasn't coming back and I'd hidden from the outside world for long enough. He'd want me to get on with my life. That's the sort of boy he was.

The doctor introduced me to classical music as we made our journey to Carmarthen, a pleasant Welsh market town on the River Towy about forty minutes' driving time from Tenby. I asked if he had something more contemporary, something with which I was familiar, but he smiled thinly, shook his head slowly and deliberately, and extolled the virtue of various composers I'd heard of but never knowingly appreciated. I half heartedly protested initially, but quickly capitulated and sat in brooding silence as he played one CD after another. He was an important man, a busy man, and he was putting himself out to help me. I didn't want to make a bad impression, and it seemed churlish to cause offence or argument over such a relative inconsequence. Listening to the various melodies was the least I could do to please him.

As we travelled east along the M4, through the worsening weather and approaching the exit lane for Swansea, I suggested we stop at a service station for lunch before continuing on to Cardiff. He didn't accede to my request, for what it was worth, but he did say, 'Oh, I think we can do better than that my dear girl. There's a pleasant pub I visit sometimes not ten minutes away. They serve an excellent lunch, as I recall.'

The doctor was true to his word and we were driving into the Red Lion's unsurprisingly quiet car park a few minutes later. I hurried into the dimly lit atmospheric building, and immediately headed in the direction of the ladies' toilet clearly located to the left of the bar.

Dr Galbraith already had a generous glass of red wine waiting for me when I returned from the bathroom, and he was sitting at a table for two within touching distance of a log fire smouldering in an imposing apparently ancient natural stone grate. As I sat opposite him and picked up a menu from the tabletop, he held up a hand to stop me. 'I've already ordered for us both my dear. The establishment serves an excellent steak. Rare, of course. It's the only way to eat it, I'm sure you'll agree.'

As it happens I didn't agree. I've always preferred my meat well done. I was irritated by his largess, and my feelings must have shown on my face because he sat back in his seat with what appeared to be a look of genuine surprise on his face and asked, 'Is there something the matter my dear? I hope I wasn't too presumptuous.'

When I didn't respond, swallowing my words, he made a show of pushing up the sleeve of his suit jacket and looking at his gold Cartier wrist watch. 'It's just that the time is getting on my dear. I thought it advisable to expedite matters in the interests of our journey.' He swivelled in his seat glanced out of the nearest window. 'I really think there's a threat of snow.'

He had a point, but would a couple of minutes really have made a difference? I considered objecting, I considered choosing a different meal to make a point, but he stood, picked up the menu and returned it to the bar. 'Would you like a second glass of wine my dear?'

'I'd like my steak well done.'

He smiled engagingly, but I could tell that I'd displeased him.

'I'd like my steak well done, please.'

'Really? Are you certain my dear? All the best chefs serve it bloody.'

I folded my arms and glared at him: furious but keen to avoid a confrontation.

This time he raised both arms in the air as if surrendering at gun point, and chortled unconvincingly. 'Well done it is!'

A small victory, but a battle I was determined to win.

We left the pub about an hour later and rejoined the M4 to continue our journey. He turned up the heating, unbuttoned his jacket, and returned to the subject of classical music before moving on to discuss my studies about twenty minutes later. He extolled the virtues of studying Psychology as opposed to Law, as he had on that drunken evening and in his subsequent letter, and outlined what he saw as the advantages of me residing in his flat rather than the halls of residence as I'd originally planned. I wasn't entirely persuaded to be honest. I was finding his demeanour increasingly unnerving despite his friendly persona, but I told myself that my temporary living arrangements would at least give me space to find my own place in my own time.

The light was fading dramatically by the time we reached Cardiff, casting dark shadows over a cold urban landscape lit by a myriad city lights. He manoeuvred through the city centre's busy traffic, and into a quiet tree-lined street lined with impressive Victorian three storey houses on either side of the road. He slowed about half way along the street, and stopped outside number 292, an imposing residence with a black gloss front door adorned with highly polished brass door furniture.

'This is it my dear. Out you get, out you get.'

Despite being divided into three flats, each with its own doorbell, the building was in total darkness. He must have sensed my uneasiness in that instinctive way of his, because he reached out to squeeze my hand and said, 'The other students won't be back from their Christmas break as yet my dear. Nothing to worry about. Nothing whatsoever! Give it a day or two and you'll be wishing for some peace.'

That made sense. There was an undoubted logic to it. But if it was true, why was I feeling so apprehensive? The halls of residence were calling out to me and I was beginning to regret acquiescing quite so readily. If only I'd acted on my inclinations.

Chapter 15

It's been a momentous day here in prison world: a good day, an exciting day; Emma's self-destructive behaviour apart, that is. I think I'll get the bad news out of the way first, before focussing on the positives. There's absolutely no point in lowering the mood indefinitely.

She cut herself again, with an outstretched sharpened paperclip this time. She must have spent most of the night working away at her wrists, scratching at the skin, picking at the flesh and sinew, because by morning her bed was so soaked in dark blood that it was difficult to tell the original colour of the sheets. How can one fragile eight stone frame hold so much of the red stuff? I shook her, shouted at her to wake up, but no response, barely a sign of life. I'm told she was rushed to the local hospital, weak but breathing shallowly. And she'll be back, of course, when the physical wounds heal. I suspect her psychological flaws may take a little longer. I'd like to think that her actions originated in remorse, but I fear they may well have had more to do with the attention it brought her than regret. At least now she's harming herself, rather than an innocent child. I guess it's the lesser of two evils. It's progress of a sort. I'm not really looking forward to seeing her again, if I'm honest, but at least I get some time to myself before that inevitable day beckons somewhere down the line.

And now for the good stuff! I'll attempt to make my recollections as big bright and loud as I possibly can, so you can get a full flavour of how it was for me: Mum and the girls were already waiting for me when I rushed into the communal starkly functional visiting room at 3:30 p.m. this afternoon. I didn't know if Mum would turn up today, let alone bring Elizabeth and Sarah with her, and my emotions

116

were virtually overwhelming when I first saw the three of them sitting there together.

Mum stood on wobbly legs as soon as she saw me entering the room, and I noticed that she looked older despite her forced quickly vanishing smile. The flickering overly bright fluorescent lighting directly above her head seemed to highlight every line, every blemish, every sunken shadow playing on her face. The girls remained in their hard red plastic seats initially, but stood stoically on either side of Mum as I approached their table, and clutched her hands tightly. It should be my hands they were holding. If only things had worked out differently.

I leant across the table to throw my arms around them all as they huddled together. And then she intervened, that same need-to-be-liked guard, out of spite, out of malice. That cow, that fucking cow!

'No touching!'

I didn't let go. What harm could it do? Such stupid pointless rules.

'I said no touching!' Louder this time, playing to her audience, wallowing in her power.

I held on, but Mum tensed inexorably. She was shaking. The woman was actually trembling, as if hyperthormic and close to freezing. I wasn't going to win this one.

'Better listen love, I think that's best.'

I slowly released my grip, took a single reluctant step backwards and sat of the very edge of my seat, craning my neck to be as close to them as possible. 'Okay Mum, if you say so.'

She nodded and smiled unconvincingly.

I took a deep breath, dabbed at my eyes with the back of one hand and looked at each of my wonderful girls in turn. Elizabeth was crying quietly and focussing on her hands, whilst Sarah was very close to tears and edging ever closer to her grandmother. Perhaps they don't look forward to their visits as much as I do.

I forced a playful grin, attempting to lighten the mood. 'Perhaps they think you're smuggling drugs in your knickers or something?'

Nobody laughed. Nobody smiled. Why would they? Such a stupid thing to say.

Mum glanced in the direction of the guard and reached across the tabletop, touching my outstretched fingers with hers. 'How are you love? Are they treating you well?'

'Not too bad thanks Mum. How about you?'

'Oh, we're just fine, aren't we girls.'

The two girls nodded in unison, but didn't say anything in response. Isn't it strange how a fleeting momentary look can sometimes say a thousand words.

'Wow, you two have grown so much.' And they had, they really had. I was missing so many milestones.

Sarah met my eyes for a fraction of a second, before looking away. 'When are you coming home Mummy?'

I bit my lower lip hard, tasting blood and fighting back the tears. What could I say? What on earth could I say? 'We don't really know, do we Mum.'

'Oh, come on now love, things aren't that bad. No need for tears. Over a thousand people have signed the petition at the last count! You'll be out of here before you know it.'

'You've been saying that for three years Mum.'

She looked flustered, close to panic. 'I've spoken to that nice MP again love. He's still looking into your case. He says you can appeal your conviction.'

'We've talked about this Mum. All the petitions in the world aren't going to make any difference.'

'Of course it will love. It's just a matter of time.'

'I've discussed it with the solicitor Mum. You know that. It's only possible to appeal if there's new evidence. I really wish there was, but there isn't. We have to accept that. Denying reality isn't good for any of us, the girls included.'

'But, Mr Bamford said…' She bowed her head, focussed to the floor and quietly mumbled the remainder of her sentence. We'd had the exact same conversation so many times before.

Not again, surely not again! It was always the same: Mum clutching at the same predictable straws, the girls trying to be positive but surreptitiously watching the clock above the door, me doubting the value of false hope whilst trying not to lower the mood still further. The four of us sat there in virtual silence after that, glancing at each other tentatively, smiling reticently, searching for the right thing to say and somehow resisting the temptation to reach across the table to link hands.

And then there she was again, that same needy guard: strutting, preening, indulging her authority to the nth degree. That cow, that fucking cow! I can hear her voice now, as if she's yelling into my ear at touching distance. 'Time! Bring your conversations to an end please. No touching, I said no touching!'

That cow, that hateful cow! My heart sank, Mum looked crestfallen and apologised for arriving late, but I fear the girls may well have felt relieved that the usual hour was over prematurely. Prison is no place for children. It's no place for family reunions. But what choice did we have? There weren't any alternatives, no better options, none whatsoever.

I stood and watched as Mum and the girls stood and walked away in a close knit huddle. Sarah looked back and raised an open hand in acknowledgement as she left the room, but neither Mum nor Elizabeth looked back. Maybe it was too much for them to bear. It certainly was for me.

Chapter 16

Dr Galbraith held an ancient black umbrella high above my head with one hand, whilst unlocking the front door with the other. 'Right then my dear, in you go, in you go, there's a light switch on the wall to your left as I recall.'

I fumbled for the switch in the orange sodium glow of the streetlamp, causing an opaque pale-blue glass clad light to burst into seemingly enthusiastic life. He handed me a single key on a red leather fob, raised a hand and pointed towards a second door half way along the passageway. 'It's the ground floor flat, the best of the three by far, you'll be glad to hear. Go in and make yourself comfortable my dear. I'll fetch your case.'

I approached the door, but waited for him to return with the suitcase rather than open it. It just didn't seem right to open someone else's door on first visiting.

'Come on, in you go, in you go, welcome to your new home. No need for formalities.'

I grinned nervously, turned the key, pushed the door open and walked in.

'I'll just put your case in the bedroom before giving you a guided tour of your new abode.'

I nodded. 'Can I use the bathroom?'

He placed a hand on each of his hips, leant backwards at a slight angle and adopted a thoughtful expression, as if choosing his words carefully. 'Now, let's make one thing clear from the start. I want you to feel comfortable here. I want you to consider the flat your home. Is that clear?'

I felt like a child in the classroom as I stood in silence.

'The bathroom is the second door on the left.'

'Okay, thanks.'

'See you in a minute or two.'

I flushed, washed my hands with scented soap, checked my hair and makeup in the illuminated art deco style oval mirror above the sink, and rejoined him in the lounge a couple of minutes later.

'Right, I'll show you where everything is before we enjoy some much needed refreshments. Is it warm enough for you?'

I nodded and smiled, warming to his convivial banter.

'Right, follow me, my dear, this shouldn't take too long.'

And it didn't. Within a short while the guided tour was over and we were sitting at an oak table in the surprisingly spacious kitchen, drinking filter coffee from pleasant chocolate brown Hornsea Contrast cups.

He asked me what I thought of the flat, and I got the distinct impression that my opinion mattered to him. That felt good. I think that's fair to say. We all need to think our opinion means something to someone. I told him I was impressed, which I was because the place was beautiful: with generously proportioned rooms, high ceilings and large sash windows through which the light would pour come dawn. Every wall was white, pristine, not a blemish, everything immaculate, everything in its place, precisely in its place. 'It's lovely, really lovely.'

He beamed. 'I'm glad you like it my dear. What did you think of the art? It's a real passion of mine.'

To be honest I hadn't really taken much note of his pictures, and I sat there with a blank expression on my face.

I thought I noticed his demeanour change just for a fraction of a second, but he relaxed his powerful shoulders and said, 'Photography is one of my passions, let me show you the photos in the lounge.'

There were large framed black and white pictures hanging vertically on each of the four walls. He placed a hand on my elbow, and gently guided me to the centre of the room so that I could revolve slowly in a circle and appreciate each in

121

turn. I didn't know what to say to be honest, they didn't seem in any way remarkable but he wanted me to like them. That was blatantly obvious. He really wanted me to like them.

We stood there staring at each in turn while I searched for something meaningful to say. 'Do they all feature the same boy?'

'Yes, yes, he's the son of a good friend.'

There was an abstract quality to the photos. The boy was clearly playing with one toy or another in each photo, but I couldn't make out his features due to defined areas of light and shade. For some reason I couldn't quantify I thought there was an unmistakable sadness about him. A sadness that still haunts me today. 'How old is he?'

He smiled warmly. 'He's five now, but he was four when I took the photos. A lovely lad, he was one of my patients for a time.'

'A patient, really?'

'Child psychiatry still forms the bulk of my work. I think I may have mentioned I lecture at the university on a part-time basis.'

'Did the boy get better?'

He paused before responding, and raised a hand to his face masking his eyes. 'Sadly not, most regrettable, It's not possible to help all my patients however hard I try.'

I sat on the white leather settee, literally lost for words. Why would he indulge such an obvious reminder of his failures? 'But, he's only...'

'Now, now, no more questions, patient confidentiality and all that!' He pushed up the sleeve of his jacket and looked at his watch. 'There's an excellent Italian restaurant not ten minutes' walk away. Why don't we freshen up and get ourselves something to eat at about sevenish? I believe it's actually stopped raining.'

I nodded enthusiastically, glad to change the subject and gratified by the prospect of a meal.

'There are a few house rules I need to discuss with you at some point, but that can almost certainly wait until morning.'

'Rules?'

'Nothing to worry about my dear, nothing whatsoever. We'll get something down on paper at some point so that everything is crystal clear to both of us. I find that's the best way of avoiding any unfortunate misunderstandings.'

'I'd like to give Mum and Dad a ring to let them know we've arrived, if that's all right with you?'

He smiled engagingly and shook his head. 'There's no phone, I'm afraid. It developed a fault some months back and I never had it repaired. I found myself rather enjoying the peace and quiet. Now, I'll change here, you use the bedroom, and we'll meet in the hallway in precisely ten minutes. There's a clock on your bedroom wall.'

Chapter 17

Mrs Martin flicked through the pages of my well thumbed personal journal, stopped, began again, and then closed the cover before looking up and handing it back to me with an outstretched hand. 'I have to say I'm impressed. You've clearly been putting in a good deal of effort. Very well done Cynthia, very well done!'

'It helps pass the time.' Why did I say that? Why be flippant? Why not accept the well-intentioned compliment with good grace?

She screwed up her face. 'Okay, I guess that's got to be a good thing, but this should be so much more than a boredom relieving exercise. Are you still finding the process useful?'

'Yeah, sorry, I'm making light of things. I don't know what on earth's wrong with me sometimes. Obviously I'm only part way into my story, there's still a lot to cover, but yes, it's making me think.'

'That's good to hear. Tell me more.'

She always used that line: tell me more, tell me more, as if nothing I said was ever sufficient. 'How best to put it? I've discovered an inner determination I didn't know existed.'

'And you've put that to good use?'

'Going over events in a logical order, one by one, who said what, who did what, what I thought, the decisions I made, it's cathartic. I'm beginning to recognise that events were largely beyond my control.'

She looked less than convinced. 'Mmm... We all make choices Cynthia. Every day we make choices that take us along one path or another. I doubt you were any different.'

I didn't like the way the conversation was going one little bit. She was correct, of course, but there was more to it than that. It was more complex, not nearly as simplistic. 'I made choices, sure I did, but I think they were reasonable choices in the circumstances. Hindsight tends to make things appear a lot clearer than they were at the time. You've said that yourself. Maybe I was a bit naive, I'd accept that much, but I just didn't see the warning signs. Why would I?'

'You don't think you were in any way complicit?'

I crossed my arms and linked them tightly across my chest. 'No, no, absolutely not! I had no comprehension of what was going on, none whatsoever.'

'And you're sure of that?'

I relaxed my arms and moved to the very edge of my seat. 'Yes, I'm certain, I couldn't be more certain. He was directing events. The man was in control.'

She smiled thinly without parting her lips. 'I've been in this job a long time Cynthia. There's not much I haven't heard before.'

The man was pure evil, the devil incarnate. I wanted her to believe me. I needed her to believe me. 'The bastard was clever, really clever, an arch manipulator, a Svengali! He charmed and twisted and cajoled and threatened. I can't properly explain it. Words just aren't enough. If you'd met him, if you'd known him, you'd understand what I'm talking about.'

'I've met manipulative men.'

'Not like this one.'

'So you're saying you were manipulated?'

'Yes, yes, gradually, minute by minute, hour by hour, day by day! He got under my skin and ate away at my self-esteem and independence. The bastard knew exactly what he was doing.'

'From the beginning?'

'Yes, from the beginning, the very beginning! From the first second he met me.'

'So, you understand that now?'

'Yes, yes, I do.'

She nodded twice and smiled, more warmly this time. 'I'm beginning to get the picture. Keep thinking, keep writing, keep making sense of events. We're making excellent progress.'

'Okay.'

She paused, as if to emphasise the importance of her words. 'Things are going well, I'm in no doubt about that, but I'm guessing it's going to get harder from here.'

'Yeah, you're probably right.'

'You think?'

I laughed despite myself. 'It's going to get harder. I know that.'

'I realise I've said it before, but remember that I'm not here to judge you Cynthia. Don't hold anything back.'

'You'll understand when I write the rest of the story. Read it and you'll understand.'

'Good, that's good, I'll look forward to it. It may not feel like it at the moment, but as I said we're making good progress.'

I got the message the first time, but her good intentions were appreciated. She glanced at the wall clock to the right of her seat. 'Right, we've got another ten minutes or so before bringing the session to a close. Have you heard anything from your family?'

I sat back in my seat, sucked in the stale prison air and tried to relax. 'Mum brought the girls to see me last visiting.'

'Ah, that's good to hear, how are they all doing?'

I exhaled with an audible hiss. 'I think they only come because they feel they have to.'

She took a white paper hankie from her handbag and handed it to me as a single tear ran down my cheek and found home on my jumper. 'It's never easy for relatives.'

I shook my head. 'I sometimes wonder if they'd be better off without me. You know, just blank me from their minds and get on with their lives, try to put what happened behind them.'

She looked perplexed. 'Now, come on Cynthia, we've had this conversation more than once. Not too long ago we sat down and read their letters together. Your mum loves you, the girls love you. That's blatantly obvious; I thought you'd accepted that.'

I bowed my head, shamed by my uncertainty. 'I know, but this place…'

'They come because they want to see you. They come because they love you.'

I agreed, more to bring the subject to a close than anything else.

'Just keep rereading those letters whenever doubts enter your mind.'

'I guess they provide a certain melancholy solace.'

'I can tell we chose the correct English teacher.'

I grinned, pleased by the compliment.

'You're loved Cynthia, that's more than many here can claim. Now, is there anything else you want to talk about before we bring the session to an end?'

'I was wondering how Emma's doing. Is she coming back?'

'You know I can't go into any detail, but I understand that she's making reasonable progress.'

'And she'll be coming back?'

'As far as I know.'

'I'm not looking forward to sharing a cell with the woman again, to be honest.'

'Just try your best to get on with her. That's all you can do. You don't get to choose your cellmate.'

'Yeah, I know that much.'

She glanced at the clock again, rose from her seat, and smiled a toothy smile. 'That's it for today Cynthia, keep writing, and we'll talk again in a week's time.'

I stood to leave, glad of the opportunity to escape to the isolation of my cell whilst I still had the opportunity. Doesn't time fly when you're enjoying yourself.

Chapter 18

Dr Galbraith entered Giovanni's Restaurant in the style of a movie star navigating the red carpet: a smile here, a handshake or kind word there. He knew all the staff by name, no hesitation, no searching his busy mind. 'How are you Piero? How's that lovely young wife of yours Antonio? Marvellous to see you again. I hope your son's feeling better after his illness. Measles wasn't it?'

'Yes, he's much better, thank you Doctor.'

'Marvellous, absolutely marvellous! Very glad to hear it.'

And so it continued. That's the sort of man he was: dripping with superficial charm. It poured out of him like a torrent, engulfing all who crossed his path.

He noticeably relaxed as the evening progressed and the lines on his face melted away. Maybe it was the red wine, maybe the toothsome food, maybe the convivial company, or maybe all or none of the above. Who am I to say? He talked of his love of psychiatry and my pending studies with an obvious passion that reignited my flagging enthusiasm for the course. He made the study of the human mind and behaviour sound utterly fascinating, and my remaining misgivings vanished like an ice cube in the hot summer sun. The more he talked, the more enthused I became and the more I realised just how much catching up I had to do if I wasn't to fail almost as soon as I began. I'd be starting the course afresh with no settling in time and no honeymoon period before the work started in earnest. I'd be at a distinct disadvantage when compared to the other students. That's the way it was. It was an undeniable truth.There was no avoiding that realisation. I needed the doctor's help to succeed.

By the time we'd eaten our desserts and were enjoying freshly brewed aromatic coffee, the doctor was still uttering much needed words of reassurance in soft reassuring tones that alleviated my anxieties very nicely. I had nothing to worry about. He was there for me. An expert in his field. It wouldn't be easy, but I was a bright girl. It was doable. He'd hold my hand every single step of the way. A bedside manner par excellence! He didn't actually say I had no hope of a favourable outcome without his tutelage, but he may as well have. It was implied. It was definitely implied and I knew it to be true.

Dr Galbraith slept on the three seater settee in the lounge that night, whilst I slept in his comfortable king size bed seemingly surrounded by oppressive framed photographs of that same unfortunate child. I'd protested half heartedly initially, I'd offered to make do with the sofa, but he insisted and I capitulated without further argument. I was his guest. He was the professor and I his student. It seemed best to comply.

I could hear that he was already up and about and making breakfast when I got up at about 8:15 a.m. the following morning. I pulled on magenta Egyptian cotton dressing gown and a pair of well worn sheepskin slippers, before making a quick bathroom visit, running a brush though my sleep tangled hair and joining him in the kitchen a few minutes later. I was met by him sitting at the table with a concerned expression on his face: a concerned look I couldn't help but notice. A concerned look that demanded a response. 'Is everything all right Doctor?'

He just sat there with an angst expression on his face, shifting uneasily in his seat but not saying a word.

Say something Doctor. Just say something and put me out of my misery. 'Look, if I've done something to upset you, just say.'

He shook his head slowly and sighed. 'I had intended to discuss the house rules later this week my dear, but perhaps now is as good a time as any given the circumstances.'

Circumstances? What circumstances? I stood and glared at him. 'Can I at least have a cup of coffee first?'

Another theatrical sigh. Infuriating!

I looked towards the kettle pointedly, and he grinned, attempting to lighten the mood. 'I suppose we can make an exception just this once. Take a seat my dear, the water's already boiled. No tips required.'

I sat as instructed and waited whilst he prepared the drinks before sitting down opposite me. 'I really would appreciate it if you dressed more appropriately before leaving the bedroom each morning.'

I laughed nervously, thinking it may be his idea of a joke, but no, not even a flicker of a smile crossed his face. He meant every pompous unreasonable word. But I've never been a fan of confrontation, and thought it best to diffuse the situation rather than tell him what I really thought of him at that precise moment. 'Okay, if it makes you feel more comfortable.'

'I really think it's best.'

Oh, he thought it was best. I'd doff my cap to the sanctimonious pig. I quietly fumed, and stood with the intention of approaching the toaster, but he pushed back his chair, jumped to his feet, and stood directly between me and the worktop. 'Let's start as we mean to go on my dear. Why don't you go and get dressed in something suitable, and your toast will be waiting for you just as soon as you're ready.'

Suitable? Suitable for what? What on earth was he talking about? I wanted to protest, I wanted to say no, I wanted to shout no, but his wild change in mood unnerved and unsettled me. 'Is there anything else you want to say?'

'Not at all my dear, not at all; now off you pop and I'll make that toast you required. White or wholemeal?'

I headed in the direction of the bedroom and shouted, 'White please,' without looking back.

'Brown really would be a wiser choice.'

Ahhh! I chose to ignore his recommendation, cursed crudely under my breath, and closed the bedroom door behind me.

Chapter 19

Emma's back, delivered to my cell by a burly middle-aged prison officer with long mousy hair, stud earrings and a midlife crisis. If only she'd taken her somewhere else; it wouldn't matter where, just not here with me. Is that too much to ask? It seems the answer is a resounding, yes, shouted from the rafters.

I made a real effort when she first arrived despite my inclinations to the contrary. I tried to be nice, I tried to hide my true feelings, I said hello, I asked how she was doing, and if her injuries were healed, but I didn't really care what she said in response, if I'm honest. I don't like the woman, I despise what she did to that innocent child and I don't trust a single word that comes out of her crafty loathsome mouth. The events that led her to my door had ruthless elusive deception at their very core. How can I take anything she says at face value? Why on earth should I? If she's capable of inducing, exaggerating and fabricating physical symptoms in a dependent child in her care, what else is she capable of? Almost anything, I presume. She successfully conned a lot of people for a long time. If lying were a competitive event, she'd be the champion of the entire world.

Anyway, for anyone who's still interested, she tells me that her wrists are healing slowly, but remain painful. Whether or not that's true, of course, is debatable. I have to admit they look well healed to me.

She told me she's to receive one to one counselling. I saw that one coming. Maybe a pragmatic structured therapeutic approach would be best. I don't envy Mrs Martin that particular task. There are limits to everyone's abilities, and I suspect Freud himself would struggle with this one even if reincarnated and dedicated to the task.

Emma has asked what I'm writing about more than once. She keeps asking, and I keep giving dismissive not committal responses that don't give anything away. I just don't want her to know. It has absolutely nothing to do with her. You'd think she'd get the message, but no, she's having none of it. 'Come on Cynthia, tell me, tell me. What do you keep writing? You can tell me, I won't tell anyone.' Hopefully she'll shut up at some point in the not too distant future and give me the peace I need to get on with it.

I don't think Emma realises just how much she's detested by the majority of other inmates. Everyone knows exactly what she did. That want-to-be-liked guard made certain of that. There'll be a reception committee waiting for her just as soon as the opportunity arises. I could warn her, of course. I've thought about it. I could tip her the wink one fine day, but what would be the point in that? It wouldn't change anything at all. Her world's about to become a less predictable and more frightening place. Natural justice some might say, but I don't see it that way. I want no part of her world, no part in her punishment. She's not a significant player in my life and I'll keep it that way if I can. Maybe I shouldn't have immortalised her on paper. I can't envisage a happy ending to her story. What about you? Would you say anything?

I plan to write two or three more pages before heading to my English class. I'm looking forward to that: the class, not the writing. Mrs Martin was correct in surmising that the process is becoming somewhat harder as my story continues. The caustic memories flood back each and every time I put pen to paper. Flashbacks, nightmares, anxiety and panic attacks are still all too regular features of my unhappy existence. I wake up drenched in sweat at about 5:00 a.m.

every morning: always early, always clammy, always exhausted, and always relieved that another night is finally over. Mrs Martin calls it post-traumatic stress: it seems it's not only combat soldiers who suffer it as I once thought. What a way to live! I'll keep writing in the hope the memories fade with time and life becomes more bearable again. Closure, isn't that what the Americans call it in that to-the-point way of theirs? Yes, that's it, I'm searching for closure. Time's a great healer, as the old saying goes, but I fear my life experiences may have changed me forever.

I've been reading and rereading Mum's and the girls' letters, as Mrs Martin suggested. And she's correct, it helps for a while. They love me and don't apportion blame. Their words convey warm affection not condemnation. Such things matter. They really matter when you're separated as we are. Yes, we only meet in that stark communal room with its peeling paint and over bright lighting, but they come, that's what matters, as unpleasant as it is, they still come. Okay, we don't enjoy the gifts that freedom would endow. We can't do the ordinary things that others take for granted. I can't take my lovely girls shopping, or to ballet classes, or collect them from school at the end of the day. I can't pop in to ensure Mum's okay and looking after herself properly, or to visit Dad's grave with flowers. I can't do any of those things and a lot more besides, but I can write to them, I can speak to them by phone when the system allows, and I can count the days until their next visit dawns. I'll keep waiting and I'll keep counting as patiently as I can. I'm loved, and that's more than many can claim. Emma, for example, doesn't receive any visitors at all. Maybe she brought it on herself, but even so, I wouldn't wish that on my worst enemy.

I'm going to have to bring this session to a close soon. These last couple of paragraphs have taken me longer to construct than I originally envisaged, and I need to get going in a minute or two if I'm not going to be late for the class. One of the guards will be putting a key in the lock and opening my cell door any time now. It's one of the features of prison life: the inescapable clanking sound of metal keys in metal locks resounding in every corner and crevice. You just can't escape it. Believe me I've tried. I'll let you know how the lesson went just as soon as I can if I think there's anything worth sharing and remember to write it down. With a bit of luck I should be able to scribble a few more miserable lines before lights out.

Chapter 20

Dr Galbraith spent the rest of the week introducing me to various psychological text books and their contents, and coaching me in the fundamental basics he deemed essential to my future academic survival. We worked hard to an agreed timetable comprising three hours before lunch time, starting at 9:00 a.m. and a further two hours from 2:00 p.m. to 4:00 p.m. each afternoon. I have to admit that I rather enjoyed the process in the main despite its arduous nature. The workload was demanding but not overly onerous when I put my mind to it, he knew his subject extremely well, he communicated the complex concepts expertly in language I understood, and there was no further talk of rules, or at least not until the Friday afternoon when he was due to leave for Caerystwyth.

I was sitting in the lounge that day, rearranging some handwritten notes in one file or another, when he suddenly appeared from the kitchen with his brown faux crocodile leather briefcase in one hand, and a look I struggled to decipher on his otherwise handsome face. I looked up and smiled, grateful for his efforts, but keenly anticipating some time to myself before the other students arrived to inhabit the upstairs flats sometime that weekend. Rather than say his goodbyes as I anticipated, however, he sat in the armchair to my right, requested that I move my notes, and opened his briefcase on the stylish French white marble coffee table directly in front of him.

'You may recall my mention of a few house rules earlier in the week.'

I took a deep breath. Be patient Cynthia, be patient. Just get it over with as quickly as possible and he'll be on his way.

'Yeah, you said something, but I thought we'd already covered that.'

He laughed in a dismissive manner that left me feeling insulted and inadequate, as if he considered my observation ridiculous in the extreme. 'Why would you think that?'

I felt under pressure to respond and felt my face redden. 'I just thought you'd explained the house rules in full.'

'Not at all my dear, I've made a few typed notes to simplify the process. I think that makes sense.'

I shook my head slowly. Was that really necessary? 'If you want me to pay rent, all you have to do is say so.'

'Not at all my dear, not at all; I wouldn't dream of it. Give me a second or two and all will become clear.'

I sat and waited with increasing impatience as he took two sheets of paper from the briefcase and handed one to me with an outstretched hand. 'Read it through carefully my dear, and tell me if there's anything that requires clarification before we both sign the document.'

This was becoming stranger and more stressful by the second. I was completely out of my depth. 'Sign it? Is it some form of contract or something?'

'More an agreement between the two of us my dear; there's absolutely no legal implications, none whatsoever. You needn't concern yourself in that regard. Just read it through carefully as I originally suggested, and we can progress from there.'

'Couldn't we just talk about it?'

He appeared utterly exasperated. 'I've gone to a great deal of effort Cynthia. I would have thought complying with my request would be the least you could do in the circumstances.'

I was ready to do what I was told and get him out of there as quickly as possible. I balanced my reading glasses on the bridge of my nose and began reading:

1. Cynthia will work hard at her studies, with a minimum of two hours home study each and every day.

2. Cynthia will consult Dr Galbraith regarding her studies as and when necessary.

3. Cynthia will provide Dr Galbraith with a weekly academic update at an agreed time, including areas of study, allocated tasks and the results of any assessments.

4. Cynthia will put her studies before socialising or home visits.

5. Cynthia will clean and tidy the flat prior to Dr Galbraith's weekly visits.

6. Dr Galbraith will do all he can to facilitate Cynthia's academic success.

I read it, and reread it, shocked that he'd write such a thing, incredulous that he'd expect me to sign it. It seemed entirely unnecessary, hugely over the top. But, he was the academic expert. And it was his flat, at the end of the day.

'I can see that you're somewhat disconcerted my dear, but I can assure you that I'm acting entirely in your interests. It's an effective technique I've used before with excellent results. You have the capacity to achieve great things but only with my help. I simply want to ensure that you live up to that potential of yours. We must do whatever it takes to achieve that outcome. Steven would want that. Of course he would. I'm doing this for both of you. I cannot stress that sufficiently.'

I smiled at Steven's memory, and nodded, not totally persuaded but near to caving.

'The first five points lead directly to point six. It's reciprocal: you do your utmost to achieve success, and I do likewise on your behalf. The agreement is simply a means of formalising that commitment on paper.'

I still thought it strange, but I accepted his fountain pen and signed, keen to get it over with, keen to see him on his way, as I said before.

'I'm delighted that you've finally seen sense my dear. It would be all too easy for a less insightful person to misconstrue my intentions and become distracted. Have a good weekend, and I'll see you again on Wednesday afternoon. We may as well make full use of your free time once term begins. I'll stay overnight and leave for Caerystwyth early on the Thursday morning. I have a clinic at ten.'

'I had thought of visiting Mum and Dad on Wednesday.'

'Work first, family second. That's what we've agreed. That's the way it has to be. Are we clear?'

I stared at the ceiling and nodded. 'Do you plan to stay every Wednesday?'

He nodded repeatedly and enthusiastically. 'I think it's advisable, at least for the foreseeable future. It will provide the ideal opportunity for a catch up face to face, so to speak. Think of it as a private tutorial session during which either of us can address any pertinent concerns and evaluate your progress.'

'I guess that's okay.'

I think I must have whispered my words ever so quietly, because he said, 'I didn't quite catch that my dear. Perhaps you could elucidate your response a little more clearly.'

I said, 'Okay,' more loudly this time.

'Glad to hear it my dear. Very glad to hear it. You won't be sorry.'

He stood, as if to leave, but sat again almost immediately and leant towards me on the very edge of his seat. 'There is one matter I've neglected to mention. Something I decided to discuss orally rather than address in writing.'

Oh, shit, surely not more rules. Where on earth was this going? His impenetrable eyes and inscrutable countenance gave little if anything away.

'You may have noticed that each of the houses on this side of the street have basements. Nothing unusual in residences of this style and period, of course. They were used as coal holes or servants' living quarters in times gone by.'

'I hadn't given it any thought, to be honest.' Why talk about the basement?

'That's a good thing: it's vitally important that you keep it that way. The cellar is my personal domain, somewhere I store various confidential files pertinent to my work. I keep the access door locked at all times. Please don't be tempted to try to open it. That's the one thing I couldn't tolerate. A deal breaker, as the modern parlance goes. Am I understood?'

I nodded, taken aback by his words and unsmiling demeanour. 'I don't think it needed saying. I've no interest in your precious cellar.'

'So you'll stay clear.'

'Yes, a thousand times, yes! You've made yourself perfectly clear. I won't go anywhere near your cellar.' I was beginning to wonder if returning to university was such a good idea after all.

Chapter 21

Emma's back in the same hospital she so recently left, but not by her own hand on this occasion. Not a great surprise, as I previously suggested. I think her demise was inevitable at some stage or other given the realities of her life here. I'm told she was targeted by a group of prison world's more vindictive residents, and violently attacked when attempting to take an early morning shower, whilst other prisoners and previously attendant guards ignored her calls for help and looked or walked away. That same needy guard I've mentioned more than once has been trumpeting the gory details of the enthusiastic mob handed assault to anyone and everyone who's willing to cock an eager ear: broken teeth, a fractured nose with the white bone breaking the skin, multiple tufts of hair torn from her bloody scalp, and a deep ten inch gash in her right buttock from coccyx to thigh, courtesy of a razor sharp blade of indeterminate type. They'll search for it half heartedly, of course, but these things are rarely found in such circumstances. All in all she's in quite a mess apparently. Terrible really! I hope she enjoys the resulting medical attention, because from what I'm told it's going to be a rather long stay this time.

I don't mean to sound callous, I really don't. I don't bear her any ill will as I may have mentioned before, but I'm not going to pretend her predicament has lost me any sleep. Not because I don't care, not because I'm an unsympathetic person by nature. I'm just not responsible for her victimisation. That's one thing I'm clear on. I took no part in the attack, and warning her of its inevitability would have served little if any purpose. Being ignored and having her food repeatedly spat in should have told her what she needed to know. She could have protested, she could have pleaded her case with prisoners and staff, she could have watched her back a little more carefully than usual, but it would have happened anyway. It was just a matter of when and how. I'm going to put her troubles to the back of my mind and forget her as best I can for as long as I can. I think that's best, and before you judge, it's practicality rather than selfishness. I just don't want to become distracted when I'm making such good progress with my storytelling. I'll be faced with her return soon enough anyway. I'll think about it then when I have no choice in the matter. Why waste my energy on her prior to that inevitable day?

Chapter 22

I was initially glad of some time to myself after the unpleasantness prior to the doctor's departure, but anyone who's lived alone will know that an empty house can be a very lonely place, particularly when you're not familiar with such circumstances. I'd just about given up on my expected housemates turning up when early on the Monday morning I was hurrying down the hall in the direction of the front door, clutching my textbooks tightly in both hands, when I heard what sounded like a boy yelling incoherently in the flat directly above me, followed by a resounding thud, as if an item of furniture had crashed to the floor. I stopped and listened to the subsequent silence, weighing up the possibilities. Someone was moving in. They'd finally arrived, that seemed blatantly obvious.

I placed my books on the bottom step of the staircase, pushed up my coat sleeve, checked my Timex, decided I had just about enough time to say a quick hello before making my way to my first lecture, and urgently ascended the stairs two or three at a time, just as the door at the top began to slowly open.

I stopped on the small landing and stared, searching for a response as the doctor stepped out of the flat and closed the door behind him. He was sweating, panting hard, his tie tugged loose, he looked agitated, and his emerging smile was less than convincing, to say the least.

I shook my head. 'Doctor, I wasn't expecting... I thought...'

His smile evaporated as quickly as it appeared. 'Shouldn't you have left for university before now?'

'I just wanted to say hello. I thought...'

'You thought, is that really such a good idea?'

'I just…'

He took a deep breath and calmed his breathing. 'It's all perfectly straightforward. No more questions, now off to university with you, and meet me in the Golden Lion's lounge bar at one fifteen. All will become clear.'

'But, I was planning to…'

'You don't want to be late my dear. Steven wouldn't want that. I'll see you at one fifteen precisely.'

He played the S card often in those days, when it suited him, when he wanted to influence me in a particular direction. And it worked. Hugely frustratingly, it almost always worked. 'I'll see you then.'

The swirling tobacco smoke stung my eyes as I entered the Golden Lion public house at about 1:10 p.m., and I paused momentarily, allowing my vision to adapt to the dim interior. I looked around the room and spotted him sitting alone at a table in a quiet corner of the room, directly below a silent wall-mounted jukebox with a handwritten 'out of order' sign pasted to its glass front. He looked up and raised a hand in acknowledgement as I approached him. 'Take a seat my dear. How about a drink to help us relax? What do you say? I was about to have another.'

'Just a sparkling water for me please.'

'Really? Are you sure I can't tempt you?'

I sat opposite him and frowned. 'I've got a lecture in a little over an hour, water will be fine thank you.'

'Very wise my dear, very wise! How about a bite to eat?'

'I ate a pasty on my way here.'

He stood, approached the bar and returned a minute or two later with a glass of water for me and a double brandy with ice for himself. 'Right, listen carefully my dear, and I'll explain the change of plans.'

Change of plans. What change of plans? I sat in apprehensive silence, waiting for him to speak again.

145

'I won't be renting the first and second floor flats for the foreseeable future despite my earlier plans. I've asked the university to arrange alternative accommodation for the relevant students. I'll send on their belongings in due course.'

Should I say anything? Yes, why not? 'But I could swear I heard someone call out this morning. I thought it sounded like a young boy.'

He laughed, head back, throat taught, virtually manic. 'Just the radio my dear! I was listening to a rather engrossing play on Radio 4 whilst moving some extremely heavy furniture from one room to another. It's about time I sorted the place out.'

Okay, I guess that made sense even if it did sound so real at the time. 'So you're leaving the flats empty. Why would you do that?'

'Your studies are progressing reasonably well overall as we've discussed more than once my dear, but there's absolutely no room for complacency. The last thing you need is unfortunate distractions.'

I wondered why on earth he hadn't talked to me before making a decision that directly affected me? 'But I'd enjoy having other people in the house. It can feel very empty sometimes.'

'The decision is made my dear. You're going to have to get used to it I'm afraid.'

And that was it. The flats remained empty for as long as I lived there.

Nothing of any great significance happened in the subsequent weeks. I worked hard at my studies, kept socialising to a bare minimum, repeatedly put off visits home on the doctor's recommendation, and met with him each and every Wednesday afternoon as agreed to discuss my progress, inevitably followed by a meal for two at the flat or one local restaurant or another. I didn't find our meetings particularly arduous, but I always hoped we would eat out rather than cook and eat in. His culinary standards were insurmountably high, as it seemed they were in all things, and I began to suspect he suffered OCD to some degree, which caused some unpleasantness on occasions. Everything had to be immaculate, everything had to be ordered and in its precise place. Even the items of food in the larder fridge and various kitchen cupboards had to be stored in order of size and type, with any labels facing outwards for easy scrutiny. He tried to make a joke of it when insisting I put right any discrepancies, but his facial muscles tightened and betrayed his true feelings. There'd be an unequivocal tension in the air, that I felt it was my task to diffuse. He even licked a finger on one occasion and ran it across the top of a picture frame before holding it out in front of him and loudly proclaiming, 'Dust! A myriad tiny particles of waste matter. You really should be more careful my dear. I have a white glove somewhere. It would be ideal for the purpose.'

I recall turning and walking away in the direction of the lounge, but he fetched a damp cloth form the sink, hurried after me and handed it to me insistently. 'I think it's best if you wipe it clean immediately my dear. Steven wouldn't want you to be slovenly, now would he?'

I was quietly seething, but softened again at the mention of Steven's name. 'I suppose not.'

'There's no suppose about it my dear. Now get it done.'

And that's how it went, week by week, month by month, the same predictable pattern right up to the 10th of April when everything changed. He was particularly complimentary of my work that afternoon, praising my efforts, expounding my virtues, with none of the usual morale sapping criticisms with which I'd become so familiar.

We finished working at just after 5:00 p.m. that afternoon, and sat together in the lounge listening to Stravinsky and enjoying a glass of his favourite French claret for the next couple of hours. There was something different about him that evening, he was more relaxed, warmer, more convivial, just as he'd been at the Indian restaurant in Tenby that first time, and I found myself enjoying his company.

We went out at about 8:00 p.m., walked off the strains of the day and enjoyed an excellent meal at our favoured Italian restaurant as per usual. He took the lead in our conversation, as was the norm, but instead of academia and my need to focus on my work, he talked of his travels and love of Rome. 'It's a wonderful city Cynthia. An education, a living museum with another architectural treasure to behold and ponder at every turn.'

'I'd love to go there one day.'

'And you will my dear, you will. And I shall be your guide.'

The evening continued in that vein, with promises to expand my education from psychology to art, to opera, to poetry and travel to distant lands. 'You've earned it Cynthia. You've worked hard, you've kept your side of our agreement. Now it's my turn, you deserve your reward.'

When we arrived back at the flat shortly before midnight, he took my coat, suggested I choose a suitably relaxing classical album to bring the evening to a close, and poured us both a generous tot of fine Hennessy brandy whilst I made a brief toilet visit to powder my nose and check my makeup.

I returned to the lounge, sat in one of the two wonderfully comfortable leather armchairs, accepted the drink gratefully and sipped at it, grimacing slightly as the strong spirit burned my throat.

'Down the hatch my dear. Down the hatch!'

I lifted the crystal brandy glass to my mouth and took a generous gulp.

'That's it my dear, that's it! Now just sit back, relax and let the music work its magic.'

And that's the last thing I remember. I've experienced drunken memory loss more than once, but this time was different. I recall getting lost in the sweeping orchestral melody, I recall downing the brandy with his encouragement ringing in my ears, and then nothing, absolutely nothing, as if I stopped existing at that precise moment.

I woke up in bed the next morning with a pounding headache and a sore back that made me wince when I moved even slightly. I peered around the room and saw that my clothes were neatly folded on a bedside cabinet, but I couldn't remember undressing. Why would I do that? It just wasn't like me to get paralytic with alcohol.

When I eventually dragged my naked body out of bed on shaky legs about half an hour or so later, I noticed blood on the sheets. I thought for a second or two that my period had started unexpectedly, but I quickly dismissed the idea almost as soon as I thought it. I massaged my head ever so gently, opened the curtains slightly to let in the subtle morning light, stood with my back facing the full length mirror on the back of the wardrobe door and began to cry silent tears that welled in my eyes, ran down my face and fell to the carpet in a steady unremitting stream. There were multiple deep bloody scratches on either side of my spine just above my reddened and bruised buttocks. What on earth had happened to me? I had difficulty computing the injuries and their significance. Steven was a gentle and attentive lover, my first. This was new territory, alien to my experience. I felt lost, confused, very close to panic and my head pounded as if a jackhammer were operating inside my skull. Why couldn't I remember? It made little sense as I began filling in the gaps. Surely not, surely not! Did I really drink that much? Was I really that legless? Did the doctor really cause my injuries? It seemed unlikely, but what other explanation was there.

I flinched and urgently grabbed a large damp bath towel from the heated towel rail in the small ensuite bathroom as Dr Galbraith knocked hard on the bedroom door and opened it without waiting to be invited in. 'Ah, I thought I heard you up and about. I'm afraid you're running rather late my dear, but not to worry. I've already been in touch with the university on your behalf and told them you won't be in this morning. A severe migraine, in case anyone asks later in the day. It seemed best. No need to thank me.'

I took a step or two backwards and clutched the towel tightly to my body. 'W-what happened last night?'

'I must be on my way my dear. I've no time to talk now. Pressure of work and all that. You have a good deal of free time before this afternoon's lectures, I suggest you use it wisely to tidy this place up after last night's revelries. It's in a shocking state, as I'm sure you'll agree. I will see you again next Wednesday as per usual.' And then he winked once before turning and walking away. 'I didn't realise you were such a passionate girl my dear. Perhaps it would be wise not to drink quite so much next time.'

I'm beginning to regret falling out with Needy Guard despite my deep loathing for every aspect of her unfortunate personality. She visited my cell early this morning, held up a large brown envelope in full view, and taunted me with it for a full five minutes or more before finally handing it over. She held it out, withdrew it, and repeated the process time and time again like a self-indulgent playground bully or a cat playing with a mouse. I could have screamed, I could have hit out, I could have lost control completely, but instead I played her game in the interests of an easy life, pleading, indulging her mindless cruelty, until I finally lost patience and sat on my bunk without moving or speaking in a silent Gandhi-like passive protest intended to diffuse her inhumanity. And it worked, it really worked, she lost interest a lot quicker than I'd anticipated and tossed the envelope onto the mattress just out of my reach. One final barb, driving home her dominance: 'There's no need to be like that Cynthia. I was just having a bit of fun, girl. Have you heard the latest on Emma?'

Every part of my being wanted to yell a stream of angry profanities and obliterate her sneering grin, but instead I forced a smile and said, 'No, I hope she's making progress.'

And then that repugnant sneer again. 'You're too soft for your own good Cynthia. The bitch will be back with you soon enough. See how you feel then. I wouldn't be too friendly if I were you. It wouldn't go down well with the rest of the girls, if you know what I mean.'

'We don't choose our cellmates.'

'Why would you? You're nothing special. You're in prison not some posh boarding school.'

I moved sideways along the mattress, inch by inch, inch by subtle inch, and reached out, determinedly clutching the envelope tightly in my right hand. 'Can I have some time alone to read my letter please? It may be from my solicitor.'

She laughed humourlessly. 'Don't get your hopes up girl, that's never a good idea in this place. Keep your head down, do your time, and pray it passes quickly. That's the best you can hope for. You should have learnt that by now. You must be a slow learner.'

'Can I have some time to read the letter in privacy now, please?'

And then a mocking curtsy. The cow, the mocking patronising cow! 'Whatever madam requires. But, you'll mark my words if you know what's good for you.'

'Thank you, I will. I'm sorry if I upset you.'

A final hoarse smoker's laugh and she left without further comment. I watched her walk away, waddling like an over plump land-bound duck, before saying a silent prayer of thanks for small mercies and tearing open the envelope, taking out my angst and frustration on the stiff brown paper.

The style of envelope had mislead me. The communication wasn't from my lawyer. There were no legal papers, no contrived formal language. Instead I discovered a single page letter from Jack in his barely decipherable scribbled handwriting with his address and telephone number, and three six-by eight-inch glossy photos of his Californian wedding ceremony in Monterey, an attractive coastal town with wonderful views of the Pacific Ocean about one hundred and twenty miles south of San Francisco.

I held the first photo out in front of me to accommodate my eyesight and laughed and cried simultaneously in an explosion of conflicted raw emotion. It looked wonderful, truly wonderful. If only I could have been there. If only, if only! Two small words of infinite meaning.

I held out the first photo at the optimum distance and studied it through my tears. It featured Jack and his new bride, resplendent in their sartorial finery, smiling, joyous on their very special day. Jack was clean shaven, tanned and glowing, exuding a youthful well-being that left me both envious and smiling. He'd come such a long way since the not so far-off days of drug abuse, and it was wonderful to witness, if only in a photographic representation of reality. At least one of us had found happiness. I guess one out of two's not too bad in this big bad world of ours. I pray it continues. Life really can be so unpredictable as I hope I've already established.

The second photo featured the blushing bride with her three attractive young bridesmaids, a photo typical of its genre, and if I'm honest not of any great interest as I don't know any of them personally. I looked at Marie for a moment or two, observed that she'd put on a little weight around the midriff, and placed the photo onto the bed immediately next to me. The third photo in contrast featured a family group, unremarkable in itself, but as I focussed on each individual in turn it left me reeling. Mum was there, in a garish lilac suit and matching hat with a large prominent purple feather, and so were my beautiful girls, standing and grinning hand in hand to her immediate left. Why hadn't they told me? We'd sat facing each other just a short time before they made the trip and they made no mention of the wedding or their planned attendance. The flights must have been booked, the accommodation arranged, their excitement levels rising exponentially, and yet they didn't say a single word. As if nothing of importance was planned. As if it wasn't worth talking about. I've never felt more excluded, so insignificant, so utterly worthless. Maybe they thought discussion of the trip would have been too much for me to bear. Maybe they thought sharing their happy anticipation would have rubbed salt in my festering wounds. Or maybe I just don't feature in their thoughts anymore. No, what on earth am I saying? I'm loved and they had my best interests at heart. Or at least I'd like to think so anyway.

Chapter 24

Dr Galbraith behaved as if nothing of any great significance had happened the previous week when he arrived at the flat early on the following Wednesday afternoon. He made a quick inspection of each room in turn, pointed out what he saw as the shortcomings, and issued words of praise and encouragement as he saw fit. Overall, he concluded, the state of the flat warranted a five out of ten star rating, not worthy of reward or sanction. I'd been lucky and had to do better in future. I found myself relieved that he wasn't overly critical, and silently acknowledged that I was becoming increasingly dependent on him for much needed validation. He was an important man, an influential man. He'd reintroduced me to the academic world, and I valued his opinion.

We spent the next couple of hours discussing craniology and its tragic historic consequences in Nazi Europe, following which he reintroduced and reinforced the importance of focussing on my studies to the exclusion of potential distractions like friends and family. It was a recurrent mantra: the work was of paramount importance, there was no room for complacency, no room for unproductive relationships, he was my mentor giving of his extremely valuable time, and his opinion mattered above all others. I was to do what he said, and do it without question. I'm not sure when I began to believe it all, but I did, I certainly did. His words became deeply ingrained in my psyche.

The next few weeks were relatively unremarkable as I attended lectures when required and retreated to the isolation of the flat at every opportunity to concentrate on my work. I was becoming more introverted, increasingly uncomfortable and lacking in confidence in the company of others. A very different person to the outgoing young student who'd arrived in Cardiff just months before.

I found myself looking forward to his visits despite the focus he placed on every aspect of my life, and I tried to put that unremembered night to the back of my busy mind.

And then it happened, the day of days, the moment everything changed forever. I rushed around the flat in a whirlwind of inactivity, watching the minutes tick by on my watch, and waiting for the anticipated blue stripe to appear in the result window of my third pregnancy test that day. Yes, there it was again, clear as day, and there was no point in denying it however much I wanted to. My usually regular period was late, the test was positive again, and no amount of wishing it wasn't was going to change that fact. I had a bun in the oven, as Jack would undoubtedly describe it.

Reality dawned with ever increasing clarity as the morning progressed. I was pregnant: expecting a child despite having no recollection of sex. Just that morning's blank confusion, the painful welts, the soiled bedclothes and his comment; his seemingly throwaway comment as if nothing meaningful had happened. It made little sense. I respected him, I was increasingly reliant on him in so many ways, but sex? Really? I just didn't see him in that way. I'd never considered sex for a single moment as far as I was aware. I wanted to understand. I needed to understand. If only I could remember something. Surely I should recall something? The smallest detail may help. He'd taught me a lot. Perhaps it was one more thing he could explain. Perhaps he could still my anxious mind.

I tried to ignore the rancid stench of stale urine permeating the phone box as I picked up the receiver, dialled, and inserted three ten pence coins into the slot with quivering

156

fingers. It wasn't going to be an easy conversation, but some things were best said. Why delay the inevitable?

'Hello, Child Guidance Service.'

'Hi Sharon, it's Cynthia, can I speak to Dr Galbraith, please?'

'He's busy with some paperwork at the moment. Can I ask him to contact you as soon as he's free?'

'I'm in a phone box, it's urgent, just fetch him, please.'

'If you're sure? You know he doesn't like to be disturbed.'

'Yes, please, Sharon.'

I frantically searched my handbag for additional suitable coins, placed them in the slot and waited. Come on Doctor, come on. How important can that paperwork be?

'Hello Cynthia, I hope this is urgent.'

It was now or never. There was no sugar coating this particular pill. 'I'm pregnant.'

Silence.

'Did you hear me Doctor?'

'Why are you telling me?'

'I'm expecting your child. You're the father! Who else am I supposed to tell?'

'Give me a second, I need to shut the door.'

'Right Cynthia, let's see if I've got this correct. You're telling me that you haven't had sex with any of the vacuous boys at the university? You're telling me that our brief single sexual encounter has resulted in conception?'

I still had some residual spirit at that stage, and I was becoming increasingly agitated by his dismissive responses. 'You're the father, there's no other possibility. Please accept that.'

'Is this something you've planned?'

157

A tear ran down my face. Of course not, of course not! What on earth was he suggesting? 'What exactly are you saying?'

'You assured me that you're taking birth control pills.'

I wouldn't do that. Why would I do that? 'I stopped taking them after Steven's death.'

'I distinctly recall your assurances.'

I must have been extremely drunk. I guess I may have been mixed up. I couldn't recall a damn thing. He had me on the defensive. 'I wouldn't say that.'

'Are you calling me a liar?'

'No, no, I wouldn't do that. But I think…'

'Think, think, you ridiculous girl! The very use of the word suggests significant doubts on your part.'

I chose not to respond, and waited for him to speak again: distressed, dejected, disconsolate.

'Let's keep things to ourselves for the moment. I think that's advisable. We can talk again on Wednesday. Perhaps you can get your story straight by then.'

I tightened my grip on the receiver and bit my lower lip hard. 'Wednesday? Can't you come before then? It's three days away. Surely in the circumstances?'

He sounded a little calmer now, his voice quieter, more reasoned. 'I'm snowed under my dear. Pressure of work and all that. I'm afraid it's completely impossible. I will see you on Wednesday as usual as per our agreement and we will talk then. That's the best I can offer I'm afraid. Now is that clear?'

'Yes, but…'

'Is that clear?' A little sterner this time.

'Yes, Doctor!'

'For goodness sake Cynthia, how many times do I have to tell you? Call me David.'

Chapter 25

I spent about twenty minutes in the exercise yard this morning, before the foreboding grey sky opened and a torrent of large raindrops flooded the concrete with about half an inch of tepid rainwater. I was rather enjoying my commune with nature despite being soaked to the skin, but the two attendant guards ushered us back into the concrete building with an urgency that far outweighed the necessity. If the rain had been scalding sulphuric acid, they couldn't have done any more. We British are so obsessed with the weather, so obsessed with petty bureaucratic rules and red tape. 'In you get, in you get. Come on, you don't want to get wet. Move! Wipe your feet before entering the building.' Well, you get the idea.

I've spent the last half hour slowly drying off in the communal recreation room waiting for lunchtime and my English class beyond. I'm on to my second notebook now and have been able to write in comparative peace despite the throng of other women chatting, arguing, playing table tennis or cards or dice, or simply going about their day as best they can within the limits of their lives. Most of them know what I'm doing and let me get on with it, in fairness to them. Lifers are accorded an undue degree of respect in prison world in a way we never would be in the world at large. It's a strange dichotomy that never ceases to amaze me. We're the high status residents best kept on side. The very top of the incarcerated tree. The women with a history of violence and nothing to lose.

Two or three of the girls have stopped by to enquire how I'm doing, or how my writing's progressing. 'How's it going Cynth?'

'What are you writing Cynth?'

'You're a busy girl!'

'Do you want to play ping pong Cynth? Come on, put that fucking book down and have some fun for a change.'

I issued brief to-the-point replies that were unlikely to offend but that conveyed the clear message that I wanted to be left alone with my reminiscences: 'I want to get on. I want to finish my story. I'll have a game in a couple of days when I've got more time.'

And they would laugh or scowl and move on, slighted but accepting. I'd like to know what they really think of me. Or maybe not, perhaps that's not such a good idea now that I think about it. I wouldn't want to get knocked back down just when I'm starting to feel a little better about myself. Self confidence can be a fragile beast.

I've received another handwritten letter from Mum, full of positive language and forlorn hope of my release, but still no mention of the wedding. Crazy really, when you think about it. It seems Mum bumped into DI Gravel in Caerystwyth a few days ago, and cornered him in a shop doorway until he capitulated and reluctantly agreed to talk to her on a rare day off. I'd like to have been a fly on the wall for that particular encounter. Mum can be quite formidable when she needs to be despite her diminutive stature. She says he told her there were some unexpected developments in my case, but that he couldn't say any more than that. Unexpected developments! I have no real idea what that means, and I don't want to get my hopes up because it could mean anything or nothing at all. Mum could have it wrong, of course, or he could have been saying just about anything to get rid of her and get on with his day despite his integrity. Who knows? I certainly don't. Hugely frustratingly, there's absolutely nothing I can do to clarify the situation however much I want to. I can't contact him, and I suspect I'm the last person he'd want to talk to even if I could. It's just a case of waiting, hoping for the best and fearing the worst. It's the only way to maintain my sanity.

Chapter 26

I have to admit that I awaited Dr Galbraith's arrival with a degree of trepidation the following Wednesday, despite or perhaps due to my need to discuss the enormity of events. The three days had passed painfully slowly as I lived with my secret. I no longer had any friends with whom to share my problems and his insistence that I refrain from contacting Mum and Dad prevented me from doing so very effectively despite their repeated efforts to contact me. Why was I so compliant to his instructions? Is that what you're wondering? Well, I'm not entirely sure to be honest, other than to say that I'd become as malleable as warm putty in his Machiavellian hands. I wanted to please him. I didn't want to disappoint him. I needed his approval. What a sad individual I'd become.

I jumped when he knocked hard on the front door at around 2:00 p.m., and opened it with my gut twisting and growling like a washing machine on the spin cycle. I just didn't know what to expect: disapproval, anger, disgust? But, no, he was standing there, resplendent in an immaculate bespoke grey pinstripe suit, holding a large bunch of red roses in his right hand and a card in his left.

'Why did you knock? You have a key.' Not obvious questions, but he usually let himself in. It was his flat, and he liked to remind me of that fact on a regular basis.

He smiled warmly. 'I thought it appropriate in the circumstances.' He held out the flowers, but withdrew his hand when I didn't accept them.

'They're for me?'

'You seem surprised my dear. Who else would they be for? In we go, in we go. There's a vase in the lounge.'

He sat on the settee and waited whilst I attended to the bouquet.

I sat in an armchair to his left, rather than join him on the sofa as he suggested. 'You seemed angry when I told you the news.'

He laughed, as if my observation were ridiculous.

'You seemed to be saying it was my fault.'

'It was something of a shock my dear. We made love once, and now there's a child on the way. Surely you can understand my initial reticence.'

We made love? He used the L word. I was more confused than ever. 'I guess so.'

He relaxed back in the seat and smiled. 'Now that I've had a couple of days to think about it and get used to the idea, I think it's good news.'

I was not expecting that! 'Really? I thought you'd be horrified.'

His smile melted away and he took on a more serious persona. 'You'll have to give up your studies, naturally. You'll need to join me in Caerystwyth where I can keep a close eye on you both, but that's easily arranged. Some things are more important than education.'

I was taken aback; he'd always stressed the paramount importance of my studies. 'You're saying you want me to leave university?'

'I've already spoken to your professor on your behalf my dear. I thought it best to put him in the picture. He was fully in agreement. Your welfare must come first. It's what Steven would want.'

I just sat there, listening, but not saying another word.

'I see no reason why you can't return to Caerystwyth with me in the morning. I'll keep your parents fully informed. No need for you to bother them.'

'I really should ring them myself. I haven't spoken to Mum for weeks.'

He took a brown plastic medicine bottle from his trouser pocket, unscrewed the top and handed me two tablets. 'Now, I want you to take two of these my dear. They'll help you relax. You've had enough stress to deal with for one day.'

'I don't need tablets.'

He shook his head and frowned. 'You let me be the judge of that, young lady. Who's the expert here? You don't have a medical degree as far as I'm aware. Now, pop them in that pretty mouth of yours and I'll fetch you a glass of cold water.'

Chapter 27

Needy Guard appeared at my cell door early this morning when I was still half asleep, banged hard on the metal grill, and tutted loudly in an exaggerated theatrical manner she appeared to find extremely humorous. 'Have you been a naughty girl Cynthia?'

I'd just woken after a long fitful night of disturbed sleep and bad dreams, and just wasn't in the mood to play her infuriatingly self-indulgent games. 'What are you talking about?'

She unlocked and opened the cell door, placed one hand on each of her fleshy hips and tilted her head sideways at an approximate forty-five degree angle before speaking again. 'Oh, I can see someone's not in a very good mood this morning. Service not up to madam's required standards? Perhaps you should complain to the management.'

'Is there something you want to say?'

Her expression hardened. 'I wouldn't be quite so cocky if I were you missy. There's a police officer here to see you.'

I jumped to my feet and followed her urgently, hopeful that Mum's conversation with DI Gravel held some hope despite my initial caution. Unexpected developments, that sounded positive didn't it? Surely it was positive. Please God let it be positive.

I entered the interview room on tenterhooks, expecting to see Inspector Gravel's craggy reassuringly knowing face in front of me, but instead I was met by a surprisingly diminutive woman in her mid to late thirties, who introduced herself as Detective Constable Meira Jones and asked me to take a seat opposite her across the small table. I felt a surge of disappointment as if struck in the gut, but I reassured myself in the way people often do. Okay, so it wasn't the inspector, she certainly wasn't who I'd hoped for, but there may still be good news. Please let there be good news.

'We haven't met before Mrs Galbraith, but I'm familiar with your case.'

I hadn't been called Mrs Galbraith in quite some time, and the name took me back, focussing my mind on the past.

'Did you hear me Mrs Galbraith?'

I returned to the present in an instant, nodded twice and waited for her to continue, full of anticipation despite the fact she couldn't have looked less enthusiastic if paid to.

'I'm here to talk to you about the recent assault on Sheila Davies.'

My heart sank, the disappointment virtually overwhelming. False hope is no hope. Why did I fall for it again? Stupid girl! When would I ever learn? 'Has she made a statement?' I knew the answer was no before asking the question. It wasn't the done thing as I've explained before.

DC Jones sensibly ignored my pointed query and spent the next twenty minutes or so asking me about 'the assault'.

I gave carefully considered non committal answers that I knew in no way incriminated me, and got the distinct impression that the officer was simply going through the motions and keen to finish the interview as soon as practicably possible. I suspect she knew the case wasn't going anywhere. I knew it wasn't going anywhere. She'd do her job as best she could before moving on to more productive cases in the world outside the walls. Cases with innocent victims. Cases that mattered involving people that mattered. Or, at least that's how I saw it.

She glanced at her watch for what seemed the umpteenth time. 'Is there anything you want to say before I'm on my way?'

'Not really.'

'Nothing at all?'

I shook my head. 'Nothing.'

She rose easily to her feet and closed her black plastic briefcase. 'Okay, we're done for now. I don't think you've got too much to worry about.'

'What are they going to do, send me to prison?'

She chuckled on approaching the exit, but glanced back before leaving the room. 'For what it's worth, I think your conviction stank. The bastard had it coming.'

I lifted my hands to my face as the tears began to flow. The kindness of strangers can be particularly poignant for the vulnerable and oppressed. 'Thank y-you.'

'Hang on in there Cynthia. You may get out of here sooner than you think.'

Chapter 28

Dr Galbraith's large imposing Georgian Caerystwyth townhouse was not dissimilar in style to his Cardiff residence, although it was retained as one dwelling rather than divided into flats.

'Let me show you around my dear. I've been looking forward to introducing you to your new home.'

The guided tour, as he called it, took around twenty minutes or so, and I have to say I was impressed. The house had generously proportioned rooms, high ceilings giving an impression of space, and large sash windows that filled it with light. There were five sizeable double bedrooms, three bathrooms, two huge reception rooms, and a large family kitchen leading to a conservatory and attractive walled garden beyond. It also had a study, and a cellar accessed via the kitchen, both of which he repeatedly stressed were his domain and his alone. He sat me at the kitchen table and drove his point home. It mattered, it really mattered.

'I do important work Cynthia. Crucial work in the interests of my young patients. Uninterrupted privacy is essential to that process. I can't stress that sufficiently.'

He paused, and repeatedly tapped the table with his right forefinger, emphasising his point before continuing. 'You will not enter my study without my prior consent.' And then he pointed at me with a jabbing digit. 'You will never enter the cellar under any circumstances. Do you hear me young lady? Never under any circumstances! I sometimes see troubled children there when they require more of my time than the clinic's busy schedule allows. Were you to interfere with that process the implications could be dire.'

'The cellar? That seems an odd place to…'

He leant towards me in his chair and stared at me unblinkingly. 'It's been converted to a suitable standard. Video facilities were installed. A useful therapeutic tool. It's more than adequate.'

'Even so, it seems an odd...'

'Are you a child care expert Cynthia?'

'No, but...'

'Am I an expert Cynthia?'

'Well, yes, of course you are, but...'

'So you acknowledge that I'm an expert in such matters.'

'Y-yes, of course. I didn't mean...'

'Then I suggest we end the conversation there before you make an even bigger fool of yourself.'

I sat in brooding silence, taken aback by the heated intensity of his response.

He shook his head slowly and laughed with an incredulous expression on his face. 'I can see you're becoming somewhat agitated again my dear. It's not good for the baby. It's not good at all. Now, what time did you last take your medication?'

He was good at shutting me down, good at making me feel foolish. And it pleased him. I didn't see it at the time, but it pleased him. And he made regular notes following our interactions. He'd take a small black notebook from the inside pocket of his tailored jacket, open it and start scribbling frantically with that favoured fountain pen of his. He did it so often that it became the norm. If I asked him what he was writing, he'd just say it was to do with his work. 'Don't worry your pretty head my dear. You wouldn't understand. I suggest you concentrate on your menial tasks. Leave more important matters to the grown ups.' The bastard, the absolute bastard!

And so it continued, we had separate bedrooms at his insistence, he continued his work at the clinic but ended his work at the university, and I stayed at the house, engaged in roles he allocated as he saw fit. These were set out in a second written agreement, which I read and signed that first evening.

To summarise what seemed an unnecessarily complex document, I was to attend to his needs and to the domestic chores. I would rise sufficiently early to shower, dress appropriately, prepare his breakfast in line with his exact requirements, and do so without making any noise that may prematurely disturb his slumber. Every detail mattered. He'd be inspecting my efforts, and the distance between each and every item placed on the kitchen table had to be exactly right. Believe it or not, he even gave me a twelve inch ruler for the purpose. I should have heard alarm bells screaming in my ears, but instead I knuckled down and got on with it.

And he really did use the ruler. Every morning he'd enter the kitchen following his early morning exercise routine, take a pristine white glove from a drawer and walk slowly around the kitchen running a finger over various surfaces. 'Not bad Cynthia, not bad at all: four out of ten on this occasion, if I'm not mistaken. I'd suggest you aim for at least a six tomorrow. That shouldn't be too much to ask, even from someone of your limited intellect and ability. What do you say young lady?'

I'd nod and say I'd try harder. I had to try harder.

And then the part I dreaded most. He'd make a show of retrieving the ruler from its prominent allocated position on the Welsh dresser which hid the entrance to the cellar, and hold it up to the light of the window, searching for any sign of greasy finger prints or dust.

'I polished it just like you said. I used one of the yellow dusters.'

'Are you sure Cynthia? Are you really sure?'

'I thought…'

He raised a hand to silence me, and approached the table purposefully. 'The position of my glass is two millimetres out of place. That isn't acceptable. It's not acceptable at all. I hope you're not nearly as slovenly when it comes to your care of the brat when it finally deems to make an appearance.'

'But I checked repeatedly, I used the ruler.'

'Are you calling me a liar?'

It was a line he used often and it stung every time. 'No, I w-wouldn't do that. I'd n-never do that!'

He shook his head and sneered. 'Oh for God's sake, stop your pathetic snivelling you stupid girl. What the hell is wrong with you? I've got important work to do; I shouldn't have to waste my time dealing with your many inadequacies.' And then he took that same brown bottle from his pocket, shook it in the air as if playing a musical instrument, unscrewed the top, and handed me two tablets with a clammy hand. 'Take your medication my dear, and please ensure that the glove is perfectly clean, dry and ironed by the morning's inspection. Surely you can manage that much?'

I had no idea what the tablets were, but I came to need those tablets. I needed them desperately, and he knew it. He'd hand them out as it suited him, like an adult to a child.

At this point in my story I want to make clear that I still possessed some spirit despite his increasing influence. I didn't roll over like a subservient puppy. I actually considered leaving more than once, before being persuaded otherwise by threats and unkept promises.

'Perhaps I should go and stay with Mum and Dad for a while.'

And he'd shake his head dismissively and stare at me as if I'd said something utterly outlandish. 'Oh, no, no, no, you're far too ill for that my dear. You require my constant expert care if you're to retain care of your brat. It's either that or a psychiatric hospital. You're a cross I have to bear. I've fully explained this to your parents more than once, as you well know.'

'But Mum said…'

He laughed expansively, seemingly amused by my argument. 'She said what you wanted to hear my dear. That's what parents do at such times. They're not as young as they once were. They can't cope with your issues at their time of life. That's what they truly feel. They have made that perfectly clear to me in our discussions on more than one occasion. That's why they haven't visited. You must have wondered. Surely you must have wondered you stupid girl?'

I stood and stared, horrified by his protestations as his version of reality sank in. Was I really that much of a burden?

'You would be well advised not to see them again without my prior agreement. Perhaps in a few months time when your mental health has improved we can revisit the situation and reconsider. It's what I want, it's what they want and I've no doubt it's what Steven would want were he able to express an opinion. Now, I hope that's clear enough even for you?'

'If you're s-sure?'

He smiled engagingly. 'I'm sure, I couldn't be more sure. If you love them as you claim, you'll leave them in peace. Now, stop wasting my valuable time and get on with your chores. I want this place immaculate when the midwife calls.'

I smiled at the idea of female company, however brief, whatever the circumstances. 'I wanted to ask…'

He approached me, placed his face only inches from mine and spoke slowly, clearly enunciating each word. 'You would be well advised to leave the talking to me my dear. I've explained your psychological frailty and it's implications to your GP in terms even that pleb can understand, but he's concerned.'

A single tear ran down my cheek and found a home in one corner of my open mouth. 'Concerned? What are y-you talking about?'

He paused, as if carefully considering his response before speaking again a second or two later. 'Will you be able to look after the brat to an acceptable standard my dear? That's what he's asking himself. There's talk of social services. Talk of a case conference. Talk of potential legal action. Talk of taking the infant away at birth. I work with those morons on a regular basis. They value my advice. They respect my contribution. And now they're talking about my child! Can you imagine how that makes me feel?'

'I'm d-doing my b-best.'

He slammed the palm of his right hand down on the tabletop. 'But it's not good enough you stupid bitch. It's simply not good enough.' Quieter this time, hissing the words, a myriad tiny globules of spittle spraying from his mouth.

I felt worthless, inadequate, desperate, very close to disintegrating completely. 'What s-should I do? Tell me what to do.'

He took a deep breath and blew the air from his mouth with a high pitched whistle. 'Just shut up, leave the talking to me, and maybe, just maybe I can rescue the situation despite your best efforts to ruin things. Do you think you can do that much for me?'

'Whatever you say. I'll do w-whatever you say.'

'That's good Cynthia, that's the response I was looking for. Maybe, just maybe I can hold things together.'

173

And that's how it continued: day after day, week after week, month after miserable month. My self-worth diminished still further and the few crumbs of praise he occasionally threw my way became shining treasures that illuminated my increasingly dismal existence. 'Please don't let them take my baby. Please, Doctor, don't let them take my baby!'

'You're not coping very well are you my dear. I'll do what I can, of course, but no promises. I'm not a miracle worker. Just keep a low profile and maybe, just maybe it will be sufficient to persuade the authorities to back off.'

'Is t-there anything at all I can do.'

He frowned and shook his head slowly. 'Just shut the fuck up Cynthia. Just shut your stupid face, take your medication as and when instructed and leave the thinking to me. There's a good girl. If you can manage that I may be able to think of something before it's too late.'

I held my head in my hands and wept. 'Thank you. Thank you so very much.'

Chapter 29

I read somewhere in what feels like another life that celebrated British premier Winston Churchill sometimes referred to his intermittent periods of debilitating depression as the 'Black Dog.' I get it, I really do. An insightful observation by an extremely insightful man. It describes my melancholy mood perfectly.

Almost a month has passed since Mum's impromptu conversation with DI Gravel; three weeks since the police officer's visit and departing words of well-intentioned encouragement. Four weeks of getting my hopes up, four weeks of denying reality, and nothing: no news, no messages from Mum or the girls, no phone calls from my depressingly, ineffectual solicitor. Why did I let myself hope again? Why kid myself? What a stupid girl! What on earth was I thinking?

And now that same black dog hovers over me, inches from my face, stalking, snarling, seeping negativity into every kink and crook of my delicate soul. I'm trying to fight it. I'm trying to get back on an even keel, but it isn't easy. It seems he's a determined beast, and I'd strangle the fucking thing if I could. I'd put my hands around its throat and squeeze, tighter, tighter, tighter, until it faded away into the distance and my mood finally lifted. Mrs Martin suggested a doctor; there was talk of antidepressants, talk of psychiatric intervention, but I didn't react well. Psychiatry's the last thing I want or need however despairing I feel inside from time to time. I like to think she understood when I explained my position and she thought about it for a minute or two. She certainly didn't argue the point with any vehemence. It's obvious really.

Instead, she made me a cup of 'Calming camomile tea,' placed a reassuring hand on my shoulder and smiled sympathetically. 'I'm sorry Cynthia, I wasn't thinking clearly. It's been a difficult week for me personally. More tablets are the last thing you need. I'm here for you. We're going to get through this together. I want you to meditate daily as I've said before, whenever you get the opportunity. And I want you to keep writing because you're doing brilliantly. Do you think you can do that for me?'

I forced a quickly vanishing smile. 'Oh, I'm sorry, what happened?'

'We're here to focus on your issues, not mine.'

Another slap down reminder that we're not friends. I never did find out what was happening in her life. Why on earth did she mention it in the first place?

'Cynthia?'

'The writing's going reasonably well.'

'That's good, that's a positive, but from what I've seen it's a lot better than just reasonably well!'

I knew what she was trying to achieve; I realised she was attempting to raise my despondent mood, but I wasn't totally convinced as yet.

'And what about the meditation?'

I realised she meant well, but come on! 'Have you tried meditating in this place?'

'What about the last thing at night, before you go to sleep?'

'Have you ever been here late at night? That's a rhetorical question, by the way. It's noisier than in the daytime.'

She nodded, acknowledging my angst. 'Look Cynthia, if there are developments in your case, that's brilliant, I dearly hope it's true, but as you know the legal wheels turn extremely slowly. It could be months before you hear anything at all. There's little purpose in torturing yourself with what ifs.' She paused, patted my knee gently and continued. 'If not, if nothing's changed, you haven't lost

176

anything. At least you're doing something constructive with your time here. There's the English classes and there's your journal. And I like to think you value our time together. All will pass given time.'

Can talking really help, even with a trained therapist? Does it really serve as a viable alternative to the aforementioned chemical lobotomy chosen by numerous other residents of prison world? Well, I think the answer's, yes. Not a resounding yes shouted from the hilltops, but a yes nonetheless. I do feel a little better after our session together. The black dog isn't dead, but he's definitely wounded. Mrs Martin dented his ardour and forced him back a few inches from my face. That's more than I expected before seeing her for the first time. Kudos to her, three cheers for Mrs Martin; I'm less depressed than I was earlier in the day and very grateful for that.

Chapter 30

On a typically wet and windy Welsh Saturday autumnal morning about four weeks prior to my due date, Dr Galbraith sat me down at the kitchen table shortly after enjoying his extensive breakfast and opened a green cardboard file on the tabletop in front of him.

'Can I get you another coffee Doctor?'

He'd given up telling me to call him David by that point, and I don't think he ever really wanted me to anyway, now that I look back on it. He revelled in his status and the power it gave him. Dr Galbraith suited him just fine.

He shook his head dismissively and made a show of shuffling through the papers for a minute or two before finally taking a one page typed letter on headed paper from the top. Why the delay? Why didn't he just do that in the first place? 'I don't require coffee, or anything else for that matter. I want you to sit there without speaking and to listen extremely carefully to what I have to say to you. It's of crucial importance. Do you understand?'

'Yes, I understand.' What else could I say?

'So, I've made myself perfectly clear?'

'Y-yes Doctor!'

'Then, you've absolutely no excuse if you don't follow my instructions to the letter.'

'N-no,'

'None at all?'

I shook my head frantically, keen to placate him. 'None!'

'Then, you accept that any negative consequences of failing to follow my instructions to the letter would be entirely your responsibility?'

I nodded without speaking, silently cursing my aching lower back, desperately wanting the interaction to end and increasingly concerned as to what he'd say next.

He held the letter out in front of him and perused the contents for a second time. 'The local social services department are becoming increasingly anxious regarding your capacity to provide adequate care for the brat when he or she arrives.'

'But they haven't seen me; only the midwife's seen me. And I didn't say very much at all. I kept my mouth shut just like you said.'

'I had no choice but to discuss your increasing reliance on tranquillisers with your general practitioner my dear. You've been going through a great many tablets. Far more than you should have. More than I could provide without raising understandable concerns. There was no other option in the circumstances.'

'I'm s-sorry. But, I only take them when...'

'You're a mess Cynthia. It's truly embarrassing. I was forced to sit down with a colleague and discuss your damned issues. I've never felt so humiliated.'

I lowered my head in shame and focussed on my feet. I'd let him down. I shouldn't have let him down. I had to think of the baby.

'And, as if that wasn't bad enough, he chose to share my concerns with the social workers. I work with those damn people on a regular basis. You've brought them to my door!' He was on his feet now: yelling, agitated, angry. 'What have you got to say for yourself? Spit it out you stupid girl.'

I fought to control my breathing, fought to control my bursting bladder, fought to find the right words. 'I c-could speak to them myself. I could try to explain.'

He laughed initially, but his expression hardened almost immediately. 'That's an outlandish idea, you moronic bitch! Ridiculous! I've spoken to them on your behalf. I've pleaded your case with the appropriate people. I've given them reassurances despite my misgivings. Do you think you could do a better job of it?'

I shook my head hurriedly. 'No, n-no, I'm not saying that!'

'So you don't think it's a good idea?'

'No! No!'

He sat back down, relaxed back in the seat and spoke quietly in hushed tones. 'I could arrange it, of course, they could come to the house, they could talk to you, but I believe the results would be catastrophic. I've done my best to minimise your inadequacies in their eyes my dear. I've utilised my expertise to paint as favourable a picture as possible in the interests of the child. I've risked my reputation on your behalf. If they meet you, if they see the state you're really in, if they witness the horrible reality, there's only ever going to be one outcome.'

I was weeping now, my chest heaving as I twitched and sweated and panted for breath. 'Do y-you think they'd take the baby?'

He remained silent for a few seconds with a blank expression on his face before speaking again. 'Oh, I know they'd take the baby. It's what they're paid to do. They'd have no other option given the circumstances. It's in your hands my dear. I'd keep a very low profile if I were you.'

I nodded anxiously and resisted the impulse to vomit.

He took his gold fountain pen from the inside pocket of his tailored jacked and began making notes in his flowing copperplate script, whilst shaking his head and frowning. 'I've been giving your predicament a great deal of thought and there may be some hope.'

I dabbed away my tears with an increasingly damp powder-blue cashmere sleeve. He was going to help. Thank God, he was going to help. 'I'll d-do anything. Please, just tell me what to do!'

He wrote another line or two in his notebook before responding. 'You must have realised there's an increased risk of congenital malformations and other developmental abnormalities associated with the use of your medication.'

'What?'

He smiled sardonically when he saw my horrified expression. 'There's been reports of respiratory and feeding difficulties in children born to mothers taking tranquillisers in late pregnancy. The brat's likely to experience withdrawal symptoms, not a pleasant process you understand. Your child will suffer. You should have stopped taking the damned stuff long before now.'

I clutched the table with both hands, my head swimming. 'But, I d-didn't know. You didn't say anything. I didn't know!'

'Are you really that stupid?'

I rose from my seat intending to plead my case, but my legs buckled at the knees and I sank to the floor.

He loomed over me, reached down, but didn't help me to my feet. 'I'm going to wean you off the drug a lot quicker than usually advisable, but needs must. I suggest we begin the process on Monday.'

I'd become increasingly reliant on the chemical cosh, and to be honest I was somewhat relieved that the planned reduction was two days away. 'It is going to be all right, isn't it? Please say it's going to be okay.'

'I'll do what I can, but no promises. Follow my instructions to the letter, and we'll see how things progress.'

I took a deep breath, sucking the air deep into my lungs. 'Thank you so much Doctor.'

He reached down again, grasped my hand and assisted me to my feet. 'Now, get up, stop your pathetic snivelling and clean every inch of this place by 11:00 a.m. at the latest. I want it immaculate: not a smear of grease, not a hint of dust. I'm seeing a patient in the cellar along with an esteemed colleague at eleven fifteen precisely. Answer the door quickly when he knocks, welcome them in, make the boy feel as relaxed as possible and then disappear. Stay well out of the way until they leave. I don't want to see you, and I don't want to hear you. Don't go anywhere near the kitchen once we're all in the cellar. Is that perfectly clear?'

I still didn't understand. Why use the cellar? Why not the study? It seemed strange, but if I'm frank, unimportant when compared to the needs of my unborn child. He was the doctor, he knew best, he knew what he was doing. He'd said it and said it. Why would I doubt his word? 'Yes, Doctor!'

He bent down and sneered, placing his face only inches from mine. 'My work is important to me Cynthia. It's vitally important. It will always come first; before you, and before the brat. Interfere, and it will not go well for you. You would be well advised to remember that.'

'Anything you say Doctor. Anything you say.'

Chapter 31

I haven't written anything for a day or two, not due to writer's block or fear of the blank page or any other such tired clichés that would go some way to explaining my inactivity, but because of welcome distractions that I found impossible to ignore.

The black dog has retreated somewhat. He's not dead, regrettably. It's not a case of RIP black dog and never to be seen again. He's still there somewhere in the background and lurching forward from time to time to snap at my heels, but he has lost some of his power. No doubt at some time in the not too distant future he'll make a resurgent recovery and gain strength again, but now is not that time. Make the most of the good times when you can. That's what I'm telling myself, and it's good advice. Mrs Martin tells me much the same thing on a regular basis.

I actually got to speak to Jack on the phone very briefly yesterday, facilitated by the wonderful Mrs Martin who allowed me to ring him from her office to thank him for the photos, after a great deal of impassioned persuasion on my part. She said no initially, she said no repeatedly, but I eventually wore her down with a combination of pleading and tears. Thank you, Mrs Martin. Thank you so very much!

It was wonderful to hear Jack's still familiar voice tinged with an unequivocal hint of American, however fleetingly, and after some heartfelt complaints regarding the early hour in California, he gave me the momentous news. My big brother is going to be a father, and it seems no one is more surprised than him. Parenthood is one of life's great rights of passage and I'm glad he can live it with someone he loves and respects as much as Marie. I very much hope they live a long life of fairytale happiness with a large pot of gold at the end of every shining rainbow. A fantasy maybe, but there's nothing wrong with wishing them well.

It's amazing what the woman has done for my big brother. She came into his life and made it a better place. How completely wonderful! I guess it's the opposite of what happened to me following Steven's death. He got Dr Jekyll and I got Mr Hyde. I suppose that's the luck of the draw. I enjoyed my brief transient time in the sun before the world became a colder darker place. I dearly hope that neither Jack nor his family ever encounter one of the vile predatory monsters that inhabit our world. Be careful who you trust, that's my advice. They can all too easily destroy your life, as he did mine.

The phone call was over far too quickly at the behest of Mrs Martin, who looked pointedly at the clock on the wall above her desk with an angst expression on her face. I said my reluctant goodbyes, put the phone down and thanked her profusely for allowing me to make the call at all. I know she was breaking all sorts of rules and she didn't need to do it. I like to think that as she gets to know me a little better she's come to like me more. But, whatever her reasons, it was an incredibly kind gesture that I've promised to keep secret to my dying day. Maybe I should have kept it to myself and not written it down at all. I plan to ask her if she wants me to remove this section if anyone else ever reads my reflections.

On another positive note, one of my English students has made such good progress with her studies that she's asked to sit a GCSE in English language in a few months' time. Rosie's a bright girl who moved from foster home to foster home as a child, after being removed from her parents' care at a young age. Unsurprisingly, she left school with no qualifications, and it's to her credit that despite the disadvantages life's dealt her she wants to put that right. I like to think it's a triumph in itself, both for her and me. I like to think I pointed her in the right direction just at the right time, and I take some pleasure in that. I've done something good that makes my life worthwhile. I'm a good person, a positive person, not one of the ghouls. Another brick in my defensive wall. Back off, black dog! Go away and stay away.

And so with the black dog growling quietly somewhere in the background, I've put pen to paper again, for what it's worth. I'll write and keep writing while the mood takes me and circumstances allow. My story gains pace from here on in, and I've got another forty minutes before lights out. I'm not entirely sure it's a good idea to address what I have to convey next before trying to go to sleep, but for good or bad I'm going to give it a try. Once you're on a rollercoaster it's impossible to get off before the ride comes to a grinding stop.

Chapter 32

When I opened the front door at 11:10 a.m. that morning, I was faced with an unremarkable looking man in his mid to late fifties, accompanied by an anxious looking boy of just four or five years with short brown hair, wearing dark blue shorts, a mustard-yellow shirt and a brightly coloured ill-fitting red woollen jumper that someone must have decided he'd eventually grow into. The man told me his name was Professor Richard Sherwood, and introduced me to the child, who said his name was Robbie in a faltering barely decipherable voice that I struggled to hear, despite my excellent hearing.

The professor continued speaking in his high-pitched musical North Wales accent as he led the hapless child down the long hall towards the kitchen. 'You must be Cynthia. Good to meet you at last. I hope you're feeling a little better.'

I wasn't sure what to say in response, and just smiled nervously at the back of his head as he strode away from me. Saying nothing had to be better than potentially saying the wrong thing again and causing an upset. Keep your mouth shut Cynthia, keep your mouth well and truly shut. Such things define me.

The professor paused in the kitchen and turned to face me, still clutching the child's hand in his. 'All ready for this afternoon?'

What on earth was he talking about? I just stared at him blankly without responding in any meaningful way.

'Oh, he hasn't told you yet. He said he meant to surprise you.'

Best not to ask. Best remain silent.

'I assume he's expecting me?'

I smiled, pleased that I could answer his question with relative confidence. 'Yes, he's waiting in the cellar. How about a drink before you join him? He said to make you both welcome.' I was keen to please. Keen to make a good impression. Please say yes, Professor, please say yes.

The boy looked back at me with pleading eyes as Professor Sherwood ignored my offer and steered him towards the cellar door.

'Would you like a drink Robbie? How about some fresh orange juice or some lovely blackcurrant squash?' Didn't all young boys like Ribena?

The boy opened his mouth briefly, but then closed it again when no words materialised. Maybe he wasn't thirsty. Maybe like me he thought it best to remain silent. I think that was probably it. Shame on you Cynthia. Why didn't you say something? Why didn't you do something? Why didn't you intervene when you had the opportunity? I let myself down that day. I let the boy down and I'll never forget it.

Sherwood stood at the cellar entrance, holding the back of the boy's jumper tightly as he tried to pull towards me. 'Perhaps later Cynthia, we don't want to keep the doctor waiting, do we.'

I shook my head in silent agreement. He was an important man. His time was valuable. Keeping him waiting was never a good idea. 'No, no, I wouldn't want that.'

And so I just stood in that seemingly ordinary family kitchen and watched as the professor led the sobbing child down twelve cold grey concrete steps towards a second door at the bottom. I felt sad for the troubled child, touched by his distress, but I reassured myself that he was in good hands. God only knew what he'd been through in his short life. God only knew why he needed psychiatric help at such a young age, but I told myself he was about to receive the help he needed. I yelled it inside my head until it drowned out my misgivings. There's nothing to worry about Cynthia. All's well with the world. I really was that girl. I really was that weak. I really was that stupid.

I turned away and rapidly retreated to the sanctuary of my bedroom, puzzled by Sherwood's comment, but keen to follow instructions. I lay back on my double bed and read Sebastian Faulks for about twenty minutes or so before resting the book on the bedside table, closing my tired eyes and falling asleep on top of the comfy soft duck down quilt.

'Cynthia! Where the hell are you girl?'

I leapt out of bed and stared at the clock on the wall to the side of the door. I'd been asleep for almost two hours. I'd stayed out of the way. I'd followed instructions. What had I done wrong this time? There had to be something. There was always something.

I heard his feet pounding on the wooden steps as he ascended the staircase. And then he appeared, kicking the door open with the point of his black shoe. 'You're not ready? Are you trying to annoy me? What the hell have you been doing?'

I knew what I'd been doing, but I had absolutely no idea what he was talking about. Should I say something in response or maintain my silence? Neither option seemed a particularly good idea. There was a shit storm coming my way.

'You've forgotten haven't you!'

I still had no idea what he was talking about. 'Is there something I should have done?'

He adopted a sour expression, and mimicked me, repeating my question in a mocking voice before adding 'We need to be at the registry office by 4:00 p.m. at the latest. Do you think you can manage that?'

I was trembling, with tears flowing down my face. I hadn't left the house for weeks. 'But, why are we…?'

He handed me three tablets, one more than usual, and told me to take them. 'Come on, swallow, swallow! We're getting married my dear, the happiest day of your life. We can start reducing your medication in the morning.'

I just stood there with an open mouth and guppy-like expression on my face. Marriage? There'd been no prior talk of marriage, had there? I was lost in a chemical haze a lot of the time, but surely I'd have remembered that. Was it possible? Maybe it was possible.

He walked towards me, pushed me back onto the bed and stood above me. 'If you're to keep your little brat, if you're to avoid him or her being taken away at birth, we need to convey the misleading impression of stable domestic bliss. We've discussed this, I've explained the position to you more than once. I can't believe I've got to tell you again.Think of our marriage as a mask behind which you can hide your many inadequacies.'

'You r-really think it would help?'

'Yes Cynthia, I've said it before and I'll say it again. It will help. You said you understood. You said you were prepared to do anything. What more can I tell you?'

I didn't remember anything at all, but that was the last thing he wanted to hear. 'What about guests? What about my family?'

He laughed dismissively. 'No guests.'

'But, my mum and dad, my…'

'You haven't seen them for months.'

'I know, but…'

'I've talked to them Cynthia. There's no easy way of telling you this. They don't want to be there.'

'They're not c-coming?'

'No, Richard and another trusted contact will act as witnesses, that's more than sufficient. The quicker we get the damned thing over with the better for everyone.'

'You c-could talk to them again.'

189

His expression hardened still further. 'Let's just forget the whole thing, shall we? It's not like I haven't got more important things to do with my time.'

'I didn't say…'

He glared at me with unblinking eyes and shook his head slowly and deliberately. 'I really thought you were committed to your child's future, but it seems I was sadly mistaken. I've gone to a great deal of trouble. I've put myself out on your behalf. And, what thanks do I get? I only hope you don't come to regret your indecision when your little one is residing with foster carers and doesn't know you.'

I swallowed the tablets urgently and fell to my knees, as if in prayer. 'Please, I don't want that. I really don't want that! I'm sorry, I'm really sorry.'

He raised his eyebrows and sighed. 'I'll give you one more chance. One final opportunity, and that's it!'

'Thank you so m-much.'

He held a finger to his lips and pointed at the clock. 'I'd be silent now if I were you. You're a mess girl. You've got less than an hour to sort yourself out. You need to attend to your appearance. I want you in the hall and looking presentable by 3:40 p.m. precisely. I do not want to be late. I do not want you to make a bad impression. Do not let me down. Do you hear me Cynthia? Do not let me down!'

My memory of the ceremony itself is somewhat hazy for obvious reasons I'm sure I don't need to explain. I can vaguely remember arriving at the registry office, I remember seeing Richard Sherwood at some point or other and I can recall returning home by taxi, but that's about it. No details, no nuances and no photos or other mementos with which to look back on the day. Not that I'd want them, of course. Some things are best forgotten.

He pushed me through the front door and into the hall when we arrived back at the house, dragged me to the kitchen by my arm, approached the sink, filled a glass full of cold water, took a single step away from me and threw it in my face. 'Think of that as the first stage of your rehabilitation my dear.'

'Why, why did…'

And then he hit me. For the first time he hit me. No more threats, no more gestures: he drew his arm back behind him and brought it around in a sweeping arc, connecting forcibly with my left cheek, causing me to stumble sideways and fall to the red quarry tiled floor immediately next to the dresser. I lay there in a huddled ball, clutching my abdomen, waiting for another blow that thankfully didn't materialise.

I was strangely accepting of the assault. I think the shock must have been alleviated by the numerous threats that proceeded it. What was my crime? What warranted such an extreme punishment? I'd broken my vow of silence and spoken to the registrar. Apparently I'd said too much. Apparently my stupidity reflected badly on him as my partner in life. 'You need to learn to keep your mouth shut my dear. I have a reputation to maintain in this town. I don't want it ruined by your stupidity.'

And then he'd write in that notebook of his before returning it to his pocket. What was he writing? What on earth was he writing?

'I'm sorry Doctor. I'm sorry, I'll try harder. I promise, I'll try harder.'

And I did, I tried, I really tried. I considered each deed carefully before acting and attempted to please him in everything I said and did. I always attempted to do the correct thing, but nothing was ever good enough for him. It wasn't remotely good enough. Whether it was cleaning or cooking or ironing or anything else, there were always flaws. There were always problems, which he was eager to highlight. He'd stand there, staring, frowning and catalogue whatever deficiencies he'd identified, invariably followed by a toxic tirade of verbal abuse, a prod or push or slap or worse.

My bruises gradually changed from red to blue to purple to green and finally yellow, before fading away completely, but the psychological scars remained and became more engrained as the frequency of the attacks increased, and I retreated further into my protective shell. My world had become a very small place, limited to life within the walls. I felt a complete failure, unworthy of love or even basic human courtesy. And he never failed to drive it home. His stinging criticisms became a mantra, the soundtrack to my life, a flood of poison words that engulfed and damaged my fragile spirit. 'I'll try to do better Doctor. I promise I'll do better.'

'Those had better not be empty words Cynthia. That wouldn't go well for you. It wouldn't go well at all.'

I carried out my domestic responsibilities as best I could betwixt wedding and birth, although it was a particularly taxing period both mentally and physically. He decided it was in the baby's interests to stop my medication completely on the day after our marriage, rather than wean me off it gradually as he'd originally planned to do. It was his decision and his alone. I had nothing to say on the matter. Nothing worthwhile to contribute. Not that he'd have listened anyway. 'There'll be no more tablets as of now. You've taken your last my dear. You may experience some minor withdrawal symptoms, it may be somewhat unpleasant, but they shouldn't interfere with your work.'

'I'll do my best Doctor.'

He laughed sardonically and sneered. 'Oh, you will, will you? Madam will do her best and I should be grateful for that.' He was yelling now, with an animalistic snarl distorting his features. 'You took the tablets, you came to rely on them, you didn't reduce the dose when you should have! Maybe I didn't make myself clear enough. Any withdrawal symptoms you experience are your responsibility and will not interfere with your work. Do you understand? Is that simple enough even for you?'

I nodded and stared at the floor. 'But you gave t-them to me. I trusted you. I didn't know what I was…' Did I really say that out loud? Did he hear my ramblings? Oh my God, he must have. Why did I say it? Why on earth did I say it?

He glowered, spitting his words, incredulous, furious, indignant with rage. 'You were falling apart you stupid girl. You were suffering memory loss. You never fully recovered from that insipid boy's death. You were in psychological crisis. Perhaps I should have let you wallow and sink, you ungrateful bitch.'

'I'm s-sorry.'

'Suck it up bitch. The coming days may give you some idea of the suffering you've inflicted on your child in the early weeks of its sad life. That's your responsibility and yours alone! Don't even think about blaming me for your inadequacies.'

As the hours passed, my body increasingly yearned for the drug, and the resulting irritability, increased anxiety, panic attacks, tremors, sweating, wrenching, palpitations and headaches well and truly kicked in. I was wracked with pain. I had never felt so low, I had never felt so ill, I had never felt so desperate. And worse, much worse, I had never felt so guilty. If my helpless baby were to suffer even a tenth of what I was experiencing, it was unforgivable. I had a great deal to answer for. Dr Galbraith told me that again and again and again. I was responsible. It was my fault. What a terrible reality to accept! My baby hadn't yet entered the world and I'd already done them irrefutable harm. What a loathsome creature I'd become.

I would have been more than happy to leave this world in favour of oblivion or whatever else followed, by that stage, but I repeatedly told myself that I had to live on for the sake of my unborn child. If I was the worthless individual he described so diligently, the child was precious and unsullied by life. I'd make their care the primary focus of my existence, my reason for living. I was determined to be a good mother despite my limitations, despite my many flaws, and that kept me going through one of the worst periods of my entire life.

Elizabeth, lovely wonderful beautiful Elizabeth, was born at South Wales General Hospital just three days after my due date, weighing in at six pounds and four ounces. Not a heavyweight, but not a lightweight either! Maybe things weren't going to be as bad for the child as I'd feared. That's what I hoped for. That's what I prayed for. I prayed and believed, but it seems miracles are all too rare. My child was not to receive one.

Dr Galbraith was surprisingly attentive and supportive during the birth, offering encouragement and kind words, charming the nurses, chatting to the doctors; so very different form the man I experienced on a daily basis. He appeared captivated as the baby eventually left my body, but his true feelings showed just for a fraction of a second when the midwife announced it was a baby girl. I couldn't even get that right. That's what he told me when we were alone that first night. 'You stupid bitch, you couldn't even get that right. I can't rely on you for anything. What the hell is wrong with you?'

Chapter 33

I was busy in the laundry by 8:20 a.m. this morning, faced with a mountain of overused sheets that I was expected to iron and fold before lunchtime at the latest. I made reasonably good progress for the first forty minutes or more, but I can only assume I lost concentration, because when one of my English students put her head around the door and shouted, 'Hi Cynth,' I placed the steaming iron down heavily on the first three fingers of my left hand. Believe it or not, as the piping hot metal plate cooked my flesh and I screamed silently inside my head, all I could think was: at least it's my left hand, it won't interfere with my writing. Some say there's no such thing as accidents. Maybe I should take the hint rather than plough on with this exercise.

I leapt backwards, knocking the iron to the floor, and stared at the burned flesh and red raw peeling skin hanging from my fingers.

'Come on Cynthia, let's get you to the sink. Quick as you like.'

I hurried after the guard and held my hand under the mixer tap as instructed. What made her think that running the hot tap was a good idea is a complete mystery to me. The pain escalated exponentially, and this time I couldn't keep the scream inside despite all my prior practice.

She turned the tap off as I urgently pulled away, apologised profusely for the error, and turned on the cold water. It stung initially as I held my hand under the freezing flow, but after about two minutes the pain began to reduce to a bearable level.

'How you doing there Cynth?'

'Yeah, not bad, the cold water is really helping.'

She smiled self-consciously. 'So, better than the hot, then?'

'Yeah!'

'Sorry about that; if you're ready we'll get you along to the sickbay.'

Not a great start, but the day wasn't a complete washout. As I focussed on an image of a beautiful tropical beach, resplendent on the front page of the calendar hanging to the right of the door, I smiled despite my pain and the unreasonably long wait for medical attention. I drank in the detail: the warm blue sea lapping a green and sandy shore fringed with palm trees and a multitude of varied multicoloured tropical flowers, and was reminded that we can seek out beauty. We can take pleasure in the small things like a kind word or friendly smile, or choose to see the sunrise, even if it is through steel bars surrounded by a sea of concrete.

And I did that day: I watched my bird as it swooped and turned and soared with seemingly infinite ease, and I felt joy. For a time I forgot my worries and was temporarily oblivious to my surroundings. I focussed on that small full-of-life creature and smiled inside. I hadn't indulged such feelings for a long, long time, and that's significant. For those few brief moments I let the light in and it illuminated my soul. I'm making progress. It's the only reasonable conclusion I can reach. I'm making progress! Maybe the black dog is more seriously injured than I originally thought. I'll carry on writing and see how things are when I've told you what happened next. Perhaps I'm being much too optimistic. That wouldn't surprise me one little bit.

Chapter 34

Within an hour of Elizabeth's birth the busy ward sister introduced us to a Dr Anne Carter, a genial consultant paediatrician with a prominent Swansea accent, whose greying hair and deep wrinkles suggested she was fast approaching retirement. She smiled warmly on greeting us, congratulated us on becoming first time parents, examined Elizabeth for several minutes in contemplative silence, and then pulled up a seat next to the clear plastic cot. 'Take a seat please, we have things to discuss.'

'Is there something wrong with my baby, Doctor?'

Dr Galbraith glared at me disapprovingly, angry, hateful, but I didn't regret speaking out. I had to know the answer. I just had to know the answer. I was the mother. Why shouldn't I ask about my child?

Dr Carter adopted a more serious persona that worried me immediately. There was a problem. There had to be a problem. I bit my inner cheek and chewed at it, willing myself not to speak up again.

She looked me in the eye, frowned momentarily and began speaking calmly and quietly, directing her words mainly at me and only occasionally glancing in Dr Galbraith's direction, despite him being seated immediately next to me.

'It's not unusual for expectant mothers to be prescribed anti anxiety medication, but regrettably it can cause problems for the child in some cases, particularly when the drug is taken in high doses and over an extended period of time as in your case.'

I'd never felt so low, the burden of responsibility virtually overwhelming.

Dr Galbraith moved to the very edge of his seat. 'I've already explained this to her, Doctor.'

He had, but it was far too late. Why didn't he explain the risks before? He should have told me sooner. I desperately wanted to tell her and alleviate my guilt. I wanted to say it with clarity and confidence. I wanted to shout it out to anyone who would listen, but instead I relaxed my shoulders, lowered my head, avoided her gaze and sat in pensive silence.

She ignored his intervention and continued, focussing primarily on me as she had before. 'Your baby has become used to the drug. We need to address that as soon as possible.'

She reached out a hand and patted my shoulder when I began sobbing. A kind woman, a good woman whom I liked immediately. If only everyone was like her.

'There's no easy way of putting this, I'm afraid. There's a significant likelihood of poor feeding with related poor weight gain. The baby's interactions with you could also be negatively affected.'

I focussed on her intently with pleading eyes, willing her to say something more positive, and causing her to smile thinly in response.

'We could potentially wait to see what symptoms your baby develops or we can begin treatment now. The latter is my preferred option.'

Dr Galbraith rose to his feet and paced the room: agitated, anxious. 'So what happens now?'

I suspect he was more concerned about me being at the hospital for any length of time than anything else.

'Please take a seat Doctor, I'd like to keep this as equable as possible. It's not in anyone's interests to heighten the tension, least of all your daughter.'

He sat as instructed. Always affable, always reasonable when interacting with anyone other than me! Creating a misleading persona; do you understand? I'm sure you understand. Why couldn't I see it? I feel so very stupid. Why on earth couldn't I see it?

'Initially, diazepam will be administered intravenously until the symptoms have been controlled for one week, at which time the daily dosage will be gradually reduced over three to four weeks.'

He shook his head discontentedly as I wept into my hands. 'That's going to be somewhat inconvenient. Can't it be done more quickly?' And then a pensive pause, the manipulative bastard. 'In the interests of the child, you understand.'

I could see that Dr Carter was beginning to lose patience and she spoke again, this time with an admirable steely determination that made me feel a little better and like her even more. 'I'm a paediatrician with over thirty years'' experience, not some kid straight out of college. I'm recommending a well established protocol that's in your child's best interests. I suggest you follow my advice.'

She was on my side. I had an ally. Three cheers for Dr Carter. She became my heroine at that precise moment. What a woman, what a wonderful woman!

I'd become expert in deciphering his moods by necessity. I could see the anger in his eyes, he was bristling, wanting to scream, but it vanished quickly. He hid it well, that devious… 'Whatever you say Doctor, whatever you say. I wouldn't dream of questioning your expertise.'

I think she may have seen through him. I think she may have encountered a man like him before at some point in her life, because she didn't melt and swoon in response to his largess as was the norm. 'Do you intend to breastfeed, Mrs Galbraith?'

I looked at him momentarily but couldn't decipher his opinion.

'Mrs Galbraith? It is the best option for the child.'

I met her eyes and nodded once. It was in my baby's interests and I was committed to being a good mother. It was my body. Why shouldn't I agree?

'Then I suggest you stay at the hospital for the next four weeks. We keep a bed available in the nurses' quarters for precisely this sort of circumstance.'

I so wanted to concur, I wanted to say, yes, I wanted to shout, yes, but would he agree? I muttered a silent prayer. Please let him agree. Please let him agree.

'Is there a problem Mrs Galbraith?'

I could see his mind racing, eyes flickering, computing his response. 'Not at all, not at all! I'll get off home in a minute or two and pack a few things for her. I think that's best.'

'You do that Dr Galbraith. The quicker we sort things out the happier I'll be.'

He just nodded and smiled warmly. Nothing more to say: no objections, no caveats, just placid agreement. What a wonderful woman, what a courageous woman! If only I'd had her warrior spirit. If only I'd had her super human strength. How different things could have been.

Seeing Elizabeth ensconced in that clear plastic cot with a tube inserted up one of her tiny nostrils, down her throat and into her stomach, was truly awful. One of my lowest points. A sight I wish I'd never seen. I strongly suspect that witnessing any child's suffering is stressful for all but the worst of this world, but witnessing my own baby's distress and feeling it was down to me, knowing it was down to me, was a horrendous burden that was extremely hard to bear. It played on my mind constantly, and I repeatedly told myself that I had to put things right as best I could. I had to be there for her. I had to protect her from this cruel world and its uncertain dangers.

Initially I was anxious about touching Elizabeth for fear of harming such a delicate creature, but I quickly gained a degree of confidence with the encouragement of the nurses, and Dr Carter, who appeared to see us as a priority case. I fed my baby as often as required and met her care needs as best I could within the limitations of circumstance. Not the best of starts for any child but I did my utmost to make up for my failures. And at least she was loved. That counts for something. She was loved.

Dr Galbraith visited the ward twice daily on weekdays, early in the morning before clinic and during the evening when his work was concluded for the day. He came more often at weekends, sometimes three times and sometimes four, but thankfully he never stayed long. When he was there he was disinterested in Elizabeth unless there were staff in attendance, and more concerned with ensuring I hadn't discussed the reality of our relationship with anyone than with her progress. I think he came more to warn me of the consequences of speaking out than anything else: 'I assume you've kept quiet about our lives Cynthia. The social services are still snooping around. They've talked of visiting the ward. One word from you could be catastrophic. You do want to keep your baby don't you?'

I'd nod frantically and say, 'Yes.'

'Then I suggest you do exactly as I say. Keep your mouth well and truly shut and maybe, just maybe, I can keep them at bay.'

'Thank you. Thank y-you so very much.'

And he'd sneer and criticise until a member of staff appeared again, when he'd become charm itself. 'Lovely to see you again nurse. Have you done something with your hair? You do a marvellous job, absolutely marvellous. Have you lost weight my dear? What would we do without you?' And so on…

Approximately two weeks after the birth I finally built up sufficient courage to phone my mum, after borrowing two ten pence coins from a particularly kindly cleaner, who befriended me and invariably enquired after Elizabeth's well-being whenever she was on the ward. 'How are you love? And how's that beautiful little girl of yours?'

The phone seemed to ring for an age before I eventually heard Mum's voice say, 'Hello.'

She sounded faltering, tuneless, not at all as I remembered her. I paused for a second or two before speaking. How would she respond? Should I have rung at all?

'Hello, who's there?'

'Hello Mum, it's Cynth.'

I could hear her breathing more heavily as she sucked in the air. 'It's good to hear from you love. It's been too long.'

I explained my circumstances, all the time wondering if I were doing the right thing. He wouldn't like it. He wouldn't like it at all.

'Is Dr Galbraith with you love?'

I shook my head vigorously. 'No, he's working, he won't be here again until this evening.'

'What sort of time are you expecting him?'

She was asking the correct questions. That had to be a good thing, didn't it? 'He usually visits some time between six and seven.'

'I'll be on my way the second I put down the phone love. Dad's at work, I'll have to collect the car, but I'll see you in about forty minutes, if that's all right with you?'

I smiled nervously. Why would she ask? 'I love you Mum.'

'I love you too Cynth. I'll be with you before you know it.'

Mum paused when she first entered the ward, but then she rushed towards me and flung her arms around me, hugging me so tightly that I struggled to catch my breath. She looked tired, older, as if life had prematurely aged her.

'Lovely to see you love. How have you been?'

I freed myself from her grip and took a backward step.
'Not great to be honest.'

'Sorry to hear that love. Things will get better, promise.'
And then a smile that melted away the years. 'Now, where's
that new granddaughter of mine?'

I led her towards the cot, hand in hand, and we stood
together, staring at my sleeping child with tears welling in
our eyes.

'She's lovely. I can't believe I'm a grandmother. I don't
feel old enough.'

I nodded enthusiastically. 'I know what you mean.'

'I have to ask love. What's the tube for?'

I'd been waiting for her to ask. Why wouldn't she in the
circumstances? The tube looked so invasive, so out of place,
so unnatural, so inappropriate. There was no way of
avoiding the subject, however difficult. 'Have you got time
for a quick coffee? The canteen should be open.'

'A cup of tea would be nice love. I've got all the time in the
world'

'Then tea it is.'

We sat together at the chipped blue Formica table,
surrounded by various hospital staff in uniforms, overalls or
white coats, and talked for the first time in months. I got the
distinct impression that we each thought the other was the
reason for our lack of contact. We both assured one another
that that was not the case, but I don't think either of us were
convinced. In fact, now that I think about it, I don't think she
believed a single word I said that day.

'We've been talking to David, love. He's been very good.
He's explained everything. You're so lucky to have him.'

'But, I...'

She raised a hand to silence me just as he would have, and
reached across the table to ruffle my hair as she had in years
gone by. 'It's all right love, no need to explain. I know

you've been ill. I hope that we can all make a new start from now.'

I bit my lower lip hard, trying not to cry.

'You're married now love, and to such a caring man.' She reached out again and touched my wedding ring with her forefinger.

'I wanted you to be there Mum, but…'

'It's all right love. Let's forgive and forget. David says that's best. You haven't been yourself; there's no point in us raking over what we can't change.'

I could see the sadness in her eyes, the lines on her face, the sallow skin fighting gravity and gradually losing the battle. 'Suppose not.' That's all I could say. A myriad words stuck in my throat. Such an inadequate response!

'Just listen to David, love. He's looking after you now. He's a wise man. He's got your best interests at heart.'

She wouldn't believe the truth even if I said it. Why would she? I was ill. A mental defective! What was the point in trying?

When Dr Galbraith visited that evening he could barely control his anger, despite his best efforts to make a good impression on all but myself. He knew, he already knew. Maybe he had his spies amongst the staff.

He made a show of seeing Elizabeth very briefly, and talked to various staff, enquiring after her progress before approaching me slowly and deliberately and pulling up a seat immediately next to me at touching distance.

I looked away, avoiding his accusing gaze as he leant forward and kissed me gently on my forehead before whispering in my ear. 'You've upset your mother.'

What could I say to that? 'But s-she wanted to…'

'She rang me as soon as she left the hospital, you interfering bitch. She's worried Cynthia. She doesn't think you're capable of looking after the baby.'

'But she didn't say…'

He laughed exuberantly at first, and then whispered again. 'She didn't want to see you. She felt she had no choice but to visit after your call.'

'But, I'm s-sure…' In reality I wasn't sure of very much at all.

'Your mother and father have already met with social services. They've offered to care for Elizabeth if she's taken into local authority care. After seeing you today your mother's convinced that's the best option.'

I swallowed hard, fighting to control my gag reflex. 'Can you do something? You're an influential man, people listen to you, surely you can do s-something?'

He adopted a contemplative expression, as if deep in thought. 'If you were to promise never to contact your mother or father again, I'll see what I can do. It may be possible to persuade them to provide you with the opportunity to prove yourself if you don't get involved in any discussions.'

My relief was virtually palpable. 'Thank you. Thank you so much.'

'So you won't go behind my back again? You won't indulge your ill-advised impulses? You won't further jeopardise the brat's future?'

'No!'

He frowned. 'And you're certain of that?'

'I'll never do it again. I promise I'll never do it again.'

He sat back in his chair and relaxed with his broad fingers linked behind his nape. 'Let's hope not Cynthia. For your sake, let's hope not.'

Chapter 35

It seems that Emma makes more comebacks than Frank Sinatra. A feeble attempt to inject a little humour into my musings, I know, but it's the best I can do in the circumstances. Please accept my apologies. Jokes have never been my strong point. I'm yet to discover what is.

   She, Emma that is, arrived this morning about forty minutes before breakfast, delivered by a flustered looking Mrs Martin, who acknowledged my obvious dissatisfaction with a subtle clandestine nod and grimace when Emma's diminutive back was turned.

   I was willing the hands of my watch to move faster and signal my escape to the canteen as she arranged and rearranged her meagre possessions and sat bunched up on the very edge of the bottom bunk, repeatedly trying to engage me in conversation despite my reluctance to reply. She is one determined lady. I limited my responses to grunts or single words initially, but she went on and on and on, until I eventually capitulated and decided to get the inevitable conversation over with as quickly as possible.

   'How are you Emma? Are you fully recovered?' Two stupid questions really, given the state of her face, but I was determined to focus on her wellbeing rather than discuss the reasons for the attack as I strongly suspected she wanted to.

   And then she began crying, and I knew what was unfolding before me. It began with a tear or two, but quickly developed into a weeping torrent of snot and tears that caused her chest to heave as she gasped for breath. She hadn't even bothered asking about my bandaged hand, but I'm a pushover, naturally empathetic by nature, and after a minute or two I reluctantly resorted to asking the question I really didn't want to ask, despite knowing that it was likely to open a door I didn't want to go through. 'What's upsetting you Emma?'

Her eyes lit up and I regretted my query immediately. Why do so many of prison world's residents suffer psychological disorders? Wouldn't a secure psychiatric hospital be a better option than this place?

'Why did they attack me? Have you seen the state I'm in.'

A misshapen nose like a stereotypical wicked step-mother in a pantomime, slowly receding bruising and swelling and a new ill-fitting denture that whistled alarmingly when she spoke. She had a point. It was a vicious assault. 'Surely you know why?'

She stood and stared at me, and I realised I should have kept my mouth shut as I'd originally intended.

'Are you saying I deserved it?'

I shook my head and checked my watch again. Why were the hands moving so very slowly? 'I'm not saying that.'

She smiled thinly and stared at me with unblinking eyes. 'Then, what are you saying?'

What to say? What on earth to say? I've got enough problems of my own without focussing on anybody else's. 'You were convicted of murdering a child Emma. There's a great many people here who find that hard to forgive.'

'I was ill, I shouldn't be here. You could explain that to the others. They seem to respect you. They'd listen to you.'

'I don't think it would make any difference. They wouldn't want to hear it.'

She started crying again, clutching at her face and tugging her greasy hair with frantic fingers whist occasionally peeping at me to weigh up my reaction. 'If they hurt me again, I'll kill myself.'

Was I being manipulated again or was she as desperate as she seemed? To be honest, I didn't know. I still don't know. 'You should talk to one of the guards. Miss Gillespie is always willing to listen.'

'I've tried that before.'

I checked the time again. Five more minutes and I was out of there. 'I know you have Emma. I know you have.'

'Maybe you hate me as much as the others do.'

This time I felt certain I was being manipulated. She was revelling in the interaction. I wanted to shut her up. I needed to shut her up. 'Why not talk to Mrs Martin? I've found her really helpful. She knows what she's doing.'

She shook her head with distain and I felt completely out of my depth. Tick tock, tick tock, only two more minutes! Pass quickly, please pass quickly. 'I'll speak to Mrs Martin for you if you want me to. I'm due to see her again in a couple of days time.'

'What the fuck is she going to do about it? I want you to talk to the other prisoners for me. I want you to persuade them to leave me alone. If I kill myself it will be your fault. Nobody else's, yours!'

One more minute, just one more minute! I'd never disliked another woman so much in my entire life. 'I'll do what I can. But don't expect too much.'

'What's that supposed to mean?'

At last, time to make a move. Thank God for small mercies. There was a loud metallic click as the cell door was unlocked and opened. 'It's time to get something to eat now. I've said I'll do what I can, and I will. Now, leave it there.'

She ran a brush through her hair and smiled. 'We can talk again later.'

I couldn't have handled the situation any worse if I'd tried. She had me exactly where she wanted me.

Chapter 36

The dark grey sky filled the air with fine winter drizzle as I exited the back seat of the Daimler with my baby clutched tightly to my chest, eighteen days after her birth. Her treatment had progressed well, which pleased me, but I found myself increasingly anxious as to what her life would bring. It wasn't the happiest of homes. I wasn't the best of mothers. He certainly wasn't the best of fathers. It was hardly the best start in life.

I was surprised to find the doctor walking alongside me holding a large black umbrella above my head as I crossed the shiny wet pavement, climbed the three familiar granite steps and stood at the front door. I thought at the time that his actions were well intentioned and on behalf of his young daughter, but later events convinced me otherwise. I strongly suspect that his actions were aimed to impress any passers-by or late morning curtain twitchers. I'm sure that you'll reach a similar conclusion given the facts.

As soon as we were in the house he told me to lay my sleeping child in her newly purchased pink cot, and to join him in the kitchen as quickly as possible. I was reluctant to separate from her, however briefly, but thought better of objecting as he stood and tapped his watch repeatedly with two fingers. He was being unusually convivial, why risk exasperating him unnecessarily.

'Sit down Cynthia.'

I pulled up a chair and sat at the table as instructed. 'Would you like a coffee Doctor?'

He sat opposite me on the other side of the table and smiled contemptuously. 'I don't want coffee, or anything else for that matter. Just shut up and listen. You and your brat are here on sufferance. If she turns out to be as useless as you, God help her.'

'I'll d-do my…'

'What part of shut up don't you understand girl?'

I didn't utter another sound.

'I'm a very busy man. My work is important to me, as you well know. I don't expect to be disturbed day or night. That's your responsibility! If you can't keep your brat quiet I'm sure there's some medication I could give her which will do the job very nicely. Like mother like daughter, eh? I suggest you avoid that if you can.'

Surely not, not after everything she'd experienced. Would he do that? Yes, yes, he probably would.

'I seriously considered outlining your responsibilities in a written document as I have previously, but I eventually concluded that it's unnecessary at this stage. I would have thought that even a simpleton like yourself can provide basic care for an infant. Animals appear to manage it without any significant difficulties. It's hardly a demanding task, as I'm sure you'll agree?'

'I'll do my best Doctor.'

And then he held a cupped hand to his left ear. 'I can hear your damned brat whining. Not a very good start is it?'

I could feel myself trembling as I struggled to control my emotions. Maybe a tablet? Should I ask for a tranquilliser? No, I had to be strong for my child. 'No, Doctor!'

'Then I suggest you shut her up before I do.'

And that's the way it continued. He came and went, working at the clinic and occasionally seeing patients at the house, sometimes with a workmate, or sometimes alone, and I cared for Elizabeth and the home, cleaning, ironing, cooking and anything else that needed doing. I did my best to satisfy his impossibly high standards, but the inspections became more vigorous, the criticisms increasingly stinging and the physical punishments more regular and forceful. He didn't hit me in the face again after that first impulsive assault, but the blows to my body hurt nonetheless. I was often bruised, but they were always unseen by others. I was entirely focussed on my duties in the interest of survival and otherwise oblivious to events around me. I didn't see, or maybe I chose not to see, what was happening in front of my face. I hate that now. I don't like myself very much when I think about it.

I'm not sorry to say that he hadn't touched me sexually since Elizabeth's unremembered conception. It's not something I wanted, certainly not something I yearned for as I had with Steven, but ten days after my return home when I was still bruised and sore with undissolved stitches, he suddenly demanded sex. There was no suggestion of affection, certainly not love, and my confusion must have shown on my face because he reacted angrily, poking me hard in the chest before plying me with a single glass of red wine that left me strangely intoxicated. 'Perhaps you need to start taking the tablets again.' And then he pushed me hard towards the bed. 'Now, just undress, lay there and keep your stupid mouth shut.'

'But, I don't w…'

He lay on me heavily and tightened his grip on my neck. 'Just shut up bitch, not another word.'

His movements were mechanical, aggressive, distanced, his focus elsewhere, and I lay there wanting it to be over, willing it to be over, with my head swimming and tears welling in my eyes.

When he'd finished he climbed off me and left the room without another word. He just pulled up his boxer shorts and trousers and walked out, slamming the door shut behind him.

The same performance was repeated more times than I care to remember in the coming weeks until about three months after Elizabeth's birth I was pregnant again.

'Let's hope it's a boy this time. Let's hope you can get that right.'

He showed no sexual interest in me from that moment and never did again.

Chapter 37

I was seriously tempted to forget my commitment to Emma in the interests of an easy life, but in the end my overactive inner voice got the better of me. It makes a habit of doing that. If only I could shut it up for ever.

I've spoken to several of the other girls over the past couple of days, attempting to coax them to leave Emma alone to live with her unreliable conscience. I chose them carefully, targeting those I thought more intelligent, thoughtful or sensitive; those I thought potentially more amenable to persuasion. But it didn't go well. It didn't go well at all. I'm not sure how hard I tried, if I'm honest. I don't know if I was truly committed to my argument, or simply going through the motions to satisfy my conscience. Maybe that's why I failed so dismally.

On each and every occasion my ineffectual arguments were rejected almost as soon as I opened my stupid mouth. Rejected with vehement anger and raised voices. 'Surely you're not siding with that cow Cynthia?'

'What the fuck are you worrying about her for you stupid bitch?'

'Choose your friends carefully Cynth. You don't want people thinking you and her are close. That wouldn't be a good idea.'

'Back off, or you may be next for a kicking.'

'Just do one. The woman's a fucking monster!'

I think it's safe to say I got the message pretty quickly. I've got enough to deal with without alienating women I consider allies or even friends. Now I've got to patch up various relationships. Perhaps I should have given up long before I did. I'll have another word with Mrs Martin when I see her next, leave the responsibility at her door and leave it at that. It's what she's paid for, after all. If Emma gets another beating, as the local parlance goes, I can at least tell myself I did my best on her behalf. I'll have to be satisfied with that.

'Did you talk to everyone?'

I blew the air from my mouth, buying time and searching for an adequate reply. Just tell her Cynthia. Just tell her. Best to get it over with. 'I tried Emma, I really tried.'

She looked truly shocked, the blood draining from her pasty prison face, as if she was expecting a very different outcome. 'What are you saying?'

'I spoke to five or six of the girls, but it was hopeless, they didn't want to know.'

She stared at me with an open mouth. 'Did you tell them I'd kill myself?'

I swallowed the excessive saliva in my mouth and looked away. How could I answer that?

She was angry now, her face reddening. 'You didn't tell them did you!'

'I did Emma, honestly I did.'

She's developed deception to an art. Why should she believe anything anyone else said? 'You're a fucking liar.'

Why is it that when you do your best for some people it comes back to haunt you? 'Not everyone lies all the time. Don't judge me by your own standards.'

'What's that supposed to mean?'

'I think you know the answer to that one.'

She spat in my face and walked away. Such a nice woman, such a delight! If only I could move out and share a cell with somebody else. I don't care who, just not her.

Chapter 38

Dr Galbraith was predictably horrified when Sarah, a second baby girl, arrived approximately nine months later; but I loved her with a burning intensity from the second I saw her beautiful face. She was so perfect, so delicate, so vulnerable, so utterly dependent on me to meet her needs. Just as it should be. Just as I liked it. 'I'll protect you from the cruel world little one. I promise I'll protect you.' And I did, I did my best, I really did, but in reality I was ill-equipped to protect myself, let alone my dependent children. I was a shadow of my former self. A servile creature so eager to please.

I should have left. I should have walked away and taken my girls with me. I should have run and run and never looked back. Why didn't I? What stopped me each and every time? It's something I've thought about time and time again. It's something I've picked at and dissected, but I can't give you an adequate answer. All I can say in my defence is that my psychological shackles were every bit as effective as any high prison walls. I was as much a prisoner then as I am now.

It was more of the same. Nothing really changed in the months following Sarah's birth, that is until one dark dank night in early February 1992, when I was faced with the first of a series of events which were to bring Dr Galbraith's true nature into sharp undeniable focus.

I was abruptly awoken from fitful sleep and unwelcome dreams by the unmistakable sound of car tyres screeching on the tarmac directly outside my second floor bedroom window. I considered pulling the warming duvet high above my head and hiding from the world, but inquisitiveness got the better of me and I jumped from bed, before approaching the window slowly and peering out nervously from behind the long heavy red velvet curtains. There was a large strangely out of place rusty white van parked outside the house in the revealing glow of the street lamps. I blinked repeatedly, casting the weariness from my eyes and closed the curtains slightly, leaving only the slightest gap through which to gape. The doctor was there standing at the front door with his keys in his hand. Nothing strange in that, nothing remarkable in itself, but he was accompanied by a second man, a middle-aged man I hadn't seen before, a man carrying something over his left shoulder. Something that chilled my blood. I could feel my gut tighten and spasm as my knees buckled and I slumped to the floor gripping the curtains with both hands. It was a child. Surely it had to be a child! A boy of six or seven years with short cropped hair and wearing pyjamas despite the bitter early hours frost. I narrowed the gap in the curtains still further and stared with unblinking eyes. The boy was either asleep or unconscious. What on earth was going on? Please don't look up Doctor. Please don't look up!

Dr Galbraith glanced up and down the quiet tree-lined street before turning the key in the Yale lock, pushing open the door and standing to one side to allow the unfamiliar man to carry the boy into the hall. He followed close behind and I heard the door close with a barely decipherable click, so different from his usual habit of forcefully slamming it shut with reckless abandon.

My mind was racing, invaded by unwelcome questions: questions I didn't want to ask, questions I didn't want to answer. Who was the stranger? Why was he bringing a child into the house at that time? Why carry him in that manner?

Why was the boy so quiet? Why so still? I shook my head vigorously, attempting to keep any unwanted conclusions at bay. Perhaps he'd been involved in an accident? Yeah, that must be it. That made sense. That would explain it. But, why not take him straight to casualty? Surely they'd take him straight to casualty. Wouldn't that be preferable? And where were the boy's parents? And why the pyjamas? I really should go downstairs to help, shouldn't I? No, if he was hurt he was in good hands. A psychiatrist was still a doctor. He'd undergone the necessary training. If the boy needed urgent medical treatment who better to provide it. And Dr Galbraith certainly wouldn't welcome my interference. That was a certainty. Best stay upstairs Cynthia. That would be the wisest thing to do in the circumstances. Best stay upstairs and do nothing at all.

I rose to my feet and crept slowly across my bedroom floor and out onto the landing, straining my ears to try and decipher the conversation emanating from the hall two floors below. Listen carefully Cynthia. Listen carefully.

'Come on Gary. Let's get the little bastard in the cellar. Get a move on man. There's work to do. We haven't got all night.'

Crude words, even for him; he was usually so convivial with his friends and workmates. And why the cellar? Maybe it was equipped with the necessary medical equipment. That would explain things, wouldn't it? In a cellar? Really? Yes, why not? He saw patients there for counselling and therapy. Why not physical injury? It was just a matter of convenience. Or, maybe my troubled mind was playing tricks on me again. Maybe I'd been dreaming. Perhaps I'd misheard the pressing barked instructions. Maybe it wasn't a child at all. Maybe the strange man was carrying a rug. Maybe I should get back to bed as quickly as possible, close my eyes tight shut and mind my own business. Maybe I should focus on my girls. Yes, that made sense. That seemed best. The bed was warm and safe, and what could I do if I went downstairs anyway? If there was a boy, he was safe. He'd receive whatever help he required. Of course he would. I had a long history of getting things wrong. Ignore your misgivings Cynthia. Push them to the back of your mind and don't let them escape.

I heard the unmistakable sound of the Welsh dresser being pushed aside in the kitchen before hurrying back to bed with my hands clasped tightly over my ears. I pictured Elizabeth and Sarah's smiling faces in my mind. Think nice thoughts Cynthia. Think nice thoughts. Don't become distracted. Make them big, make them bright, make them loud, and don't let them fade. That's it Cynthia, that's it!

I returned to bed and lay perfectly still with reality crowding in on me and demanding to be heard like a thousand trumpets in every corner of the large bedroom. Was the boy something to do with my husband's work? That provided a viable explanation, didn't it? That seemed reasonable. Either he'd been involved in an accident or that explained it. He was the doctor. He was the expert. He'd said it repeatedly, time and time again. Are you a child care expert Cynthia? Are you at the top of your profession Cynthia? No, I'm not, no I'm not! I never said I was. Think nice thoughts Cynthia. Think nice thoughts.

I didn't see the boy leave the house the next day, and to be honest I pushed him from my mind over the next couple of days as I got on with my chores, attempting to alleviate the doctor's dissatisfaction and wild mood swings, and minimising any potential conflict in the interests of my lovely girls. It was as much as I could do. As much as I could cope with.

But then, one evening later in the week I was forced to think again as the boy with short cropped hair was brought back into sharp focus. I snuggled up on the brown leather three seater settee in one of the two sitting rooms, with the girls cuddled up closely on either side of me, and paid only passing initial interest to the BBC Welsh evening news as an attractive young female newsreader with a black bob summarised the day's key events at the start of the programme. The volume was turned down low for fear of disturbing Dr Galbraith who was working in his study at the other end of the hall, and I strained to hear as the presenter talked of a missing boy in the Caerystwyth area. I can safely say that she had my undivided attention almost immediately. I swallowed hard, held a single finger to my lips and turned to smile nervously at both my girls, keen to reassure them but also keen to listen. 'Shhhh girls! Mummy wants to hear the television.'

I watched intently as an unshaven dishevelled-looking police officer with greying hair and wearing a well-worn threadbare Harris Tweed jacket and poorly adjusted rugby club tie that looked as tired as he did, introduced himself as Detective Inspector Gravel, the lead officer in the case. A distraught and obviously exhausted father named Mike Mailer shuffled uneasily in the seat next to the officer and spoke in an emotionally charged faltering voice, pleading for the return of Anthony Mailer, his missing seven-year-old son. 'If you have my son please don't hurt him. Please let him go. Please contact t-the police at the earliest opportunity.' He'd made his statement. He'd stuck to the script, and then it all became too much for him. I felt his pain as he rose from his chair and rushed away from the cameras with tears pouring down his morose face. Yes, I felt his pain, I empathised with his suffering, but I chose not to make the links. I refused to make the links. Think nice thoughts Cynthia. Think nice thoughts and silence your troubled mind.

The inspector continued despite the impromptu interruption, explaining that the unfortunate boy had been

219

abducted from his home in the early hours, two days previously. He was taken from his bed by a person or persons unknown. And if that wasn't bad enough, as if that wasn't horrible enough to ponder, his mother had been viciously attacked and remained in intensive care at South Wales General. The police suspected her attacker or attackers had abducted the boy. What an awful possibility, what an awful reality: that poor woman, that poor child! I was fixated on the screen and couldn't look away however much I wanted to. Don't think it Cynthia. Don't dare think it. It wasn't the same boy! Surely it wasn't the same boy? He was a doctor, a therapist, a healer. He helped troubled children. He'd written articles. He'd spoken at conferences. He was dedicated to his work. Why would he abduct a child? He liked boys. He wanted boys of his own. Of course he wouldn't abduct a child, would he?

And then a photo of the missing boy flashed on the screen. A colour photo of a slightly built young boy with short red hair and freckles, wearing his primary school uniform with obvious pride. He filled the screen and spoke to me. He yelled at me despite my reticence. He was smiling in the photograph, but there was an unmistakable sadness about him. It must have been his eyes. I think it was his eyes. Or was I in the realms of fantasy again as the doctor so often claimed. I could have been. My judgement was less than reliable. It was hard to tell sometimes.

I blinked and stared and blinked and stared again, fixated on the screen. Don't look away Cynthia. Be brave Cynthia. Please don't look away. Was it the same boy? It could be. It definitely could be. He was within the same age group. He could have had red hair. It was a distinct possibility. It was difficult to tell in the lamplight.

I wanted to look away. I was desperate to look away. I rushed forwards and switched off the TV at the mains with frantic fingers. I flicked the switch, tore out the plug and threw it to the floor. Maybe the father wasn't as nice as he seemed. Maybe the mother was an abusive parent. Yes, that would explain it. It must be something along those lines. It had to be. What other explanation was there? Even if the doctor had the boy it must be for very good reasons. Think nice thoughts Cynthia. Think nice thoughts.

I knelt on the carpet immediately next to the television and held my arms out wide in front of me. 'Come on girls, down you come and give your mum a nice big hug.'

Chapter 39

Oh my God, oh my God, what a truly awful morning! I've seen some terrible things in this life of mine and I'll add this one to the list. If our brains had a delete button, I'd be pressing it repeatedly: delete, delete, delete! It brought back some ghastly memories, an abomination from my past, and for an awful moment I was back there again in that terrible place. Some things are impossible to forget.

After a typical night of wails, laments and whimpers I woke to see Emma hanging from the window's steel bars with a single blood stained bed sheet secured tightly around her scrawny neck. I leapt from my bunk, forgetting I was five feet above the ground, and fell heavily to the concrete floor, twisting my ankle in the process. Adrenalin, it seems, is a highly effective painkiller and I didn't feel a thing.

Emma's face was red, veering on purple, her tongue hung grotesquely from the side of her mouth and a thin line of drool spilt down her chin. I approached her quickly, hopping to accommodate my injured leg. At first I thought she was dead and feared I was at least in part responsible. I held a hand up to her neck and felt for a heartbeat whilst shouting for help at the top of my voice. I thought she was dead. I really thought she was dead. Was she really that desperate? Had I let her down that badly?

I took repeated deep breaths and stumbled backwards, frantically grasping at the sheet in a hopeless attempt to loosen the tourniquet around her throat. Not again, surely not again! And then the cell door opened and I urgently stood aside as two uniform officers rushed forwards towards her.

Just for an instant the world stood still, as if in slow motion, and the scene became crystal clear in my mind. The tips of her feet were on the floor. They were definitely on the floor. She was supporting her own weight. The attention-seeking cow was supporting her weight!

The larger of the two guards, an experienced women in her mid-forties named Jacky, griped Emma around the waist with two strong arms and lifted her easily from the floor as the second guard who was younger and new to my wing, struggled to untie the sheet from the bars with tears welling in her eyes. And then I saw it: a flicker of a smile playing on Emma's distorted hateful face as she was lowered gently to the floor. The cow, the manipulative cow! It seems there are no lengths to which she won't go to gain attention, whatever the effect on those around her. She just tosses the grenade and revels in the devastation. How can anyone be that selfish? How can anyone be so self-obsessed? Does she bring anything positive to this world? I can't think of anything just at the moment.

Emma may have fooled the guards as they resuscitated her selflessly and rushed her from the cell with the aid of a stretcher, but she wasn't fooling me. I just stood aside and watched, despising her in a way I never had before. I know exactly what she was doing. I recognise the self-obsessed. I recognise the self-serving. I've been there and seen it before.

I have the cell to myself again, and I'm happier for it. Everything's relative and it's important to remember that. Be grateful for the little things. The things that make our lives better, if only slightly. And so I'll make the most of my comparative privacy while I can for as long as I can. Maybe this time she won't be back. Let's hope not anyway. I'll say a silent prayer along those lines with the hope that the great puppet master in the sky listens to my pleadings, takes pity on me again and sends Emma somewhere else to serve the remainder of her sentence, along with other broken individuals in need of fixing. It would be better for her and it would be better for me.

What on earth led Emma to so desperately crave attention at any cost? What on earth goes on in that troubled head of hers? I guess that's another story, and I should focus on my own. I hope that this time the doctors identify her true-self and facilitate appropriate intervention away from here, anywhere away from here. There's been far too many crises in my life already as you're about to find out.

Chapter 40

Events moved quickly during that turbulent period, and just a few days after that poor desperate father appeared on the Welsh evening news, they took a further dramatic turn for the worse. I'd been up from bed for about an hour and was putting the finishing flourishes to the doctor's breakfast: checking and rechecking that everything was right, everything in its correct place and at the correct distance, when at precisely 6:30 a.m. there was a forceful knock on the front door that reverberated around the large house and left me close to panic. Who on earth would disturb our household at that hour? Dr Galbraith wouldn't be ready to get up for another hour, and I'd need all the available time to prepare for his eventual appearance.

Whoever was at the door knocked again and kept knocking: harder, harder, harder. I slipped on the bare tiles as I rushed down the hall, slid the last few feet on my stockinged feet and collided with the door. I turned the key in the lock with quivering fingers, turned the handle and took a single step forwards, staring with an open mouthed expression when I urgently opened the door. There were five people crowded around the entrance, three uniformed police officers: two females and one male accompanied by an overly excited Welsh Springer Spaniel, and two men in plain clothes, one of whom I immediately recognised as the tired detective inspector who'd so recently appealed for any information relating to Anthony Mailer's recent disappearance. He stood at the front, clearly in charge, and held up his warrant card in plain view.

'Mrs Galbraith? Mrs Cynthia Galbraith?'

I narrowed my eyes to virtual slits, closed my gaping mouth and said, 'What can I do for you?' more concerned about the early hour than the reason for their unexpected visit.

'My name is Detective Inspector Gravel. We're here to speak to your husband. Where is he?'

I didn't move an inch. I just held my ground like an overly obstructive doorman at a Cardiff nightclub, fixed DI Gravel with a determined glare and said, 'I can't let you in. My husband wouldn't want to be disturbed. Not at this time of the morning! I haven't even had the chance to finish preparing his breakfast as yet. You'll have to make an appointment like everybody else.' What a ridiculous thing to say! How very stupid! Was I really that obsessed with meeting my husband's unreasonable expectations? Sadly, it seems I was.

The inspector didn't look happy. He didn't look happy at all. 'Get out of my way Mrs Galbraith.'

Why didn't I just stand aside and let them in to get on with whatever they were there to do? I should have let them get on with their job. But instead, unbelievably to me now, I took a single step backwards and attempted to slam the door shut, connecting violently with the inspector's right knee as he stepped forward and placed his foot in the door. Why did I do that? I really shouldn't have done that. What on earth was I thinking?

The second plain clothed officer, who I later learned was DS Clive Rankin, moved forward quickly and pushed the door forcefully with both hands, causing me to stumble backwards and yelp as I landed heavily on the tiles, which seemed to excite the dog still further as she bounced up and down on the spot.

DI Gravel rubbed his leg with one hand as he pushed past me and into the hall. He turned back, bent down, offered me his open hand and assisted me to my feet as the remaining officers accompanied by the dog crowded into the hall behind him. 'You have two daughters Mrs Galbraith. I'm going to give you one final opportunity to tell us where your husband is before we search every inch of this house. Where is he Mrs Galbraith? Now Mrs Galbraith!'

My two lovely girls suddenly appeared at the top of the stairs and called to me as I pondered my next move. I felt utterly conflicted, my mind racing, faster, faster, careering out of control. Why were these unwelcome strangers in my home? Could it be something to do with the young boy I'd seen carried into the house a few days previously? I looked towards my daughters, then at DI Gravel, and then at my girls again, before finally turning away from the officers and approaching the staircase. The girls had to come first. Surely they had to come first. Whatever he said, whatever he did to me, they had to come first. Like it or not he'd have to deal with getting up early for once in his life. He'd have to address whatever it was these people wanted face to face. I began slowly climbing the stairs and said, 'He slept in his study last night. It's the second door on the right down the hall,' without a backward glance.

I descended the stairs reticently, holding Sarah up to my chest with one arm whilst gently guiding Elizabeth with the other. 'Come on girls, everything's going to be just fine. These nice people are here to speak to your father.'

'Stay with the mother and kids until someone arrives from social services Pam. Keep them well out of the way. Rankin, with me! The rest of you can start searching as soon as Galbraith's arrested.'

Why on earth did he say that? Why the talk of social services? I felt increasingly close to panic as the metaphorical storm clouds closed in. He'd been correct all along. I was an inadequate mother, unworthy of my daughters. Don't take my girls. Please don't take my girls.

We were ushered into the sitting room to the left of the front door by a friendly female officer in her thirties, who instructed us to take a seat, smiled warmly and told us to call her Pam.

'Please don't take my girls. I'll try harder. I promise I'll try harder.'

She looked confused by my reaction and uttered words of reassurance: apparently kind words that were pleasing to the ear. But I didn't trust her. Why would I trust her? He'd told me repeatedly to question the intentions of anyone in an official role. 'Be extremely guarded Cynthia. Think carefully before speaking, and that's if you have to speak at all. They may well appear pleasant enough on face value, they may even appear to have your best interests at heart. But it's a mirage, an illusion they seek to create. They'll lull you into a false sense of security and pounce, using anything and everything you say against you in court. Don't trust them for an instant if you want to keep your brats.'

I heard his cyclic mantra resounding in my head as clearly as if he were speaking directly into my ear. I focussed on his words, listened intently and kept my mouth tightly shut just like he told me to. Be careful Cynthia, stay tight-lipped, that's for the best.

'Is there anything you want to ask me Mrs Galbraith?'

I clutched my children tightly on either side of me, shook my head and strained my ears, keen to get any clue as to what was happening down the hall.

The police didn't knock this time. They just opened the study door and burst into the room. I could hear DI Gravel's raised voice and was surprised by the ferocity of his words.

'Wake up Galbraith, it's the police!' He was assertive, disrespectful and seemingly in control. I couldn't quite believe it. I'd never heard anyone speak to the doctor like that before. He'd called him Galbraith. Not Doctor, just Galbraith! A small part of me revelled in his attitude, but maybe the doctor would pounce suddenly and devour him.

Dr Galbraith began speaking, and I feared that nothing had changed. 'Please accept my sincere apologies gentlemen. I have trouble sleeping on occasions. I sometimes take a tablet. Tell me what can I do for you both?' I guess he must have been sleeping when the CID officers entered the room. It wasn't unusual for him to sleep in the study.

'You're under arrest Galbraith. Put the cuffs on Sergeant.' They were arresting him. They were actually arresting him. Perhaps I'd be next. Oh my God, perhaps I'd be next. Criminal neglect, that's what he said they'd call it. Say nothing Cynthia. Not a word, not a single word.

'This has to be a mistake.' The doctor sounded rational, sure of himself. A mistake, that made sense, it was probably a mistake. They'd pay a heavy price for their error.

'Have you got something to say for yourself Galbraith?' There it was again: the implied lack of respect. Maybe it wasn't a mistake after all?

'Do you know who I am?' He sounded incredulous but I thought I identified a degree of anxiety in his voice. Just for a moment, just for a fleeting moment!

'I know exactly who you are you smug bastard. My officers are going to search every inch of this fucking place, and you're going to be locked up. Still feeling quite so confident?'

And I don't think he was. I really don't think he was.

'Sorry about the inspector's language Mrs Galbraith, I'll have to wash his mouth out with soap and water.'

I forced a half-hearted smile in response to her well-intentioned humour and kept listening.

'I really fail to understand the reason for your hostility. You can search for as long as you wish. There's absolutely nothing to find.' He sounded calm, assertive, his usual confident self.

'Shall I take him to the car boss?'

'Leave him to me Clive.'

229

And then I heard a mind-blowing commotion as Inspector Gravel manhandled my husband through the study door and down the hall with such speed that he struggled to keep his footing.

I peered around the doorframe and stared, confused by events and not quite able to believe what I was witnessing. The officer rushed him down the hall, pushing him repeatedly in the back with his right shoulder if he slowed.

'Come back into the room and take a seat please Mrs Galbraith.'

I was transfixed, very close to panic but unable to look away as DI Gravel stopped abruptly on reaching the front door, and shouted back into the house, 'Rankin, bring that computer for the tech boys to have a look at. Pam, you stay with Mrs Galbraith and the kids for the moment. Social services transport's on the way. I want this fucking place searched from top to bottom. If you find anything of interest, anything whatsoever, I want to hear about it immediately. Are you all clear?'

There was a chorus of, 'Yes, sir.'

'Sit down Mrs Galbraith, I won't ask you again.'

I did as I was told this time and watched from the settee with my arms around the girls shoulders. They were well used to shouting and to sitting in complete silence, seemingly unaffected by such dramatic events, which when you think about it was a problem in itself.

I turned in my seat and watched from the front window as DI Gravel frogmarched the doctor out of the house, down the three granite steps into the quiet early morning street and flung him into the back seat of the police car with such force that he skipped across the seat and hit the inside of the opposite door. DS Rankin followed closely behind carrying my husband's desktop computer in both arms.

'Put that fucking thing in the boot Clive. Let's get this cunt back to the station.'

'Don't listen girls.' Such a nice way with words!

DS Rankin closed the boot, climbed into the driver's seat and started the diesel engine, whilst the inspector sat in the back within touching distance of the doctor. I didn't know it then, but my world had changed forever.

Chapter 41

The previous chapter wasn't easy to write. The memories are still surprisingly raw given the amount of time that's passed. The creative process brought this world's insidious dangers into starkly sharp focus again. I've been experiencing repeated debilitating headaches since, and the horrors of the past are dwelling on my mind almost constantly as I go about my busy day. The black dog is gaining strength again, gaining strength and stalking me determinedly. What if Jack's infant encounters one of the Galbraith's of this world? What if my lovely girls encounter another man like him but with different deviant tastes? Oh my God! It just doesn't bear thinking about. I know our families are more guarded than most as the result of our experiences, but is that enough to protect them? Please let it be enough.

I was seriously tempted to bring the entire writing process to a premature end and flush the torn pages of my notebooks down the nearest toilet, but I remembered Mrs Martin's words of encouragement and decided to continue despite my exploding anxieties. She did say it wouldn't be easy, she did say there'd be rocky ground along the way, but that it was a road worth travelling. Let's hope she's right and the demons are eventually defeated. Rocky ground is one thing, but this feels more like insurmountable cliffs. I'm approaching the critical part of my tale now, and so those cliffs are likely to become higher still. There are towering mountains on the horizon. I'll just have to see if I can climb them.

Chapter 42

An ageing British racing-green Volkswagen Golf arrived at our Caerystwyth town house only minutes after my husband's enforced departure, driven by a young girl in her early twenties, who the WPC told me was a social services children's resource centre worker named Karen Giles.

I tightened my grip on the girls' shoulders and pulled them closer to me, as the officer opened the front door and asked the social worker into my home uninvited by me. 'All right Karen. Good to see you again, how's the family?'

'Not bad thanks Pam. You're looking tired, I hope you haven't been overdoing it again.'

'It's these early starts. You know what it's like. Come on in, I'll introduce you to Mrs Galbraith before heading back to the station.'

'Do they know what's going on?'

'I've told them the basics, but a fuller explanation wouldn't do any harm in the circumstances.'

I listened carefully to their very ordinary conversation, trying to make sense of events, and acutely aware that those events were largely beyond my control. The two women seemed so amicable, so very human, so unthreatening, but I had to be cautious as per his instructions. Not a word out of place Cynthia. Not a single word.

The social worker walked towards me, shook my hand limply, smiled and said, 'Nice to meet you Mrs Galbraith. You must be Elizabeth and Sarah. I've been looking forward to getting to know you all.'

I had never been so wary. I wanted to speak to them. I wanted to reach out and connect with another human being to plead my case, but they were behaving just as he said they

233

would, with their ready smiles, kind words and insincere manipulative pleasantries. Don't fall for it Cynthia. Don't fall for it. Keep your stupid mouth shut. Not a word, not a single word!

The smarmy social worker smiled again, keen to ingratiate herself still further and pull me into her caustic web. 'I'll be taking you to Caerystwyth Children's Resource Centre this morning Mrs Galbraith. The girls will be interviewed by a police officer and child protection social worker who are specially trained to work with children. The interviews will be video recorded and could potentially be used in evidence if there's any suggestion of relevant criminal activity. You'll be interviewed by a detective, but she'll explain more about that when we get there. Now, is there anything you want to ask me before we get on our way?'

I shook my head unhappily and avoided her eyes. The shock of information was mind blowing. Things seemed to be moving at breakneck speed and threatened to overwhelm me completely. 'Do we have to go?' I knew the answer was yes before asking the question, but I asked anyway in the forlorn hope I was wrong. It seems I... Well, you know the rest by now.

'Please fetch your coats. It's cold outside, and time we made a move.'

I said nothing more, no objection, no argument. What was the point? I followed her orders like a lamb to the slaughter. It was happening exactly as he said it would and there was nothing whatsoever I could do about it.

A Detective Constable Myra Thomas introduced herself with a fleeting smile and ushered me into a small dusty cluttered office at the children's resource centre about an hour and a half later. 'Have a seat please, I'll fetch us both a hot drink before we make a start, tea or coffee?'

Was someone really going to make me tea? A nice gesture, or was it another trick? He'd said that they'd be devious. He said they'd pretend to be nice. Yes, that must be it, another transparent ploy to get the better of me. 'Tea, please, no milk or sugar.'

'Try to relax Mrs Galbraith. I'll be back with you in two minutes.'

Relax, how was I supposed to relax? My mind was exploding with questions I couldn't answer. How did the girls cope with their interviews at such a young age? What were they asked? What if anything did they say? He'd told them never to speak of our home life, he'd repeated it time and time again as they sat and listened in total silence, but did they understand his cautionary advice sufficiently to resist skilled interviewers? Were they old enough to understand the risks and implications? What if they said something? Oh my God, what if they said something? What if they described me as a bad mother? What if I said something inappropriate? I could lose them forever.

DC Thomas pushed the door open with the tip of her fashionable black suede ankle boot and handed me a white pottery mug filled almost to the brim. 'There you go. Now, let's make a start.'

I rubbed my tired eyes, smearing black mascara across one cheek.

'What's wrong Mrs Galbraith?' What did she mean by that? Could she read my thoughts? The doctor often claimed he could. Maybe she was no different. It was hopeless, absolutely hopeless.

'Can you hear me Mrs Galbraith?'

And then I spoke out instinctively without thinking, without engaging my brain. 'You've been so kind.' It was okay to say that, wasn't it? I hadn't let anything slip. There was no harm in that.

She leant towards me and handed me a Kleenex paper hankie taken from a packet in her handbag. 'You've had a difficult day, you're bound to feel emotional. Anyone would in the circumstances.' What a nice thing to say, it seemed she understood. Perhaps it was okay to talk to her after all.

'I saw my parents. They collected my daughters after their interviews. I don't see very much of them anymore. I hadn't seen my dad since leaving for Cardiff.'

She looked genuinely surprised. 'Really? Why's that?'

It seemed like an innocuous enough question. Why not answer? 'I let them down. They choose not to keep in touch.'

The detective looked at me quizzically. 'But they seemed absolutely delighted to see you earlier today. Your dad seemed overwhelmed with emotion. He could hardly contain himself.'

'It's all a show, they don't really feel like that.'

She shifted uneasily in her seat. 'Why do you think that?'

'My husband explained it to me. He's a clever man and understands such things. He speaks to them on a fairly regular basis. They just can't cope with my inadequacies.'

She shook her head slowly. 'Are you scared of your husband Cynthia?'

I didn't expect that one! I'd said too much, far too much. It was spilling out of me like a flood despite my determination to remain tight lipped. Time to think. I needed time to think. I nodded ever so subtly and whispered, 'He wouldn't want me to talk to you about that.'

'Dr Galbraith is in custody. It's safe to talk. The more you tell me the better. He can't hurt you anymore.'

I took a deep breath and steadied myself, making a show of sipping my hot tea before biting my lower lip and looking away.

'We need your help Cynthia.'

Now, that got my attention and I sat up in my seat. Why would anyone need my help, of all people? 'Really?'

236

'A child is missing. A seven-year-old little boy called Anthony with short red hair and freckles. His mother was attacked and he was taken from his home in the middle of the night. It was an extremely violent assault. She was left for dead. We believe that your husband had something to do with the attack and the boy's abduction. Have you seen Anthony? Can you help us find him?'

Oh my God, oh my God! Think nice thoughts Cynthia, think nice thoughts.

'Can you help us Mrs Galbraith?'

I closed my bleary eyes tight shut and began repeatedly rocking back and forth in my chair. It was too much to contemplate. Too much to handle. I was like a rabbit caught in the headlights with nowhere to run.

'Did you see him? This is your opportunity to tell me what you know.'

My mind was doing somersaults, attempting to compute the information but failing dismally. Maybe I should tell the nice officer what I'd seen and heard. I wanted to, I really wanted to. Perhaps I should follow my instincts. It would feel so good to help. But hold on! What would the doctor say if I did the wrong thing again? What would he do to me? Surely if he had the boy it must be for extremely good reasons. He was an important man with an important professional role. Perhaps it was better to say nothing, rather than say or do the wrong thing yet again.

'Speak to me Cynthia.'

I parted my lips as if to speak, but then reconsidered. He could tell the police everything they wanted to know if he chose to. It was probably best to leave the talking to him, and say nothing more.

'Mrs Galbraith?'

I ignored her prompt, closing my mind for fear of saying the wrong thing again.

'We suspect that Anthony is in terrible danger. We're talking about a child's life. Can you help us find him?'

I bit my lip again, harder this time.

'Look at me Mrs Galbraith. Open your eyes, please.'

I opened my eyes slowly and stared into space, avoiding her inquisitive gaze.

'I am going to ask you again. Was Anthony Mailer at your home?'

I clamped down my teeth and tasted blood.

'What is it you're afraid of? If you know anything, anything at all, you must tell me.' She was getting agitated now. Just like him, just like him! It seemed she wasn't so nice after all. Keep your mouth shut Cynthia, keep your mouth tightly shut.

I closed my eyes again, acutely aware of the accusing shadow of my husband looming over me and cautioning continued silence. She's trying to catch you out you stupid bitch. Don't trust her for an instant. You've said too much already. Not another word, not if you want to keep those brats of yours. Not a single word!

'Do you know anything at all Mrs Galbraith? Can you help us find Anthony?'

I met the detective's pleading look for a fleeting moment and shook my head vigorously, attempting to persuade her to bring the interview to an end.

She persevered for another twenty minutes or more before reluctantly accepting defeat. I was just glad it was over. So very glad it was over.

And then she smiled warmly and placed what I suspected was intended to be a reassuring hand on my left shoulder. 'I'm going to make a phone call to find out if my colleagues have finished searching your house. I'll take you home just as soon as I can. Is that all right with you?'

'I haven't got a key.'

'You don't have your own key?'

238

'I've never had one.'

'I'll ask one of my colleagues to drop one off.'

I nodded, grateful for the kindness. 'Okay, if it's not too much trouble.'

DC Thomas took a red Parker pen from her black leather police issue handbag and asked for my home number.

We left the resource centre about an hour later, after the various search officers had left my home. I sat next to her in the front of the unmarked CID car and asked if they'd found anything significant. She chose not to answer. I still didn't know if there was anything to find.

The detective kept her eyes fixed on the road rather than turn to face me. 'What do you think they may have found?'

I shrugged my shoulders noncommittally and said nothing more. I'd said too much already; how stupid could a person be?

She repeatedly asked me the same unanswered questions during the twenty minute journey, and I felt genuinely relieved when we finally arrived at the house and she chose to remain in the car. She handed me a small white card with her name and telephone number on the front as I exited the vehicle. 'Contact me any time if you need to talk.'

'When will my husband be home?'

She smiled reassuringly. 'He's still being questioned, as far as I'm aware. It could be some time, and that's if he comes home at all.'

I had a skip in my step as I opened the door. How good would that be: just me and my lovely girls. Or was that too much to ask for? Yes, it was probably too much to hope for. He'd explain himself, he'd outwit them, he'd win in the end. He always did. Why should this time be any different?

I jumped, spilling a small amount of my elderberry tea into the white saucer when the phone rang out and shattered the

239

silence later that evening. I entered the hall in response to the demanding ringtone, picked up the receiver tentatively and held it to my ear. Please don't be him, please don't be him.

'Hello Cynth, it's Mum, is that you love?'

Should I say anything in response? Maybe or maybe not, I'd made enough mistakes for one day.

'Say something Cynth, the girls want to hear your voice.'

My breathing became more laboured and my eyes filled with salty tears. 'Are they with you now?'

'Yes love, it's on speaker phone. They can hear everything you're saying. They want to say hello. They're missing you love.'

She sounded so gentle, so caring. Perhaps it was for the girls benefit rather than mine.

I heard Elizabeth and Sarah yelling 'Hello' in excited voices, encouraged by their grandmother. 'Can they come home Mum?'

'Give me a second love, I'll just give Dad a shout. We need to talk privately. I'll put the girls on.'

'Good night Mummy!'

My eyes flooded with tears again. 'Good night you two, sweet dreams, be good for Granny.'

'Hello.'

'Yes, I'm still here Mum.'

'Dad's going to read the girls a bedtime story while we talk.'

I smiled, recalling my own happy childhood. 'That's nice!'

And then a brief silence before she spoke again. 'I'm worried about you love. What on earth's going on in your life? The police and social services haven't told us very much at all.'

I shook my head, wanting to tell her, but doubting her true intentions. 'When can the girls come home? They're my daughters, not yours.'

'I know that love! I'm on your side.'

Really? I hoped so. I really hoped so. 'Bring them home first thing in the morning. I'll have their breakfast waiting.'

I could visualise her shaking her head in that maddening way of hers. 'It's not that simple love. The social worker explained that if we didn't agree to look after the girls until told otherwise, they'd be placed with foster carers.'

I felt as if my fragile world was dismantling still further. 'They can't do that.'

'They've applied for some sort of legal order love. There's going to be a meeting. The social worker's going to discuss it with you once they know what's happening with the police.'

I didn't want to hear it. I just couldn't accept my new reality. Think nice thoughts Cynthia. Think nice thoughts. 'I just want them home!'

'Talk to the social worker love. Hold on, I've got his number here somewhere.'

I didn't want to talk to the social worker, or anyone else for that matter. I just wanted my girls home with me at the earliest opportunity and for us to be left alone to get on with our lives as best we could. I slammed the phone down and screamed: louder, louder, louder. The doctor had it spot on all along. They were all liars, they were all against me, and they all wanted to take my children. Or at least, that's what I thought at the time.

Chapter 43

My porridge was cold, lumpy and particularly unappetising this morning, as it often is on Mondays for some inexplicable reason, but that apart it's been a pretty good day. Things progressed as per usual until about 11:00 a.m. when one of the senior guards rushed into the laundry where I was busy ironing again despite my recent accident, and announced that the governor, no less, wanted to see me immediately. I felt somewhat anxious as I rushed to keep up with her as she negotiated various corridors before stopping abruptly on reaching the governor's never seen before polished dark-oak door. I had no idea why I'd been summoned and my nerves almost got the better of me as she knocked reticently and waited for a woman I could only assume to be the governor's secretary to shout 'Come in!' after a few seconds of painful silence. Getting that nervous made little sense given my situation and the limits of potential sanctions, but I think the scenario spirited me back to the headteacher's office following some minor misdemeanour or other years before. Isn't it strange how our past shapes and torments us when we least expect it.

'Cynthia Galbraith to see the governor.'

The slim middle aged secretary looked up from her typewriter and pressed the red plastic tannoy button to its left. 'Cynthia Galbraith to see you Mr Thompson.'

I stifled a nervous giggle. Pathetic, I know, but there you go. It felt so like school.

'Send her in Joe.' I assumed it was short for Joanne, but who knows? I never did find out for certain and I guess it doesn't matter anyway.

She pointed at a second oak panelled door located just a few feet behind her desk and said, 'You can go in now.'

The governor was sitting expansively in a brown antique leather swivel chair behind a large modern desk, when I entered the room and stood before him. Why do such people need such huge offices? I know it's a status thing, but really, what a ridiculous waste of space. Isn't the title, power and salary enough?

'Take a seat Cynthia.'

Cynthia: my first name, and take a seat in one of his padded chairs. Now that surprised me. I was expecting to be left standing there wishing the floor would open up and swallow me whole whilst he said whatever it was he had to say for himself. But instead, he smiled warmly and called to his secretary, asking her to make two cups of coffee. He didn't actually ask me how I like my coffee, I guess that would have been a step too far, but it was coffee nonetheless. The officious assistant with her brash and superior persona was making coffee for a prisoner. I bet that stuck in her craw. Wonders never cease.

'I suppose you must be wondering why I've asked to see you?'

I nodded as the secretary reentered the office in snooty silence and placed a tin tray holding two cups of black coffee, a jug of milk and a bowl of brown sugar next to the desktop computer. 'Will that be all sir?'

'I'll need you to take dictation in about an hour, but that will be all for the time being. Close your door on the way out please.'

He turned back to face me and looked me directly in the eye. 'Help yourself to a coffee.'

I was all fingers and thumbs as I poured a splash of milk and sugar into my cup and stirred vigorously.'Thank you, it's appreciated.'

And then a flicker of a smile played on his lips before he spoke again. 'I've had your solicitor on the phone this morning: a Mr Breen. He seemed a pleasant enough man.'

I moved to the very edge of my comfortable chair and took a deep breath before raising the cup to my lips, swallowing a mouthful of sweet coffee and savouring the rich flavour. 'What was it he wanted?' I was hoping for something positive; praying for something positive.

'It seems there's been some developments in your case.' There was that phrase again. All I could think was: developments, what developments? Somebody tell me before my head explodes.

'I'll leave the specific details to your lawyer, but suffice it to say he considers them significant.'

I resisted the impulse to protest. I wasn't any clearer than when I'd entered the room. 'Can you tell me any more, please?'

'I'm sure your solicitor will put you fully in the picture just as soon as he sees you this afternoon. He'll be here around two. I'll ask Jo to ensure there's a room available. Now, Mrs Martin tells me you're writing a journal.'

And that was it: he directed the conversation away from my question and never went back to it. He was in control. He was in charge. Like it or not, I'd just have to wait until the afternoon's meeting. Be patient Cynthia. You've waited three long years. What difference would another couple of hours make? I'd just have to be patient and let the minutes tick by.

I thought my solicitor looked older and somewhat jaded as he shook my hand firmly at 2:00 p.m. that afternoon. His brown hair had thinned alarmingly since I'd last seen him, and his previously boyish face was finally showing its age. Isn't it strange how we expect people to appear as they were when we last met them, even when it was years previously. I guess he was making similar observations about me. Perhaps it's best not to think about it too much. I'm not getting any younger either.

'Good to see you again Cynthia. How's life treating you?'

A stupid question given my living arrangements, wouldn't you agree? 'Could be worse.'

'Please take a seat, and I'll explain what this is all about.'

I sat as instructed, my gut doing somersaults with the expectation of it all.

'How long has it been?'

'Three long years.'

He took a cigarette from a packet of twenty and offered me one before lighting the tip and sucking at it hungrily as the poisonous fumes spiralled into the air and stung my eyes. 'I thought so.'

'Look, can we forget the small talk and get on with it.'

He took another drag and nodded twice. 'Do you remember Detective Inspector Gravel?'

Just tell me, whatever it is just tell me. 'Yes, of course I do.'

'He called to see me at my office first thing yesterday morning.'

'And?' It was too important to be patient for a second longer.

'The new owners of Galbraith's Caerystwyth town house have been pulling up floorboards as part of a central heating project.'

I was beginning to wonder if I was going to like what he said next one little bit.

'They found a large collection of files, photos and videotapes.'

I breathed a sigh of relief. I thought they'd found a body. 'The police know exactly what he was. It'll be more of the same.'

'Oh, it was, no surprises there, but there was one different file. A file dedicated to you.'

I had absolutely no idea what he was talking about. 'Why me?'

'Everything you said was true.'

I shook my head incredulously. 'Well, I know that, but nobody believed me at the time did they!'

'He kept a complete written record of everything he did to you. They'll believe you now.'

'Does it change anything?'

He stubbed out his cigarette and smiled. 'Yes, I believe it does. I need to sound it out with the barrister, but I'm quietly confident that with your agreement we have grounds for appealing your conviction.'

It sounded like good news but I wasn't ready to throw my figurative hat in the air just yet. 'What sort of stuff did he record?'

He pushed up the sleeve of his navy pinstripe jacket and checked his stainless steel wristwatch. 'I'll drop you a line sometime in the next couple of days to put you fully in the picture, but I want to spend our remaining time today discussing where we go from here.'

I looked at him with pleading eyes.

'I've got to be out of here in twenty minutes. Shall I make a start?'

I nodded reticently, making the best of the situation. 'Okay.'

'As I said, I believe we have grounds to refer your case to the Criminal Division of the Court of Appeal. It's a lengthy process, but the sooner we start the quicker you may be out of here.'

'You think there's a real chance I'll be released?' Please say yes, please say yes.

He paused and adjusted his paisley tie, collecting his thoughts before responding. 'Look Cynthia, the new

246

evidence is a significant breakthrough, there's no denying that, but there's no guarantees. As you know courts can be notoriously unpredictable. I need to do the groundwork in consultation with Mr Brown, make the relevant application and see how things progress from there.'

'So they could decide to overturn my conviction?' This was getting more exciting by the minute.

'Slow down, there are various possibilities.'

I was afraid to ask my next question for fear of him saying something I didn't want to hear, but I formed my hands into small tight fists and asked it anyway. 'Can you spell them out for me?'

'I don't think it likely, but they could decide to dismiss the appeal.'

'And?'

'They could allow the appeal and direct that you're acquitted on the basis of the new evidence. They could allow the appeal, and substitute your murder conviction for a lesser charge open to the trial jury at the time of your trial. Or they could allow the appeal and direct that there is a retrial.'

Why are such things always so frigging complicated? 'What do you think is the most likely option?'

He checked his watch again, pushed back his chair and stood to leave. 'Either reducing your conviction from murder to manslaughter or a retrial. But, I'll be able to give you a better idea once the barrister's had a chance to review the papers.'

My eyes lit up as I felt the adrenalin surging through my system. 'Can you put a figure on it?'

'If I were a betting man I'd say seventy-five to eighty per cent in your favour. But as I said there are no guarantees. I've got to make a move Cynthia. I'll drop you a line as soon as I get the chance.'

I loosened my hands and relaxed back in my seat. Things were looking up at last.

Chapter 44

I got up at precisely 5:30 a.m. as per usual on the morning after the doctor's arrest and hurried down to the kitchen on autopilot after a brief bathroom visit, to prepare his breakfast in line with his exact requirements. I rushed around in a whirl of frantic activity, checking that everything was ready, everything in its place, everything at the correct distance, when it suddenly dawned on me: I was alone in the house and there was absolutely nothing I needed to do. He wouldn't be coming down the stairs, he wouldn't suddenly appear with his criticisms, complaints and threats or worse, and I felt grateful for that brief reprieve. He'd be back of course, I couldn't let my standards slip, everything had to be perfect for his eventual return, but I could make the most of my free time and enjoy a quick cup of herbal tea before getting on with the housework and trying to forget that my girls were not with me as they should be.

I became increasingly anxious as the hours ticked by, fearing that every car that past, every sound and every shadow signalled Dr Galbraith's imminent return to the house, full of recriminations and spewing hate. I watched and waited with bated breath, hiding behind the banality of familiar household tasks until the phone rang out loudly in the hall at just after 12:00 p.m., causing a lump in my throat and a knot in my stomach that twisted and ached with ever increasing force as I tried to decide on an appropriate course of action. Should I answer? It could be the social worker my mum mentioned. I should answer, of course I should, it could be news of my girls. But hold on, what if it was the doctor? What if it was him? Don't be him, please don't be him!

I rushed in the direction of the phone and clutched at the receiver for fear of the caller bringing their call to an end before I had the opportunity to answer. I held the phone up to my ear with one hand, wondering if I was doing the right thing, whilst clutching the small hall-side table with my free hand, fearing my trembling legs may give way at any moment. Please don't be him, please don't be him!

I steadied myself and whispered, 'Hello.'

'Mrs Galbraith, is that you?'

I recognised DI Gravel's robust worldly voice as soon as I heard it, but I couldn't find the confidence to speak.

'It's Detective Inspector Gravel, we met at your home the other morning.'

He knew it was me. There was no hiding in silence. And it could be news of Elizabeth and Sarah. I had to say something. Come on Cynthia, say something. 'I remember.' Pathetic, I know, but it was the best I could do.

'I'm not in the habit of doing this, but the circumstances are exceptional.'

Doing what? What on earth was he talking about? I tightened my grip on the phone, willing myself to speak again. 'Does my husband know you're calling?' I was very much hoping the answer was no. He wouldn't like it. He wouldn't like it at all.

'He doesn't, and that's a good thing. He's just finished in court. He's facing some extremely serious charges. But, for some inexplicable reason he was given bail.'

'Bail?' I knew exactly what bail meant, but I didn't want to believe he'd be coming home anytime now. Oh, my God, he was coming home.

'Please listen to me very carefully Cynthia. He's been released and there's fuck all I can do about it. You haven't got much time. He's a very dangerous man. He's been charged with some truly horrendous crimes against children. You need to get out of there before it's too late. Why not go to your parents' place? Your daughters are already there. You need to…'

I didn't hear the rest of DI Gravel's seemingly heartfelt plea. I decided I'd heard enough and put down the phone, determined to face reality however difficult, however traumatic, however onerous. I think the inspector's call proved a watershed moment for me. A wakeup call that forced me to consider whether the missing boy was a victim of my husband's violence as I was, and still in my home. It was a distinct possibility, and I had to know. This time I had to know the truth. There'd be no more denial. Be brave Cynthia. Please be brave.

I slumped at the kitchen table with my head in my hands and stared at the Welsh oak dresser for at least five minutes or more before eventually building up sufficient courage to act. I'd been passive for too long. Much too long. The worm had turned.

Even then I considered ignoring my newly found inclination to act, but that small voice inside my head became louder and insistently urged me on. Why on earth had it remained silent for so long?

I rose to my feet, slowly approached the dresser one cautious step at a time and urgently searched in the left hand drawer with trembling fingers. Where was the key? Where on earth was the key? It had to be there somewhere. Yes, there it was, there it was. Get a move on Cynthia, get a move on! I had to act quickly before he returned to the house and silenced that small voice forever.

I placed my shoulder against the side of the heavy dresser, using all my meagre weight and strength to gradually push it aside. Come on Cynthia, you can do it, push harder girl, just push harder.

And then it moved, inch by reluctant inch it moved, suddenly without warning. I stood facing the partially unencumbered clandestine door, sweating profusely, panting hard, willing myself to move, and then I stepped forward, spurned on by that same small voice and bold images of the young boy and his desperate father flashing repeatedly behind my eyes like a cinematic film. I gripped the door handle tightly in my right hand and slowly turned it. You can do it Cynthia. Come on, you can do it.

I stared down at twelve cold grey concrete steps and towards a second white painted steel door beyond them. Why another door? Why did he need a second door? What was it hiding? I could still run, couldn't I? Of course I could, it was still an option. It wasn't too late. But what if the boy was down there and needed my help? No, not this time, there'd be no running this time. You can do it Cynthia, come on girl, you can do it. Be brave Cynthia, down you go.

I took my first tentative step, fearing I may lose control of my bladder at any second and flood the steps with yellow liquid. I paused on the second step for a second or two, breathing deeply, panting, contemplating retreat despite my newfound determination, but then I rushed quickly to the bottom two or three steps at a time without allowing myself sufficient time to think of the danger and potentially change my mind.

Come on Cynthia, open the door. You can do it, open the door. I held the key to the lock, dropped it to the floor, bent down, picked it up and tried again. My hands were shaking. It wouldn't open. No wonder it wouldn't open. They were shaking too much.

I tried again, holding the key to the lock with one hand whilst steadying it with the other. A part of me wanted it to stay locked forever, but it didn't, oh my God it didn't! There was a loud metallic clunk that made me jump as I finally turned the key in the lock. That's it Cynthia, that's it! I'd done it. It was unlocked. Come on Cynthia, push it open. What are you waiting for? Maybe there's nothing to see. Push the confounded thing open.

I threw the key to the floor and pushed the door inwards, slowly, inch by cautious inch, before peering into the darkness with nervous eyes. It was pitch dark, far too dark to see anything at all until my eyes adapted to the gloom. Maybe that wasn't such a bad thing. Maybe I should turn and run before switching on the light. No, not this time, there'd be no running this time.

I placed my hand through the doorframe and groped for a light switch. Yes, there it was, there it was, you can do it, Cynthia, flick the switch. Be brave! You can do it, flick the switch.

I finally turned on the light after two fumbled attempts and took a single step backwards as a blindingly bright fluorescent light burst into seemingly enthusiastic life and flooded the room. I shut my eyes tightly, shielding them from the sudden intense electric glare, and then took two small steps forward and slowly opened them, squinting into a large glaringly white space.

At first I didn't see the naked young boy hanging from the bloody black steel shackles secured to the wall to the side of the door, or the video equipment, or the black leather bondage hoods, or the razor sharp scalpels and car battery and other instruments of torture, or the rusty metal meat hook fixed to the ceiling above a stainless steel drain and sloping tiled floor. On first impressions it was a strange, cold, clinical space, and despite the putrid smell of human waste, I felt strangely reassured by the room's initial scientific, lab-like appearance. It was all white tiles, every conceivable surface covered in polished white titles stained with blood and gore. Like an operating theatre. A lot like a hospital operating theatre. That's what I told myself, but I was clutching at straws, desperate to deny the horrendous reality unfolding before me. Desperate to close my eyes and escape the truth. That's the only explanation I can come up with for my ridiculous thoughts. I was clutching at straws.

Desperately clutching at straws! Maybe people were wrong after all: maybe the doctor was misunderstood rather than criminal, maybe the cellar was something to do with his work, just as he insisted. I wanted it to be true. I so wanted it to be true.

I took another step forward with a newfound confidence born of determined denial, and slowly scanned the room with rapidly blinking eyes. When I first saw that poor emaciated young boy for the first time I just stood and stared, desperately wanting to believe that the horror before me was a product of my vivid imagination rather than grim unrelenting reality. I walked towards him, lifted a hand to his freckled face and touched him gently on his right cheek. I felt his warmth with my finger tips and sighed. He was real. There was no room for denial. He was definitely real. This wasn't work. It wasn't science. This was why men joined the vile bastard in the cellar from time to time. This was why they sometimes brought young boys with them. That's why I'd been ordered to stay away and keep my mouth tightly shut until they left. It all seemed so blatantly obvious, so clear. Why hadn't I seen it before? Had I subconsciously chosen not to see it before? The doctor was a monster. They were all monsters. There was no denying the awfulness of what they'd done.

I placed the palm of my right hand ever so gently on the boy's bare chest and held it there for a few seconds, desperate to confirm that the warmth I'd felt in his face indicated life rather than further self-deception on my part. Yes, there was a heartbeat, a faint but definitive heartbeat! Thank God, he was alive. The boy was definitely alive.

I urgently struggled to free him from his metal shackles in a hormone fuelled frenzy, until my painted nails were broken and my fingertips bled. But my efforts were utterly hopeless. I'd never felt so useless. Stupid girl, stupid girl! I could hear him saying it.

I slumped at the boy's feet in a pool of intermingling body fluids and wept uncontrollably… No amount of endeavour on my part would suffice, however hard I tried. And even if I did finally manage to get him down from the wall, which appeared a lost cause, there was no way I'd be able to carry him to the door, let alone drag him up the concrete steps to the kitchen. I just didn't have the physical strength required. Do something Cynthia, don't just sit there, do something!

I lifted myself to my feet, oblivious to the stench. He needed urgent help. I needed urgent help. I had to get to the phone before that evil bastard returned to the house. It was my only chance. It was the boy's only chance. Come on Cynthia, run, run as fast as you can.

I turned away from the boy and rushed towards the steps without looking back at him. Why hadn't I told the inspector what I knew? Why on earth hadn't I told him of my suspicions? Stupid girl! I should have told him. It seemed so obvious now. Why didn't I tell him when I had the opportunity? I heard the doctor's mocking voice in my head again, louder, louder, louder until it threatened to overwhelm me completely. Stupid girl, stupid girl! Why can't you ever get anything right? Just ignore him Cynthia, he's a devil, a vile evil freak of nature. Ignore everything he says. Just ignore everything he says!

I slipped on the final step and stumbled into the kitchen, but stopped suddenly and listened, desperately hoping I was mistaken. The key in the lock, the front door opening, the door slamming shut, the heavy footsteps on the hall tiles. He was back. Oh no, he was back! Where could I run to? Where could I hide? What could I say to placate him? Hold it together Cynthia, hold it together, now was not the time to panic.

I took repeated urgent gulps of stale air and pictured the poor emaciated young boy hanging from the bloody black steel shackles in that terrible place, the hell within a hell

Galbraith had created. I decided at that instant that there'd be no retreat. If I was going to die I'd die fighting. If the boy were to die it wouldn't be for want of effort on my part. Be brave Cynthia, he'll be here at any second. Please be brave!

I listened as the monster's footsteps got closer, closer, closer. And then he appeared: tensing and relaxing his powerful muscles, loosening his broad shoulders, and forming his hands into the weapons that were entirely familiar to me. He stared at me from just inside the door, then at the displaced dresser, and then at me again. Be brave Cynthia. The boy's relying on you, please be brave!

He walked towards me, yelling: louder, louder, louder, until I thought the room itself may be shaking. He looked incredulous, shocked, filled with incessant rage. 'What the hell have you done you sanctimonious bitch?' I hate that word, I so hate that word.

I willed myself to move and edged slowly along the worktop, inch by inch, inch by cautious inch. Come on Cynthia, nearly there, nearly there. You can do it, look him in the eye, don't show your fear.

And then I moved quickly with my eyes focussed on the prize, and grasped a nine-inch filleting knife from a knife block on the shiny black granite work surface I'd polished a thousand times in a hopeless attempt to please him. Hold it tightly Cynthia, ever so tightly. It's your only hope. Don't drop it, please don't drop it!

I couldn't let him reach the steps. I had to impede his progress in any way I could. It was my only hope. It was the boy's only hope. Come on Cynthia, be brave, you can do it.

I manoeuvred past the dresser in a cautious sideways motion whilst holding the knife out in front of me with both hands clutched tightly around its metal shaft. That's it Cynthia, keep going, one more step, one more step, you can do it.

The doctor narrowed his hateful eyes and growled like the beast he was as he rushed towards me, striking the left side of my head with a powerful blow, as I stumbled backwards and thrust at him ineffectually with the blade.

I lost my footing and hit the door frame hard, before falling forwards and slumping to the floor: shaken, trembling, absolutely terrified but no less determined. Don't give up Cynthia, the boy's relying on you. Your daughters need you. Fight for your life.

I felt physically sick as the doctor approached me, raised his leg high behind him, and kicked me forcibly about six inches below my left armpit, before stepping over me and striding towards the first of the cellar steps.

I'd never felt such pain and I'd never felt such fear, but the small but determined voice in my head urged me on. I gasped for breath, my ribs screaming as I lifted my bruised and broken body onto all fours. Come on Cynthia, it's now or never.

The room was swimming in blurred focus as I stared at the doctor's broad back and crawled forwards as quickly as I could until I reached him. Faster Cynthia, you can do it, faster, faster!

I lifted my right arm stiffly, wincing with pain as I plunged the knife deep into the back of his left thigh with as much force as I could muster, jolting my wrist violently when the steel tip struck the bone. The doctor screamed horribly, injured but far from beaten. He kicked out with his uninjured leg, landing a painful blow on the very top of my head with the heel of his shoe, as I grabbed at his legs in a determined but ineffective attempt to further impede his progress.

I cried out, stunned, dazed, the room a myriad tiny stars, but I didn't let go. As he shook me off and raised his foot to stamp down on my head, I grabbed the cloth of his trousers, extended my free arm and plunged the blade deep into his thigh for a second time. I knew it was do or die. I knew there was nowhere to run. It was fight or flight and flight wasn't an option.

He swivelled and span despite his injuries, freeing himself from my fragile grip, and kneed me hard in the face, fracturing the bridge of my nose and leaving me close to unconsciousness with blood pouring from both nostrils. He looked down at me and sneered as he had so many times before.

I watched as Dr Galbraith hobbled across the kitchen clutching his severely injured leg and tied a tight tourniquet high on his thigh above his wounds before limping towards the cellar steps with blood soaking into his trousers. He clawed repeatedly at his head as was his custom when stressed, and I knew in that instant that there was still hope. There is always hope.

Just as he was approaching the bottom step, I lifted myself to my feet with the aid of an overturned chair, spat a mouthful of warm blood to the floor and stumbled unsteadily in the direction of the steps, taking what seemed an age to hobble to the bottom. Come on Cynthia, keep going, you can do it, one step at a time, you can do it.

When I finally reached the cellar the doctor was standing at a wall-mounted medicine cupboard, drawing a clear liquid into a syringe. I stood and stared like a mute statue as he turned away seemingly oblivious to my presence, and fast approached the helpless boy with a cold determined expression on his face. I had to do something, and quickly. It was now or never. As I stumbled in his direction with the knife held tightly behind my back, he stopped, suddenly aware of my presence. He turned towards me and stared, seemingly shocked that I'd dared to enter his secret domain, shocked that I hadn't surrendered to his dominance, shocked that I dared challenge him at all.

He shook himself as if waking from a trance, met my eyes, and smiled: mocking, cynical, dismissive. 'Your timing couldn't be better my dear. You're just in time to watch the little bastard breathe his last breath. And then, once you've helped me dispose of the corpse, it will be your turn to die. A welcome release from your worthless life, I expect. But, don't think it will be over quickly. You're going to suffer. I'll make certain of that. I'll take my time and indulge my inclinations until you beg for mercy. But, don't worry yourself my dear, that's for later.'

His words, as chilling as they were, strengthened my resolve. I'd never felt so scared, I'd never felt so alive and I'd never felt so ready to fight. I took one step forwards, then another, then another, and reached his side just as he was about to insert the needle deep into the boy's bare distended stomach. The doctor seemed strangely oblivious to my presence as I gripped the knife in both hands, lifted it high above my head and brought it down into his muscular back with all the destructive force my diminutive frame could muster.

He dropped the syringe, lost his balance on the filthy once white tiles, and hit the wall hard before slumping to the ground. I'd done it, I'd actually done it, but it was far from over. As I stared down at him he began to move, just slightly, ever so slightly, and I took my opportunity whilst I could. I raised that razor sharp knife above my head for a second time and brought it down into his upper chest with all my strength.

There was disconcerting sucking sound as I pulled the bloody blade from his body and stood above him. Was he dead? He was, wasn't he? Surely he was dead. I was praying he was dead.

I should have walked away at that precise moment. I should have rushed for the phone to summon help. But for some inexplicable reason I had to know. I just had to know if he'd breathed his last. I knelt at his side and stared at his seemingly lifeless face for a full minute or more, before reaching out nervously to feel for a heartbeat. Was it over? Was it really over? Surely it was over. Please let it be over! I had to be certain. Like it or not, I had to be certain.

As I leant close to him he opened one eye, quickly followed by the other, and snatched at my face with flashing teeth, only falling fractionally short of my nose. I had to be fast, I had to react quickly, and I did, thankfully I did. My adrenalin fuelled reflexes served me well and I leapt backward causing his attack to fail. As he reached up grasping for my exposed throat I jumped to my feet and brought the blade down forcibly, before repeating the process time and time and time again until his face was a bloody mess, totally unrecognisable as the man who'd brought so much misery and torment into so many innocent lives, mine included. And then it suddenly dawned on me. This time it was over. It really was over. Exhaustion overtook me at that instant and I slumped to the floor next to his corpse.

I don't know how long I lay there amongst the gore. All I know is that he was dead, it really was over, and in that instant all was calm and contentment despite the horrors all around me. I was alive, the boy was alive, and our world was a better place. A safer place.

I was strangely unaware of my injuries and the knife held in my hand as I hurried up the steps in the direction of the hall. The knife fell to the floor and made me jump as I picked up the phone and dialled the emergency services, urgently requesting the police and an ambulance.

I wandered into the lounge, exhausted, caked with blood and excrement, but truly elated. I lowered myself slowly to the floor and unlocked an old oak cupboard with bloody fingers that were no longer trembling. I took my favourite LP from the record collection I hadn't dared play since leaving Cardiff years before, and rose unsteadily to my feet. I smiled contentedly, took the record from its wonderfully colourful atmospheric sleeve, lifted the record player's plastic lid, placed the disc on the turntable, waited patiently for the needle to make contact with the black vinyl, and turned up the volume to maximum. I sat back down on the sumptuous soft woollen carpet with a newfound energy coursing through my body, and listened happily to the songs of my carefree youth, whilst waiting for the emergency services to arrive.

Chapter 45

Mrs Martin met my eyes, held her gaze for a fleeting moment and smiled with warmth and affection. 'I heard about the appeal. It's fantastic news. I'm delighted for you.'

She looked genuinely pleased for me. As excited as a child on Christmas morning. 'Yeah, I don't want to count my chickens and all that, but my legal team are really hopeful. They tell me I've got an eighty per cent plus chance of being released in the coming months. That's as good as it gets, apparently.'

'Pretty good odds, I'd say.'

'It seems so. Fingers and everything else crossed!'

'So where did they find the file?'

'The new owners were renovating Galbraith's study and found it under the floorboards along with some other papers and several videotapes he was particularly keen to hide.'

'And he'd recorded everything he did to you?'

I nodded in contemplative silence before speaking again. 'Yeah, point by point in specific detail. He was always making notes: always scribbling in that notebook of his or on one piece of paper or another. The scheming manipulative bastard! It seems I was a long term project. An ordinary typical young carefree student to psychologically destroy day by day and study along the way. He planned everything from the very start, every destructive move, every step from the first time he saw me in Cardiff at the age of eighteen. I was a disposable lab rat in his eyes, and nothing more.'

'And he killed Steven?'

I felt a deep pang of regret as I nodded my head. 'Oh yeah, he ran him down in the street as if he were worthless. What a piece of work!'

'And the girls, where did they fit in?'

'He wanted boys for his own deviant purposes. The girls were an inconvenience.'

'That's terrible!'

'And of course a wife and children helped give the misleading impression of happy middle-class respectability. We were camouflage: a mask behind which he could hide his true nature from the world.'

'So the three of you served a dual purpose.'

'It seems so: readily available research material and effective concealment in one useful package. What a way to think; what a way to live your life.'

She blew the air from her lips with a high pitched whistle. 'Psychopaths never fail to amaze me.'

'He brought nothing but pain and misery into my life. I'm so very glad he's gone.'

'Hoorah to that!'

'And all those unfortunate boys, it's truly horrendous what they went through. No child should have to experience such horrors. The filthy bastard even maintained meticulous alphabetically ordered files detailing the violence inflicted on each victim. There were numerous videos and photographs taken over the years. One child from a local children's home even died on film. If only he hadn't gotten away with it for so long.'

'How long was it?'

'Over thirty years! It seems he began offending shortly after qualifying as a doctor.'

'So he kept up the deception, helped some patients he saw and targeted others that met his victim profile. What a terrible betrayal of trust!'

We nodded our mutual agreement before I spoke again. 'Yeah, together with his accomplices; it seems there was a paedophile ring operating in the Caerystwyth area for generations. Galbraith was a lead figure before his arrest.'

'Look Cynthia, I have to ask. Did you ever find out what happened to Anthony and his mum?'

I smiled, recalling our brief meeting the previous summer. 'Oh, yeah, Anthony's mother, Molly, first visited me after I'd been here for just a few months. It was great to see her. She wanted to thank me in person for saving her son's life.'

'And you did Cynthia. I've no doubt Galbraith would have killed him were it not for you. That's something to be proud of. I'm surprised you haven't mentioned her visits before now.'

'I assumed you knew, to be honest.'

She shook her head. 'It's the first I've heard of it.'

'Molly threw her arms around me when we first met, before being ordered to sit by one of the guards. I like to believe we had an immediate affinity born of adversity. We both wept uncontrollably, but they were tears of shared empathy rather than sorrow. A release of painful pent up emotions that were particular to us and only to us. This may seem ridiculous, but it was like greeting an old friend or family member rather than a stranger.'

'It makes absolute sense. It's not ridiculous at all.'

'I guess you're right.'

'So how were they coping after their ordeals?'

I smiled again, more convincingly this time. 'They'd done even better than I could have hoped.'

Mrs Martin swivelled in her seat, reached down behind her and switched on the kettle for the second time that afternoon. 'Tell me more. It's nice to discuss some positives for a change. Let's make the most of it whilst we can.'

'Molly was barely conscious when her daughter found her battered and bleeding, but she regained consciousness after a couple of days on the intensive care ward and made surprisingly rapid physical progress once told her son was alive and safe. I think the news was just the tonic she needed, infinitely more effective than any medication the doctors could offer.'

'And her injuries?'

'She said her head and facial injuries gradually mended after surgery. I don't know what she looked like before the attack, but she looked pretty good when I saw her, everything considered. The reconstructive surgeon did a tremendous job. The scars were barely visible by the time we met.'

'Another courageous woman!'

'You won't hear me arguing. She actually grinned and told me that dental implants funded by her criminal injuries compensation payment looked better than her original teeth. Talk about a positive attitude.'

'And what about the psychological effects? They don't always heal as quickly as the physical injuries, as you know only too well.'

My mood became more sombre and I felt my facial muscles tighten as unpleasant memories played on my mind. 'We've got a lot in common. Galbraith hovered between us like a third presence we couldn't extinguish. Our world has become a dangerous place where monsters lurk in the shadows. He haunts our dreams and waking hours, sometimes appearing in our thoughts when we least expect him. Evil called our names and tainted our lives with a toxic stain that's impossible to wash away completely, however much we'd like to.'

'You speak with passion and eloquence Cynthia.'

'I think the writing's reignited my love of language.'

She smiled but the expression quickly left her face. 'Has Molly received counselling? Community services can be somewhat erratic at best.'

'She saw a psychologist who specialises in working with victims of violence on a private basis.'

'And it helped?'

'It seems so. She still sees her from time to time, as far as I know.'

'It sounds as if she's in good hands.'

I sipped my second cup of pleasant, calming camomile tea and smiled warmly. 'We both are.'

She looked back at me and self-consciously adjusted her fringe. 'Thank you so much, that's very nice to hear. You're too kind.'

'There's an unmistakable glimmer of light at the end of what's been a very dark tunnel.'

'Well, let's ensure that light gets brighter and brighter and becomes a shining beacon of hope for everyone who sees it.'

'I'm beginning to think it will.'

'And what about Anthony?'

I refocussed on the past again and for an awful moment I saw him hanging from the bloody black steel shackles in that terrible place, that monument to evil.

'Cynthia?'

I opened my eyes wide, instantly back in the room as the image gradually faded and returned to the past. 'Molly thanks God each and every day that Anthony doesn't remember a thing from the time he went to bed on the night of his abduction to the time he woke up on the children's ward days later. He awoke as if from a bad dream he couldn't recall.'

'In time he's likely to require answers, but I guess that can wait until he asks those questions himself.'

I nodded again, concurring with her assessment. 'He'd lost a great deal of weight and strength, but he gradually recovered with the help of physiotherapy and his mum's home cooking. He's back to his old self apparently and playing rugby again.'

'That's really good to hear. Did Molly ever get back together with that ineffectual husband you mentioned? Not that it really matters one way or the other.'

'Yeah, it's not a relationship made in heaven, but they were making a go of it the last time she wrote to me. She says she may even trust him again given time.'

'It can be strange how life works out sometimes.'

'Galbraith's dead, seven of his fellow offenders received lengthy prison sentences, it could have been a lot worse.'

'Things can always be worse.'

I nodded once and smiled despite or perhaps due to the burdensome nature of the subject matter. 'I want to say how grateful I am for your help Mrs Martin. You've been a lifesaver. Thank you so much.'

She leant forwards, reached out and squeezed my hand tightly before releasing it and sitting back in her chair. 'That's wonderful to hear Cynthia, but I think it's about time you called me Mary.'

'Ah, I got there in the end. Mary it is!'

Epilogue

I finally decided to publish my memoir after being persuaded by my mum, of all people. She read it shortly after my successful appeal and release, and convinced me it was a tale worth telling a few months later. I sent samples of my work to various literary agents in large brown envelopes adorned with brightly coloured first class stamps, but they either sent rejection letters or didn't bother replying at all. Eventually, when I'd almost given up on the idea of a book, a London based publishing house asked to read the entire manuscript and offered me a reasonable deal three weeks later. I'm not expecting to sell many copies, but if a few people read it and take my cautionary message on board to some degree, I'll be gratified by that. I've been told more than once that the book is a celebration to the human will to survive and overcome, even when faced with the greatest adversity. Whether that's true I'll leave it to you to decide. I still don't trust my judgement to any great degree.

I should probably mention that I'm back living with Mum and my wonderful girls in Tenby. I have a part-time job at a local restaurant run by a lovely English couple from somewhere in Sussex, and I spend as much quality time as possible with my girls, swimming and the cinema being particular favourites. No doubt it will take some time for us all to get properly used to each other's company again, but things are progressing pretty well everything considered.

I still suffer nightmares, I still feel on edge a great deal of the time, and I still find it almost impossible to trust others, particularly men. I repeatedly remind myself that there's a great many good guys out there in addition to the monsters, but Galbraith made a deep psychological impression that's extremely hard to erase. Thankfully, my memory of him isn't in such sharp focus as it once was, but I doubt if it will ever fade away completely and join the previously proactive black dog in virtual obscurity.

I've kept in occasional touch with Molly Mailer and have invited her family to visit during the summer months when they can take full advantage of everything Tenby and the surrounding area has to offer. She says they'll come in August, but that they'll rent a caravan near the beach rather than stay with us at the house. I think that makes sense, everything considered. They may or mayn't actually turn up, of course, I'll just have to wait and see.

I keep in regular contact with Jack and his family. He's never been happier. His little girl is almost two now, and I hope to visit and meet her one day when I've saved enough money for the return journey to America. The girls will come with me, of course, but I don't think Mum will make it this time. She says that one journey to California is enough for one lifetime and that she was never that fond of flying in the first place. She's relying on Jack, Marie and little Stella to make the long journey to Wales at some point in the not too distant future. I feel sure they will.

I received an untidy, barely decipherable letter from Gloria a couple of months back, completely out of the blue. It seems the English lessons I provided had little positive effect in her case, given the multiple spelling errors. I was delighted to hear from her, but disappointed to read that she's back in prison for another nine month stretch. It seems she never did kick the drug habit, and in truth I doubt she ever will. I suspect that the toxic chemicals she injects so keenly are a form of self-inflicted therapy she can't do without for very long however hard she tries to resist their destructive allure. I like to think that one day she'll have her own Mrs Martin and surprise me, but I won't hold my breath. I'll say a prayer for her occasionally and leave it at that.

I never did find out what happened to Emma or Sheila, and to be honest that's just fine with me. All in all, I'm a great deal happier than I've been for quite some time. I've no idea what the future holds, of course, but I now feel able to face whatever it brings with real optimism rather than the dread I so recently felt. I haven't decided if I'll carry on writing just yet. I've considered putting pen to paper on more than one occasion, but I'm not sure if I've got anything else worthwhile to convey. And so, I'm just going to get on with my life for now, love those who matter most and do the best I can with the cards I'm dealt. If I do decide to write another book and anyone actually thinks it's worth publishing, I like to think you'll be one of the first to know.

Cynthia Jones
14, February 1997

A note to the reader

Thank you for reading: When Evil Calls Your Name. I'm always interested to know what readers think of the book, and I'd be grateful if you'd leave a review on Amazon.

John Nicholl
30, November 2015

Also by the author:

White is the coldest colour

Lightning Source UK Ltd.
Milton Keynes UK
UKOW04f0919220216

268852UK00005B/359/P